COLD CASES AND BITTER ENEMIES

J.M. DABNEY

HOSTILE WHISPERS PRESS, LLC

Cold Cases and Bitter Enemies

J.M. Dabney

Hostile
WHISPERS PRESS

Copyright © 2022 by J.M. Dabney

Hostile Whispers Press, LLC

ISBN: 978-1-947184-57-2

Print ISBN: 978-1-947184-58-9

Photographer/Illustrator: Golden Czermak (FuriousFotog)

Cover by: J.M. Dabney at Hostile Whispers Designs

Edits by: AlternativEdits (Laura McNellis)

REMEMBER:

This book is a work of fiction. All characters, places, and events are from the author's imagination and should not be confused with fact. Any resemblance to persons, living or dead, events or places, is purely coincidental.

PLEASE BE ADVISED:

This book contains material that is only suitable for mature readers. It may contain scenes of a sexual nature and/or violence.

For my readers who make telling my stories worth it.

COLD CASES AND BITTER ENEMIES

COLD CASE UNIT BOOK 3

An unknown enemy wanted to take everything from us.

Graves

I'd spent all my forty-plus years paying for mistakes when I'd simply been human. Living in the shadow of my friend's happiness grew harder every day. I didn't mind being the odd one out. I didn't mind being considered the unlovable strait-laced-ish one to their mayhem. Acceptance after a lifetime of not measuring up was nice. I'd found my rhythm and my place among the weirdness of my unit. That was until Marcel Douglas, the new ego-maniac in Homicide, decided he had to pick apart every case I'd left behind.

Douglas

Leaving Chicago hadn't been in my plans, but my daughter needed me. I'd do anything to make her happy. When her mother was transferred overseas, I'd moved so my daughter could stay with her friends—the place she'd come to love. Being at the bottom of the hierarchy and earning respect didn't sit right with my pride. I wasn't afraid to admit that. And I'd made one hell of an enemy. Graves and his Cold Case Unit frustrated me, and I didn't understand their methods. A series of body dumps brought me back to Graves for help, but he wasn't feeling charitable.

We'd thought we were our biggest and bitterest enemies until the threats came. Could we work together before the man gunning for us could finish the job?

GRAVES

COLD CASE
UNIT

M y partner, Stevenson, slouched down in his chair on the other side of our pushed-together desks, and I kept throwing paper clips at him as he whispered into his phone. The big, blond menace wasn't exactly hiding the fact he was dirty talking to his boyfriend, Doc. I rolled my eyes as I tried to focus on the case file in front of me. He winked at me as I threw another clip particularly hard.

"Should I speak up, Graves?" He smirked, and then his expression completely changed. "Aw, baby, you know I wouldn't do that to you. You're only mine."

"You two are disgusting." I pushed up from my desk and escaped. At least the senior Detectives Robert and Remy Kauffman were at the courthouse that day. I couldn't deal with those lovebirds either.

I exited the building from the basement entrance where our Cold Case Unit was housed and circled the precinct to where I knew the coffee truck was parked at least until lunchtime. When I'd transferred to the new unit with three of my fellow Homicide Detectives, we'd caused a stir. But when Robert and Remy had taken over a serial killer case that they'd found hidden in the cold case files, I guess I'd enjoyed the interplay between them and Stevenson.

I shoved my hands in my jean pockets. Over a year after being transferred, I still wasn't used to not arriving at work in a suit and tie. We didn't hold to a dress code unless we had to do interviews, check out leads, or the dreaded court dates. Spring was almost in the air, and the slightly chilly breeze raised the hairs on my bare arms.

In my mind, I pictured how I looked and what my parents thought about my new career path. Being the only child of the District Attorney and State's Attorney, I was an embarrassment. I mentally grimaced as I remembered the first Sunday dinner after I'd taken my place in Cold Case. They'd liked the media coverage on us busting a serial killer who had terrorized our city for a decade. But now that I wasn't on a straight path to captain, hell, they'd hated the fact I'd become a cop.

My career aspirations should've been much loftier. Maybe a State's Attorney like my mother or a run for a political post, mayor, governor. But even before joining the academy, I'd never wanted any of those things.

"Graves."

Dammit, I pretended I hadn't heard the bane of my existence yelling my name and focused solely on the line that would lead me to the caffeine I needed.

"Graves, I know you damn well heard me."

I stopped mid-step and turned on my toes to face Marcel Douglas, one of the newest Detectives in Homicide. The tall, Black man was about a head taller than me, which was unusual since I was almost six-two. He wore a suit the way a male supermodel did, and I hated him on sight for looking perfectly put-together. He had a shaved head and a perfectly groomed beard. I couldn't find a flaw except for the crinkles at the corners of his eyes. He'd picked up some of my cases when I transferred. We'd also inadvertently worked together when he'd found information on a cold case Stevenson investigated. I'd attempted to avoid him since.

"You bellowed, Detective?"

"Is it a requirement of the Cold Case Unit to be a brat?" he asked as he lifted a heavy brow and kept his hands in the pockets of his slacks.

"That would be Remy. The rest of us are pretty normal, except Stevenson."

"Speaking of Stevenson, I've been trying to get through to Doc for over an hour."

"Mid-morning phone sex."

He groaned and rolled his eyes. "Of course. I don't even want to go by the morgue anymore. I've heard things that would make a damn phone-sex operator blush."

The frustration in his tone almost made the corners of my lips twitch. There were occasions that I really did love my friends. I kept it low-key, but they became the family I'd never had. Why they had to bring in Douglas, I didn't know. Oh, yeah, I knew, the fact Douglas drove me crazy. It was particularly amusing to my friend, Vega.

"What do you need from Doc?"

"Just wanted to double-check his findings on a killing at Bella Notte."

"Bianchi's club?" I'd known Carmine Bianchi since my days where I'd been assigned to the Organized Crime Squad back when I earned my detective shield.

"Yeah. A body was found in the alley about a week ago. Seemed straightforward enough, but Doc had a theory that it was a body dump."

"Doc's right."

"How is Doc always right? He's gotta be wrong sometimes."

"Doc's never wrong. You haven't learned that yet?"

"No one is that good. It's impossible. How do your and their methods even work? There's no rhyme or reason to it. It's illogical."

"That's more a nonsensical or philosophical discussion for Doc or his fellow genius, Vega. Not everything has lateral movement toward an answer. Sometimes you just have to throw knives at a wall and hope a few of them stick."

"Exhausting."

"Yes, you are. May I return to getting my coffee and hoping Stevenson and Doc's little daily foreplay ritual has ended by the time I get back?"

"You have a set-up in Cold Case that would make a barista jealous."

"But Stevenson is there."

"Okay, I'll give you that one."

I frowned at him and his failure to continue with our argument. He lived to argue. He thought we exhausted him, but I couldn't be in the same space with him for more than ten minutes before I wanted to scream. I turned and crossed to the truck, rolling my eyes when I felt him behind me.

"Weren't we done?"

"You're not the only one who wants coffee, Graves, us lowly detectives in Homicide don't get all the perks that Cold Case does."

"Oh, you mean, the heat that's iffy. Probably a ceiling and shelves full of black mold. Or how we're the ghouls in the dungeon?"

"Are you always this argumentative, or am I just exceptionally lucky?"

"Most would say it's my winning personality, Douglas, but to be honest, it's just you."

"Brat is definitely on the employment requirements for the

dungeon." He muttered, and I didn't give him the satisfaction of a reply.

"Simon, what can I get you today?" Jeff, the usual barista, greeted me.

"My usual, please. All the caffeine and sugar." I lifted my arms to lay them on the small counter as I rested my chin on my forearms.

"Triple or quad?" He grabbed a large cup and turned away.

"Quad shot today. I'm having to deal with Stevenson."

Jeff chuckled. "Last I heard, he's practically moved his office to the morgue to be near Doc."

"Only if I could be so lucky."

"Don't hate on the adorable man. When I saw him and Doc at Xanadu a few weeks ago, no one else existed. Doc has that man wrapped securely around his little finger."

Xanadu was a local kink-friendly club. I'd been invited to go a few times, and even though it wasn't my scene, they dragged me along. For a while, I hadn't thought it was Stevenson's scene either. But it was odd what we learned about people we've known for years. I wasn't the social type. I preferred my space. Yet my friends said I needed to be more sociable, and they'd taken it upon themselves to make sure it happened. As much as I complained, I'd never admit how much I loved the people watching when they took me out. It was better than being home alone all the time.

"Could you add a large black coffee to that order? I'm paying." Douglas stepped up too closely behind me.

"Personal space, Detective." I straightened to put a few more inches between us, but the side of the truck and the mass of Douglas's body wasn't allowing much of that.

"Shut up and say thank you for the coffee." He leaned down and ordered in my ear.

"Thanks." I hissed through my clenched teeth.

"That sounded like it hurt, Graves. Simon, huh?"

"It's Graves. Use it."

"Maybe, maybe not."

"Simon, are you going to be at the Outreach Saturday?" Jeff asked.

"Yeah, I'm babysitting for Saffy and Major, big date night. Aria is amazing. Have you seen her?"

"Yes, Graves, I have, and I was shocked when they told me they had a regular babysitter in the guise of a taciturn detective."

"She's the best baby. I was going to go to the Outreach for dinner and then let her run around in the playroom for a bit."

"Maybe I'll meet you there for dinner. They're trying out a new menu, and I have to see Boss. He has a few applicants for another truck. I'm expanding to the other side of the city. A lot of new construction."

"Well, text me. I have to pick Aria up at six. I have about five hours to kill that night."

Jeff shook his head at me as he turned around with the two to-go cups in his hands and set them on the counter.

"Large, quad shot with five pumps of caramel and three sugars. One large black coffee." Jeff gave Douglas the total, and I stepped out, finally taking a full breath without being sandwiched between him and the truck.

The politeness ingrained in me didn't let me run, but the part of me that didn't like the man's presence made it hard to stay. I took a sip of my coffee and let out a blissful sigh at the strong, sweet brew. I had the syrup at our coffee station, but I just never got it right.

"How are you not bouncing all the time?" he asked, complaining.

"I could chug this and still take a nap."

"Babysitting, huh?"

"What of it? Major and Saffy are doing great. He got a job doing studio musician work through a reference from Vega's wife, Cash. Major's still a little overprotective since she got hurt, and with his benefits and the work, he said he made enough to take care of his girls."

"I wasn't saying anything bad, just didn't see you as a fan of kids."

"I do have nieces and nephews through Robert and Remy." I turned to head back to the basement entrance.

"You're always running or arguing. I'm an asshole, Graves. I never claimed not to be. We got off on the wrong foot because I couldn't see how your thought process worked."

"You called my work shoddy, Douglas." I snarled at him.

"And I think I've tried to apologize more than once."

"Oh, was that what you called what you attempted to do, apologizing? You called me illogical and asked how I became a detective."

"I apologized afterward."

I shook my head and quickened my steps.

"My legs are still longer than yours. Are you going to hit a full sprint next?"

I came to an abrupt stop and turned and tilted my head back to look at him. "Douglas, we're not friends, we don't work together, and why the hell are you following me?"

"I'm hoping to steal Stevenson's phone so I can talk to Doc without an interruption."

I peeked at my watch to check the time. "Good luck with that. He's probably already gone and on his way to the morgue. Nine AM is their usual coffee date."

He cursed loudly. "I'm never getting that man's full attention."

"If you have a *Daddy* voice it might work in your favor. Doc seems to respond to that, but Stevenson might take offense."

"Is that what would work with you, Graves? A *Daddy* voice?" His tone softened but strangely held a deeper rumble, and he smirked at me.

"Even if I were gay, which I'm not, you wouldn't be my type. Good day, Detective." I left him standing there and was thankful when he didn't follow. Just because I worked with a unit of all gay and bisexual people didn't mean I was. The assumptions were made, and there was nothing I could do about it. And in my parents' eyes, it was another failure on my part. I'd long given up on pleading my case.

2

DOUGLAS

The call came in at two AM, and I'd rolled out of bed, left a note on Savannah's nightstand, and drove across the city to the crime scene. Thankfully my daughter was self-sufficient about getting up and dressed for school on her own. She shouldn't have to be an adult already. I'd swore my kid would be a kid once she lived with me, but I was completely failing at that.

My black SUV came to a stop just outside yellow crime scene tape and the strobe light show of red and blue. The address was becoming all too familiar. *Bella Notte*. Bianchi was connected. Hell, the man didn't make a secret of that. I didn't know if I believed he didn't have anything to do with the previous body. No matter what Doc or Graves had to say about the medical examiner's findings.

Shit, as if just thinking about them conjured the two men, as I ducked under the tape, I saw Graves stood beside the body as Doc crouched beside it. Doc was scribbling notes on his clipboard. I'd learned quite a bit working with them on a murder and missing person's case months previous. I could even say I'd made a few work friends, but Graves still rubbed me the wrong way, and if his attitude was proof, he felt the same toward me.

"What sin did I commit?"

"You're just lucky, Detective." Doc tipped his head back and batted his lashes.

I grinned as I thought about how hard it was to keep that brat in line. I glanced at Graves to find him staring at his phone with dark circles under his eyes.

"Missing Homicide, Simon?"

"Graves," he corrected me. "And no, someone handed over my card, and here I am. Princess brought a client back here about twelve-thirty and saw taillights as a nondescript sedan with no plates or covered ones squealed tires out of here. She's giving her statement now since I gave her the go-ahead."

I still didn't understand the power the Cold Case Unit wielded within those forty blocks. That night wasn't the first time I arrived to find Remy, Stevenson, or Graves, for that matter, already at the scene. The people around there didn't put that much trust in law enforcement, but it appeared every one of them always had a card to hand over.

"Another body drop, Doc?" I didn't hide the skepticism in my tone.

"He's been dead by my calculation for at least three hours before it was called in. No ID on our victim, and there was some serious damage to his fingertips. I'll try to pull them once I get him back to the office."

"Dental records?"

"If you can find the teeth, Douglas."

Dammit, just like the first body we'd found.

"Bianchi is waiting inside with a few uniforms. He's not happy." Graves seemed almost amused by that.

"Want to join me, Simon? Work on those rusty skills of yours?"

"Graves." He enunciated, but I had no intention of correcting myself. His snarl and anger were too much fun. "But since I have nothing better to do. Doc, Stevenson's waiting to escort you back to the morgue?"

"You know he is. He's currently asleep on the gurney. We had a late night."

"When don't you two have a late night?"

"That is true, Graves, and don't be jealous." Doc batted his lashes.

"When do you plan to start the autopsy?" I asked

"Probably eight AM. I still have to finish photographing and sketching the scene. My assistant has it set up to scan the alley for a 3D representation for a recreation. If I decide to start earlier, I'll call."

"Okay, I'll probably be at the office after I'm done here. My daughter won't be expecting me home for breakfast." I said goodbye to Doc and walked toward the back entrance of the club.

"Daughter?" Graves asked.

"Yeah, teenager, Savannah just turned thirteen." He didn't ask any more questions as we entered the main room, and I scanned the brightly lit club, the spotlights almost blinding.

It was easy enough to spot Bianchi in a horseshoe booth with a drink in front of him as he scowled at the uniformed officers.

"How do you want to work it?"

"You're asking my opinion, Douglas? Will wonders never cease?"

"Quit being a bitch. This is apparently your territory. Inside intel would be appreciated."

"Bianchi doesn't respond well to good cop-bad cop. Be straightforward with him. I won't say he'll give you what you want, but he'll definitely be more respectful."

I nodded, and we approached the table. I frowned as the mob boss's face lit up.

"Graves, hey, honey."

"Hey, Carmine. Been good? How's the husband?" he asked as

he slipped into the booth, and Bianchi ordered someone to bring an espresso. "Didn't your youngest, Sylvia, just have a birthday? Sixteenth, right?" They were goddamned besties.

"Never have a daughter, honey, sons, breed like bunnies when you know it's going to be a boy. Girls. I got grays. All the grays."

"Your own fault, Carmine. You and Stephen spoiled her rotten."

"That's all my husband's doing. I wanted to send her off to a nunnery in the middle of the Antarctic. What was that boarding school you went to, honey?"

"It was an all-boys one, would defeat the purpose of keeping her safe and chaste, but probably wouldn't keep her anymore chaste at an all-girls school either."

"Your humor has not improved. Your close association with Remy has ruined you."

"You still love me, though."

"That's debatable."

Graves let out a carefree laugh and thanked a twinky server in skintight clothes when he dropped off the small cup and saucer with a lemon twist on the side.

"Carmine, this is Detective Marcel Douglas. He's new in Homicide, started after our crew transferred."

"Nice to meet you, Detective. I see you haven't made friends yet. Get used to being handed the Cold Case cards."

"I'm starting to understand the rumors and the power they have. I'll adapt."

"Have a seat. Something to drink, coffee? I'm sure you want to ask me some questions."

Again, I was suspicious. Mob-connected men weren't so quick to talk to cops, and I glanced at Simon as I slid into the spot across from him. He was casual, not an ounce of tension existed, and the ever-present twin indents between his brows were nowhere to be seen.

"I'm good. I'm sure you're ready to get home."

"My husband is sending me texts every five minutes. He's anxious when I'm not home, even though I hired him a complete team of bodyguards. Are you married, Detective?"

"No, divorced. We were both in the military."

"Then you understand the worry?"

"Yes, sir, I do. You wouldn't meet with me when we found the other body."

"I wasn't here that night. I was actually out of the country. Family trip to celebrate the birthday. As Graves pointed out, my daughter just turned sixteen. Nothing my security team and managers couldn't inform you of."

There was that fond glance at Graves again. There was a story there, yet I was unsure if I wanted to delve too deeply into why he and a mob boss were close enough to remember children's birthdays. I'd learned from working with Remy and Robert and their team that sometimes it was best not to ask too many questions.

"It would be pointless to ask if you have enemies?"

"Everyone has enemies, doesn't matter if you're me or a PTA mom, those women are vicious. I offered Stephen a bulletproof vest for meetings." Bianchi chuckled and I noticed his body language had changed once Graves sat down. He was relaxed and open. Not an ounce of defensiveness in his posture.

"Did you know the victim?"

"They asked me to look at him, but he doesn't appear familiar. I will say, though, whoever dressed him did a spectacular job. Hand-stitched. Not many places have that quality of work anymore."

"Hardleston, he'd be a good place to start, I don't think it's his work, but he'd know who," Simon suggested.

"Our Graves here has excellent taste, and don't let the lowly cop job fool you."

"It's not lowly, Carmine, be nice." That was the first time I heard the edge to his voice since we'd entered the building after

I'd used his first name. There was something going on there, and I was going to find out what.

"Drink your coffee, honey," Bianchi ordered. "He needs a keeper. Type A personality, perfectionist...they never know what's good for them."

"Don't listen to a word the man says," he said to me and then glanced back at Carmine. "Keep your suggestions for your pet and leave me out of it."

"I apologize, Graves, sincerely." There wasn't an ounce of sincerity in his tone, and everyone within listening range knew it.

Graves snorted and shook his head. "I'd believe it if you weren't smirking and plotting as we speak. Did they show you photos of the last victim?"

"Yes, another unknown, cheap suit. Those two didn't run in the same circles, or they were in different ranks. Graves, you know me. I run my clubs. I've stepped back from the business in order to give my husband and children a more normal-ish life. Our sons are living the freedom of college, with bodyguards, of course, because, let's face it, I'm still paranoid."

"Doesn't mean they aren't still gunning for you."

"Very true, Simon. But what's the point of warning me with the bodies of men I don't know? You talked to Seamus yet?" There was amusement when Bianchi asked.

"No. And this isn't my case, and I'm not going to."

Bianchi laughed loudly. "Aw, still smarting from the affectionate ass pat?"

"That wasn't affectionate, Carmine. That was about a second smack from spanking."

"Oh, you should've seen your face. The pictures were legendary."

"Just because my friends are on the LGBTQ spectrum doesn't mean that I'm looking for a boyfriend. The minute I took this assignment, every horny criminal and crime boss in the city saw a target on my ass."

"Can't blame us for looking."

"Behave and talk to Douglas. I'm getting a refill." Simon slipped out of the booth and picked up his cup and saucer. I tracked him until I saw him lean on the bar.

"We need to buy that boy a sense of humor," Bianchi whispered affectionately. "I'm sorry there's not more I can give you. I can write a list of enemies that are probably in the thick file you already have."

"What do you think is going on?"

"I have no idea, Detective. I've slowly withdrawn from that life over the last year or so. I still own my clubs, but we have strict no weapons, drugs, or criminal business policies. Believe me when I say I don't know why me or my club would be targeted. I'd understand if young men in my employee were dumped, but this isn't logical."

"A lot about this city isn't logical." I glanced at Simon.

"Don't break your heart on that one."

"No intention, and he isn't my type."

"Tall, leanly muscled model beautiful men with a permanent five o'clock shadow and an ass you could bounce a quarter off, aren't your type? You're an exceptionally unique man then, Detective."

"I hope your husband isn't a jealous man."

"My husband has checked him out more than I have." He reached into his pocket and removed a business card. "Here, this is my personal contact info. Please don't hesitate to call me directly if you have further questions."

I took the card and stared at him. "I still don't understand why you're so cooperative."

"You were in the military. You had a wife. That's a dangerous profession for a family man. When I took over for my old man at twenty-one, I had no intentions of coming out or much less carrying on the family name with some woman I didn't love. Fifteen years ago, I met a sweet, single dad raising five kids on his own after his divorce. I fought with family tradition and machismo, but in the end, him and his children were everything to me. Leaving a life behind that I never truly wanted wasn't all that much of a hardship."

"If you think of anything else, let me know."

"Of course. I'm going home to my family. It's well past time I tuck my husband in."

I stood and waited for him to exit the booth, and I offered my hand. "Thank you for your time, Mr. Bianchi."

"Please call me Carmine. Any friend of Graves's is a friend of mine."

That went a bit far, but I didn't bother correcting him. "Carmine." I waited for his security to escort him out, and I shifted to see Simon carrying on a conversation with the same young man who served him.

He was casually leaning against the bar, and I slowly closed the distance between us until I was a few feet away from him. I stood back to listen in on the conversation.

"Is he still on the couch?"

"Graves, you know he is. We've been together for two years. He should know our anniversary by now."

"Honey, you're dating a firefighter. Most of those guys can't remember their own names after a shift."

"Don't take the side of the first responder." The kid pouted and leaned into Simon's space.

"Just go home to Tyrone, move his blanket and pillow back to the bedroom. Your last boyfriend forgot he had a boyfriend. Remember, he tried to explain why blowjobs aren't cheating during said blowjob."

I covered my nose and mouth to hide my snort.

"Did you have to remind me of that one?"

"Yes, yes, I did. Because I became an unwilling hostage negotiator trying to talk you out of the Xanadu bathroom stall."

"You did, didn't you?"

"I did. And the sad part was I think that was the highlight of my night." Simon tweaked the man's cheek.

The young man affectionately tugged at the front of Simon's t-shirt.

"You're too handsome and understanding to be single."

"Honey, you're probably the only one to think so."

"I think your partner is waiting for your attention."

I smirked at the kid as he grinned at me around Simon's shoulder, and the grumpy man was instantly back. Fuck, I had to figure out how to make up for being an asshole. I wasn't interested in having a best friend or someone to go out for beers with, but a friendly working environment wouldn't kill me.

"You want to have breakfast?" I asked without too much thought.

"I could eat. I think I had a handful of dry cereal before I went to bed, and then my phone went off."

"Is there a place open this time of night?"

He nodded. "And it's gourmet."

I shook my head at his tiny smirk, and then I was following him back outside. The scene had been cleared of the body. Although, the forensic team was still hard at work.

"We're not going far. You can leave your vehicle. They won't clear the scene for a few more hours, at least. I parked at the Outreach and jogged over," he said as we stepped out onto the main strip.

I stood back as he greeted people as he passed. There were even a few hugs exchanged. He confused me. He seemed so closed-off and a bigger asshole than me. Then I overheard conversations, saw him interact with a crime boss like they were old friends, and showed affection to people who more than likely were a week or more overdue for a shower. And he didn't even hesitate.

Before I could comment, we stepped up to a classic 50s style diner and walked inside.

"Mama Sue, feed me."

"Boy, you need to find you a person to be your keeper because I ain't it." A plump older woman in a uniform slammed her fists on her hips.

"But, maybe sexy, older women are my thing, ya know? Maybe I've always secretly wanted a sugar mama."

I laughed behind him as he threw himself around the woman and pressed his face into her neck.

"You're a brat. You've learned some bad habits from those friends of yours. You were such a good boy before Remy and Doc."

"I'll tell them you approve. I brought you a newbie. He hasn't experienced the three AM hangover special yet."

The woman tsked at me like I'd caused a personal offense. And with them still attached to each other, I was led to a corner booth up front. The space was narrow and looked to be constructed around an old subway car. Once we were seated and she got our drinks and food orders, she left us alone.

"What's a three AM hangover special? And you don't look like the hangover sort."

"I'm not, but it's big and greasy and adds five miles to your morning run. Stevenson brought me here one night after we became full-time partners."

"What's with you and Carmine?"

"Oh, long history, back when I first started. I worked Organized Crime. It has a shit turnover rate, so they cycle people out to stave off burnout. Bad man, but his family comes first. I respected that, and he respected that I never used his children in a power play."

"You're not sleeping enough, sweetie." Mama Sue patted Simon's cheek. "Make sure he gets home safe, newbie."

I chuckled as she filled out coffees and walked away.

"You're not so bad when you're not fighting me, Simon."

"It's Graves, Detective. Use it."

"Maybe, maybe not."

Our shared meal was relatively quiet, not even any snark, but maybe that had more to do with the fact the leanly built man ordered enough food for a damn army. He didn't seem like the greasy diner food type, but I'd come to meet the Cold Case Unit guys with preconceived notions from rumors around the precinct. I'd learned a lot about their loyalty to each other. The passion they had for the victims. I had to respect them for that. And while I'd gotten friendly with the rest of the guys and somewhat with Vega, Graves and I seemed to go at each other at the least provocation.

I just had to find out what it was about the man seated across from me that put me so on edge. A part of my issue was I couldn't figure him out. He was a series of contradictions. I'd seen them when we'd run into each other and also on the rare occasion we worked together. He made me question myself, and at forty-eight, I thought that was a thing in the past.

Mama Sue interrupted my contemplation to refill our coffees, and I went back to finishing my too early breakfast and ignoring my odd feelings about Graves.

3

GRAVES

COLD CASE
UNIT

I leaned back against the brick wall in the alley behind Bella Notte and cast my gaze right and left, I should've left it alone, but I couldn't. Most people assumed I missed Homicide and I kind of did, but not in the way they thought. It was puzzles, and I'd always loved those, jigsaw to crosswords. They said everyone needed a hobby.

There were no bigger puzzles than cold cases. It was a challenge. Yet Homicide was about the race. Following the leads before they ran out. Statistics showed you had forty-eight hours to find a suspect before your odds of finding them became harder.

I'd found the adrenaline rush of it addictive. My nose wrinkled at the scent of days' old trash. Moldy and musty air that you knew would stay in your nose long after you escaped the space. I leaned my head back against the cold wall and let out a heavy sigh as I tried to calm my mind enough to work.

"Not the place for hookups now, my friend."

I grinned at Carmine's voice and turned to find him, the flare of matches lit the broad angles of his face as he lit his cigar. "You know I don't do hookups." Hell, I didn't do sex. I'd kept that revelation to myself. With my asshole friends, they'd give me shit for being a virgin barreling towards middle age. *Asexual.* That label had come up in overheard conversations about the LGBTQ-plus community over the years. I'd listened close without seeming to be, and then I'd caved and asked Vega and Doc questions .

"This I know. So, if you're not looking for a body to pass the time, what *are* you doing here?"

"I don't know."

"Not an answer, honey."

I sighed as I shoved my hands in my pockets and pushed off the wall with my shoulders. "I'm just not getting it. You're the target."

"Obviously."

"But why? I mean—" I paused to take a breath. "You have more enemies than you can count. Wouldn't it be easier to just take the kill shot and be done with it? Why the production? Why not just kill you and take the credit for taking down the last Bianchi boss?"

"You're the detective. I'm just an old mob boss in retirement."

"Carmine, as much as I adore you, don't play that bullshit with me."

"Fine. I've come to enjoy a life of a certain status, but you know I don't run whores or drugs. That was my old man, not me. I keep a toe in but leave the messy work for others."

"Anything remarkable lately?"

"No. Seamus and I are at odds, but that's not unusual."

Seamus Finnegan was a relatively new face in the city. He was a brute where Carmine was all elegance. Seamus didn't have the patience for an operation like that. He'd drop the bodies at Carmine's feet while looking the man in the eyes.

"Also, this isn't his style."

"No, it's not. Your detective is a rather handsome man." The subject change was abrupt and classic Carmine.

I shot him a killing glare to find him smirking at me. "He's not mine. I can barely stand him."

"My father said love and hate are the same things. It's just a matter of what you want more. Do you want to fuck them or kill them? But to be honest, some of the best sex is hate sex."

I couldn't help the laugh that slipped free. "Remind me never to take dating advice from you."

"You'd have to date in order to require advice. You look like shit, Simon, but you're looking a lot happier in the last few years. As odd as it is, we're friends and share a mutual respect. My children and husband have always adored you. If you ever need anything, you can always call."

"Thanks."

Back in the day, I would've bristled from that offer. For as long as I could remember, I'd needed to be above reproach, and that was never more apparent than when I became a cop. I was under the expectations of my fellow and superior officers. But also, my parents wouldn't abide by the scandal attached to their names. They loved to remind me they'd worked too long and hard for me to ruin that for them.

"Any time, as I said, we're friends as suspicious as that has made you to Internal Affairs."

"They never focus on the ones who actually need closer examination."

"Because they don't understand the profound power that trust and respect possess. I think Douglas gets it. But as with all men who don't fully understand, he's suspicious. I did some digging. He took a hit coming here. He had an established career, on his way up the ranks, but came here for his daughter."

A cold chill went up my spine. I didn't like Douglas, but that didn't mean I wouldn't protect his daughter if I needed to. Carmine was a powerful enemy to have, but I'd destroy it all if he even had a moment's thought about touching her. "And I don't have to remind you she's off-limits."

"It pains me after our long association that you think I needed to be reminded." Sincerity filled his voice.

"Just making it clear. Shit." I jerked my hands from my pockets and forced my fingers through the curls that had escaped the careful styling. "Children."

"What?"

"What's the cruelest way to send a message?"

"Ah. Attack one's children, but they're not mine, and none of my men recognized them. And my father's been gone way too long to father those young men."

"True. I don't know. You know how my brain works."

"Throwing those knives, Simon?"

"It's how I work best, even if I don't let people see my process."

"Are you missing Homicide that much?" he asked me.

"No. I have no regrets about transferring out but something about all this…I can't let it go. There's…I don't know. A piece is missing."

"The piece is the why."

"That, too." My phone beeped in my pocket, and I pulled it out. "Graves," I said without checking the number.

"Detective, I'm getting very tired of hitting walls with your name on them."

I rolled my eyes at Douglas's annoyed-sounding voice, and Carmine chuckled. I was about to answer my newest enemy when I froze as lips pressed to mine.

"Be a good boy. I'll see you soon."

I stared at Carmine's disappearing back.

"Why is Carmine Bianchi telling you to be a good boy? And did he…fuck! I don't want to know. Just get your ass here. I'll text you the address." The phone was still against my ear when he disconnected the call.

I shook my head as the notification pinged, and I checked the address. I was close by and made my way to the scene. I really had to stop handing out my cards. I also had to stop hanging out with the pain in the ass crime bosses that wanted to do some matchmaking through jealousy. Yet nothing Carmine did surprised me anymore.

The strip was lit up, and I barely noticed the first responder vehicles off to the side in a paid parking lot. My SUV rolled to a stop. I opened the door, slid from my seat and pulled out my badge on the chain from under my jacket. I stood back for a few minutes to watch Douglas and Davian go toe-to-toe. My friend barely came to the big detective's chest.

"Well, Detective, you sure make friends everywhere you go."

"Graves, you know this one?" Davian asked.

"Unfortunately. Are you okay, honey? Let me see." I grabbed Davian's face and checked the damage. "Good thing you're a pro at cover-up." He had the start of a black eye and some dried blood around his nostrils, but he seemed okay. I released him as I turned to stand beside him.

"You know I've had worse." I caught his expression as I glanced at him as his eyes went skyward, and that made his thick, fake lashes flutter.

"Why am I lucky tonight?" I asked as Douglas growled and crossed his arms over his chest as he looked at us like he wanted to bust us both.

"Roo is sick. I didn't want to call Remy to leave her."

"It's fine, just tell me what happened?"

"I ran out of condoms, and I was headed to the Outreach. I saw two big guys, complete muscle, but looked like they stepped off the screen of a mob movie. Next thing I know, I'm getting hit, and I take off running. I didn't even see anything until I came out of hiding and found the body. Doc wasn't on duty tonight."

"You need to see a paramedic?"

"No, but my night is over with. I'm going home to a bath, chocolate, and Idris Elba."

"Sounds like a plan."

"Was that so hard to say? Couldn't you tell me you didn't see shit but two guys in suits?" Douglas's bass voice dipped even lower with his frustration.

I snorted as Davian raked his gaze over the detective and sucked his teeth with disgust.

"Is your name Kauffman, Graves, Stevenson, or Warner?" He didn't even pause. "No, it's not. Can I go now?"

"Yeah, come down to the precinct tomorrow, today, whatever, and give a statement. Are you okay with that?"

"For you, Graves, anything."

"Thanks, honey. Have fun with Idris."

"You know I will." Davian sent Douglas one more dirty look, and I watched him until he disappeared.

"This isn't your crime scene," he yelled at me as he closed the few feet that separated us until he loomed over me, but I refused to react.

"And you're not making friends."

"I don't need to make friends. I have a job to do."

"Well, you're doing a really shoddy job."

"You've just been waiting on this. I don't need you or your unit's damn permission to talk to witnesses to a crime. That isn't how shit works."

"Well, down here, that's the only way it works." I turned to walk off.

"You fucking crime bosses now, Simon? Is that what does it for you?"

I stopped mid-step and pivoted on my toe. "What the fuck did you just say?"

"You heard me. You're not an idiot. No wonder he was so friendly. I bet you gave it up easily, too."

"Listen, asshole, who I fuck or don't fuck has nothing to do with you. Carmine could bend me over in the middle of his club, and you still wouldn't get a fucking say. Now, do your goddamn job and stay out of my way."

I didn't run back to my vehicle, but I didn't pause as he yelled my name as the people at the scene stared between us until I was safely in the driver's seat and headed home. I was several blocks away before I noticed the death grip I had on the steering wheel. I should've knocked his fucking teeth out, but decorum won. Next time, I didn't know if I'd be able to control myself.

4

DOUGLAS

COLD CASE
UNIT

I'd come home from the crime scene and barely took time to remove my tie and jacket, before grabbing a beer and plopping down at my kitchen table. I'd fucked up, and I'd known it as soon as the accusation was out. Hell, I didn't understand why I'd even said it, but then he'd squared up, and I'd doubled down. I didn't know what had come over me. I'd heard Carmine's voice in my ear telling Simon to be a good boy, and Simon wouldn't even be civil to me. Yet as soon as I'd seen him, he looked mussed and happy. His carefully styled hair showed off beautiful black curls, and I wondered if Carmine had tangled them around his fingers, and I got pissed. I didn't even like Simon in that sense. Although, that didn't explain my anger at Carmine's voice and the obvious sound of a kiss.

All I could picture while waiting for Simon to arrive at the scene was the image in my head that I'd interrupted them. Carmine and Simon curled up in bed, cuddling, and I'd wanted to rage at or hit something. Instead, I'd accused Simon of fucking the man like I was a jealous lover or boyfriend.

"What did you do?"

I jerked my head up to find Savannah standing in the kitchen doorway. "Hey, why aren't you still asleep?" She was wearing pajama bottoms and a tank top, her hair piled in a messy knot on the top of her head. Even at thirteen, I could still see her as a three-year-old in her princess nightgown and asking me to read her a story.

"It's Friday night, teenagers we do that, ya know, stay up all night, but it's been a long time since..."

I playfully growled at her. Donna and I'd never planned to have kids, so when we were both thirty-five, and a sudden illness caused us to panic, we'd rushed to the doctor. When they told us she was pregnant, we'd been shocked. That didn't mean we hadn't been happy, though. And our daughter loved to point out we'd be eligible for Social Security by the time she graduated high school.

"You can stop there."

"So, what did you do?" she asked again as she came to sit down at the table. I lifted my arm, and my fingers tucked a stray curl behind her ear.

"Why do you think I did something?"

"Because you always have that look when you're feeling guilty. It can be a fight with mom when y'all were married. A case you didn't think you were solving quickly enough. It's always the same look."

"I got frustrated with someone and said some shit I shouldn't have."

"Say you're sorry." I smiled at how simple she'd made it sound.

"Sweetie, all I've done is try to apologize to him since shortly after we met and got off on the wrong foot. And I keep fucking it up."

"Am I finally going to meet a boyfriend?" She batted her lashes.

I'd never been out because of being in the military, and then I was married to her mom for twenty-one years. Being Pansexual was more something I just was but never really had practice at.

Yet when we'd had the sex talk with Savannah, we'd told her who she loved, no matter their gender, was all about making her happy and that I was Pan. As a biracial kid, she already had to deal with racism. Our home was always love is love.

But I also hadn't dated since the divorce. With retiring from the Marines and the new career path, relationships weren't on the top of my to-do list.

"He hates me."

"That's because you were probably an asshole." We'd never corrected her love of profanity inside our houses. Her mother and I weren't the best role models when it came to language. Outside of our home, Savannah was a perfectly polite kid. "Mom has had two boyfriends since the divorce and several dates, and what have you had...nothing."

"You're just vicious tonight." I tapped my half-empty bottle on the table.

"Blame it on the hormones. We girls get like that sometimes."

"We do not stereotype in this house." I smiled as she giggled at me.

"What does he like?"

"Coffee. His nieces and nephews. Something called a three AM hangover special made by a waitress called Mama Sue. He loves giving me shit."

"The giving you shit is probably his favorite thing."

"Probably, I wouldn't put it past him." Not many men would go up against a man my size, but Simon hadn't backed down once. His skin had flushed, and his green eyes had darkened with fury.

"What's his name?"

"Simon. He's a detective in the Cold Case Unit. I took over some of the cases he left when he transferred out of Homicide."

"Did you pick them apart?"

"Am I that predictable?" She nodded enthusiastically. "You're not good for my guilt right now."

"Not part of my job. What is part of my job as your daughter is helping you make up for being an asshole perfectionist."

"Oh, wise one, how would you suggest I do that?" I asked as I leaned my forearms on the table, and she mirrored me with a small smile.

"Do something he totally doesn't see coming."

I groaned. "That's how I got in trouble in the first place."

I can't seem to help myself when it comes to Simon. I'd always found I could hold my temper in any situation, but with him, I wanted to push. He was confident in his job. He had a weird, found family, but I couldn't fault the way they were with each other. I'd seen it when Doc had delivered a baby of a few friends in the morgue, and they'd rallied to get the homeless couple housing and everything they'd need. It was like they hadn't even seen it as them doing more than what needed done. It was completely selfless, and it didn't make sense to me. When they came together when Doc was taken by a suspect who turned out to be a former boyfriend of Doc's, they'd had sources from everywhere going above and beyond. That wasn't just co-workers. That was family and loyalty above all else.

"What else does he like that you didn't mention?"

I bent my arms and scrubbed my hands over my beard, and reminded myself I needed to make time for a trim. I thought about her question, and the conversation I overheard came back to me. "The Outreach. He's supposed to be there tomorrow night." I knew he was babysitting but would that work in my favor?

"Why don't we go?"

"We? I didn't agree to a *we*." Simon wasn't a potential boyfriend. I'd do with one less enemy, though. I'd go, I'd say sorry, but I didn't want my daughter involved. My luck, she'd like Simon and then take his side, not what I needed in my life.

"Come on. You have an adorable daughter. How can he stay

mad at you with me around? He'll have to listen and not fight because I'm there."

"You think that'll work?" I couldn't believe I was considering bringing her into the mix. It wasn't her place to make things right. Again, I reminded myself of my promise to let her be a kid, but she kept wanting to fix things. That had always been her personality, and as much as we fostered her strong individuality, we always wanted her to take time for herself and not worry about everyone else. Fuck, she was just like Simon, and I was screwed.

"Can't hurt to try, and I really want to meet the guy who stands up to you."

"I see your logic now." I knew there needed to be an ulterior motive.

"It's flawless." Fuck, now she sounded like Doc.

"I'm not so sure about that. You really want to go?"

"Yeah. The Outreach is pretty well-known around here. They're always on the news. Mom used to mention it, and some of my friend's parents volunteer with some of the programs. I'd like to see it."

"Okay, we'll go, but don't get your hopes up that anything is going to get fixed. Now, go to bed. You're a teenager, but you need sleep, and I'm not far behind. I thought Chicago was bad for the middle of the night calls."

"Yeah, and you need to do something about this," She tugged the hair on my chin. "All that gray, you're looking pretty old."

"That's what happens when you're almost fifty with a teenager."

"That was uncalled for." She huffed as she got up. "At least do something with yourself. How do you expect to get a boyfriend looking like that?" she asked as she motioned toward me, and then she was gone.

"I love you, too," I yelled as I collapsed back and finished off my lukewarm beer.

I had to figure out what this antagonism I had for Simon was. The man was gorgeous. He really did look like a model. I knew he was in his early forties. I think his file had said forty-three, but it definitely didn't look like he was. He had that tall, lean frame that spoke of hours working out. Yet, with the schedule he kept, I didn't see him spending much time in a gym.

Okay, he was fucking beautiful, especially with those curls he hid. I just had to make up for my mistake. Even if I was attracted to the odd man, I couldn't take this unwanted development out on him. I didn't have the time or energy for a partner.

I'd thought about finding someone, most single people did, and it would be easy enough to find a hookup to take the edge off. I just didn't think it was in my makeup. I'd happily stayed married to Donna for all our years together, but we'd grown apart during our separations. One of us was always deployed while the other took care of Savannah. We co-parented like a dream team, our divorce had been amicable, and we'd remained friends and teammates through it all. I missed that, the companionship. The easy intimacy. The hours of being together when we had the time for just us.

That's what I wanted back, but I didn't know how to find that again. I wanted permanence and commitment. I was almost fifty and didn't have time for games. At the thought, Simon formed. I snorted at my own stupid thoughts. I'd do well to remind myself to ignore my mid-life crisis and focus on my job and trying to make friends with the impossible man.

5

GRAVES

COLD CASE
UNIT

I patted Aria through the sari wrapped tight around me,
holding her securely to my chest. Before I headed to dinner, I
was checking in at my office. I was the programs director on a
volunteer basis. It wasn't like I needed to sleep or anything, but
Boss had asked me to join the Outreach board along with him,
Remy, and Doc. I liked it, and it made me feel useful—like I was
doing something good with my life.

"Graves, rescue mission." An amused voice yelled from the
daycare area, and I groaned. I left my office and walked down the
hallway to find Claudia grinning at me.

"Why me?"

"Because you and Doc are the only ones who can talk her out."

"Amber?"

"Yes, she tried to be brave again and froze midway. She only
has like four feet to crawl before the first exit. You know she'd
have a meltdown if we went. So go." She crossed her arms over
her chest and nodded toward the maze of tunnels secured to the
walls and with steel supports.

"Fine." I debated removing Aria from my chest, but she was
sleeping, and I hadn't arranged for her bottle to be warmed yet.

Hearing her cry killed me. I crossed the room and stepped into the ball bit that we sanitized and refilled every hour. They were germ factories, but the kids liked them.

I knelt down, took a deep breath, and entered the tunnel of doom. I knew the exact spot she always froze. And I couldn't help but smile as I caught sight of the three-year-old curled into a ball.

"Hey, sweetie, tried to be brave again?" I asked as I reached her and twisted onto my side.

"I was doing it."

"I know you were, and I'm so proud of you for being so brave and trying. But it's almost dinner time, and Mrs. Janice will be looking for you." Her foster mom was a great woman but was overwhelmed with settling twins. They were working on getting a better schedule.

"I can do it."

"I know you can, but would it make you feel better if I held your hand as you did? Baby Aria is going to want her dinner soon, too." She nodded. "No, you have to say I can. But if you don't want me to touch you, what do you say?"

"No."

"That's right, and no always means no." The Outreach taught consent and anatomical names for their body parts. It was safest for the children when no cute names were used, and their personal space was respected. The establishing boundaries were an important part of our childcare programs.

She nodded and held out her hand, asking me to hold it, and she moved to her knees. The trip was awkward, but we finally made it to the exit. And as I waited for her to go down the slide, I realized the indignity I was about to face. I flipped to my back and went headfirst into the ball pit. When I looked up, Amber was standing over me, grinning.

"Thank you."

"You're welcome. Now go find Mrs. Janice so you can have

dinner before going home." She nodded and took off running, and then my life descended into hell.

"Now, I show up, and what do I see, but Graves playing in the tunnels."

"I was on a rescue mission, Douglas. It was important work." A girlish giggle came from my left, and I turned my head to find a young teenager watching us. Great. I went back to glaring at Douglas. "Are you stalking me?"

"No. My daughter wants to meet the man who can stand up to me. Do you need help? Seems you have precious cargo."

"Yeah, thanks." He bent and grabbed my wrist, pulling me easily to my feet, and I instantly released his hand. "Amber tries to be brave and go through the tunnels alone. She always freezes at the same spot. Doc and I are the only ones she allows to get her out, and we respect our children's consent." I patted Aria as she shifted. She was a little over one, but Saffy still nursed and used an attachment parenting method. That meant being close to someone made Aria feel safer, and Major letting me babysit outside the apartment was still new.

He gave me an odd look and then motioned the girl over. "This is Savannah. She was curious about you and the Outreach."

"First timer, both of you. You want a tour?"

"That would be great." She seemed excited, and I promised myself to keep my snark to a minimum. It wasn't her fault I didn't like her father, and she seemed genuinely interested in our place.

"Okay, let's go to my office for Aria's diaper bag and then we'll start the tour and end it in the cafeteria."

"Your office?" Douglas asked behind me as they followed me down the hallway.

"Yes, I'm the programs director for daycare and afterschool, the support groups, and for our community closet. I'm one of the board members for the Outreach. This is where I spend all my time if I'm not in the dungeon." I picked up the bag and turned to find Douglas staring at the pictures on the wall.

"You smile." He grunted as Savannah elbowed him in the side.

"On occasion. Let's get to that tour. I didn't see what the menu was for tonight, but they always work hard on it."

I gave them the usual tour we used for donors, starting with the afterschool area with couches and games. On the opposite wall of the remodeled warehouse was a line of rooms for our groups and classes.

"So, you do support groups, too?"

"Yes. We have alcohol and drug recovery groups two times a week after nine so they're not here when the children are. The chain-smoking outside the exit alone is enough to choke you. We also do childcare for expecting and new parents, sexual health, and other support groups such as grief and chronic pain."

"What are those rooms?" Savannah asked.

"Those are our laundry that's free to use, and the door beside it is our community closet. Anyone can come here during any working hours to wash clothes or to find a new outfit, but we offer vouchers for interview clothes through a few partner businesses if needed."

I showed off our training areas for getting certified in a trade and answered questions. I grinned at Savannah because she was constantly asking them after each area. Douglas trailed behind as she stuck close to my side. I loved how impressed she seemed by everything. Teenagers weren't usually this happy to get pretty much what we considered the selling pitch.

"And this is where most of the action happens. We have a community grocery store that our Kitchen Manager Bart keeps stocked. It helps stretch assistance and benefits." I pushed open the door into utter chaos, but it was controlled. Bart ran the kitchen like the drill sergeant he used to be.

"Bart, what's good tonight?" The local culinary school had

people volunteer every Saturday for credit and work experience before graduating.

"Everything. They sent their best tonight." He said that about them all, but he was rarely wrong.

"This is Savannah and her dad, Detective Douglas. I'm giving them the gold star tour."

"You're the best at them, honey."

"Marcel," Douglas corrected, and Bart held up his gloved hands when Douglas offered his hand for a shake.

"Nice to meet you both. Honey, sit in Olive's section, please. It's her first night, and so nervous she's barely holding up."

"I'll take care of it." On the way out of the kitchen, I checked Olive's assigned area on the schedule.

I motioned them to follow and into the massive cafeteria that was set up as a restaurant dining room. I went through the tables to the smaller section in the back that they saved for training waitstaff.

"Since you're here, you can have dinner." I took a seat, making sure Aria wasn't too close to the table. I set her bag in the chair beside me, and they sat across from me.

"And you work as a detective and do this full-time?" Savannah asked, and I noticed Douglas was still studying me.

"Most of the time, in the last few years, this place has expanded so much that Boss couldn't do it on his own. Remy and Doc were always on the board, but I asked Boss if there was anything I could do. We split the programs about sixty-forty. Volunteers help with our overhead and let us stretch our money further."

"Good even, evening." Bart wasn't exaggerating—she was about to pass out.

"Olive, love, look at me." I waited and held out my hand. "May I?" She took it. "You're doing an amazing job. It's your first night, and you have the script, a few more Saturdays, and you'll be a pro." She nodded. "No, Olive, repeat it for me."

"A few more weeks, I'll be a pro."

"That's perfect. Now, all you have to do is hand us the menus and read the script."

Olive passed out the menus with a smile that was a little forced, but that was okay. "Good evening, I'm Olive. I'll be your server tonight. May I start you off with drinks?"

"Savannah, something to drink?"

"Sweet tea." I ordered the same, and Douglas ordered a soda.

"I'll be right back with your drinks and to get your order."

"You've got this, Olive."

"Thanks, Simon." She grabbed my hand for another squeeze and walked away.

"Training?" Douglas asked.

"Yeah. We open up our cafeteria every Saturday night as a full-service sober restaurant. People who work get paid minimum wage, and when they apply for jobs, they have work experience to put on the applications. A lot of jobs with livable pay don't usually hire someone with no experience or address. So, we also run training from kitchen staff to computers, and we have a fully running mailroom."

"There's no prices." Savannah commented without looking up from the menu.

"People pay what they can. Don't have any money? Free meal. For me, I estimate what I'd normally spend and pay that, plus a tip to whatever server. Mainly Bart tells me who's new, and I sit in their section to give them a great first night experience."

"All free?" Savannah huh'ed, and I nodded.

"Yes, people can come in, use our shower facilities, community closet if they need or want to and then have a real sit-down meal with respect. The kitchen is all volunteer-run, but we also have spots open for job training. They can learn free of charge in exchange for volunteer hours. So, what do you think, Savannah?"

"I like it. Some of my friends have parents who donate or volunteer."

"Don't mention names because I probably won't know. I don't work with the public a lot, but since everyone around here considers me the normal pain in the ass, I get stuck with the tours. I don't have tattoos or any extra holes in my face. Only one chance to make a first impression."

Olive made it through dropping off drinks, taking orders, and seemed a little more relaxed.

"Could you have Bart break out one of the bottle warmers for me?"

"Give me Aria's bottle. Bart already has one set up for her." I pulled out the bottle Saffy packed for me and handed it over. "He's preheating."

"Thanks." I smiled at Olive, and then she walked away from the table. I brought my attention back to my unexpected dinner companions.

"You're your own community." Douglas looked at me.

"Pretty much. We're pretty self-contained in our three warehouses. It's not perfect, but we've learned to work together. I'm not going to say we don't get trouble on occasion. What we do here threatens the status quo."

"Everyone seems to be doing a great job."

I loved how Savannah seemed to get more impressed by the minute. I took pride in the Outreach. Sometimes with my job I felt like a failure when I couldn't solve a case. Yet I could come to the Outreach and see what all of us accomplished together—as a community.

"Thank you. We try."

Douglas seemed about to talk when I had chubby arms wrapped as far around me as they would go.

"Amber, where's Mrs. Janice?" She shrugged.

"Wanna eat with you."

"Did you ask, or did you just run?"

"Amber, you can't run off like that. Simon, I should've known." Janice had a baby on each hip, and who knows what smeared over their faces.

"Hey, Janice, you have your hands full. If you don't mind, she can sit with me. We'll come get her plate. Excuse me." I stood. "May I hold your hand?"

"No means no?"

"That's right." She took my offered hand, and we followed Janice to get Amber's plate.

"I'm sorry she interrupted your dinner."

"No interruption, and you could use a little help. When you're ready to go, you can come get her."

"Thank you, Simon. I'll get used to twins soon. Dan covered an evening shift, and he's a lot of help when he's home."

"It's fine, just breathe, me and Amber will be just fine." I picked up her plate of chicken nuggets and fries and led her back to the table.

Once again, Douglas was studying me like I was a piece of evidence that didn't fit with the rest. I didn't share this side of my life with anyone but my friends and the people I met at the Outreach. At work, I was the perfectionist, the kid of the District Attorney and State's Attorney. But here I could play with the kids and interact with everyone without the expectation of me being one thing. It was like when I decided to stop buzzing my head and let the curls do what they wanted. Jeans and t-shirts instead of the suits that I'd normally worn in the past.

"It seems we have another guest for dinner."

Douglas stood and went to help get Amber seated, and as he went to pick her up, she held out her hand and said no.

"We don't pick up or touch without consent here. You must ask, and if she still says no, we respect her decision. Gentle parenting-childcare and consent is one of our standing rules."

"I'm very sorry, Amber. I'm Marcel. May I help you into your chair?"

She looked at me for help. "It's your choice."

"Okay, but only lift." He lifted her as I placed her plate on the table.

The rest of the evening went along with polite conversation between Douglas and me, friendlier talks with Savannah, and taking care of Aria and Amber. I was relaxed by the time we parted ways outside the Outreach, and he and his daughter went in the opposite direction than me. I didn't see us being friends, but it would be okay. I had enough people anyway, but him aggravating me less would be nice.

6

DOUGLAS

COLD CASE
UNIT

Monday morning, I strolled into Homicide with a travel mug of coffee and an actual full nights' sleep. That hadn't happened in months. I'd even had the energy to take Savannah out to spend time with her. She was too used to a military officer and cop's schedule to be phased by much. Her friend group even allowed her to spend nights at their place if I said it was going to be an all-nighter, and she didn't want to stay home alone. The neighbor across the hall was nice enough to check in and keep an eye on my daughter when I couldn't.

I'd kind of thought the weekend would help me figure shit out, but I was even more confused when it came to Graves than I was before. Savannah liked him, and I had to keep reminding her the grumpy man wasn't a potential boyfriend for me that she could torture. She pouted and told me I wasn't fun and disappeared to her room.

I couldn't quite get the two sides of Graves to mesh. The way he was at the Outreach, with Olive and Amber. I hadn't expected to show up and be led to the daycare to find him coming down a slide into a moat of colorful plastic balls with a baby strapped to his chest. Although, I'd admitted to myself that it was cute, even when he glared up at me as he waited for me to be snarky.

His voice had carried through the tunnel, and he'd been gentle and nice. He'd focused on Aria and Savannah during the tour, never getting frustrated with all my daughter's questions. The program he and his friends ran was at a scale not even the bigger cities had. As we'd sat down to dinner, I'd studied the room. People of every kind were seated at the tables. A homeless person who got the same attention and service as we had. I'd even seen Olive try to give back a quarter a man left as a tip, but he refused.

I'd tried all day Sunday to compartmentalize Detective Graves with Simon, and I couldn't do that.

"Detective, Graves dropped off an envelope on your desk about an hour ago." I nodded at the young detective a few desks over and picked up the manilla envelope in question. I set my mug down and opened the clasp. I pulled out several sheets of paper, and there was a handwritten note on top.

Douglas. Davian's statement. He had a family emergency and called me yesterday. Nothing mind-blowing, but that was kind of a given with what he said at the scene. There's a list of tailors included. Hardleston recognized the stitching and said it could be one of two places that contracts to the same person for alterations. Pictures of the suit are included.

He was doing my job for me. I should have called and yelled at him, but I didn't have the will to do so.

"You hanging out with the fairies in the dungeon now, Douglas?" Stelman was an asshole, and I hadn't liked him from the beginning.

"You're assuming I'm not one of the *fairies*?" I smirked at him as his face turned red, and I didn't miss the gay slur he uttered under his breath as he headed in the opposite direction. I was too damn old for the bullshit. I was an almost fifty-year-old Black, Pansexual man. If they wanted to start shit, they were more than welcome. Yet they had to learn I wouldn't stand by while they did it.

"Douglas," Captain Tyson yelled from his office. The man had one volume, which would put a bullhorn to shame.

I left the information on my desk and made my way to his office.

"You wanted to see me?"

"Yes, close the door behind you."

Closed-door meetings were never good.

"Ignore, Stelman. It's just a matter of time before he loses his teeth or his badge. What do you have on the Bianchi case?"

Just the mention of his name irritated me because he was too close to Graves. I still wasn't over what I'd overheard. "Not much."

"Did Graves talk to him for you?"

"Is it well-known that those two are best friends?" I sat down in one of the chairs in front of his desk and rested my chin on my upraised hand.

"They ran into each other a lot before Graves moved here from the Organized Crime Unit. Graves couldn't be dirty if he tried, and them being friends…we never have issues with Bianchi when he comes up in a case. Bianchi is polite."

"I'm sure the case has something to do with him. He claims he doesn't know the victims. And as much as I don't want to, I believe him. Doc said their fingertips were destroyed, and there were no teeth for dental impressions."

"Professional?"

"That's what I'm thinking, but I have no evidence."

"See if Graves will help you out." Tyson leaned back in his chair.

"I don't think that's a good idea."

"It's no secret you two aren't friends. But if you can seduce one of my best detectives back out of the basement, I'll owe you." The man winked, and I couldn't help laughing.

"I think he loves the basement." Graves seemed so suited for the job, passionate, and I wouldn't try to talk him into coming back.

"Remy took all my best people. Losing them had my solve rate go through the floor in the last year. I don't know what the hell they did, but…" He threw up his hands.

"I know. I went looking through some of their cases. I can't figure out their formula."

"Are you getting the cards yet?" He leaned back heavily in his chair and studied me with way too much amusement.

"Friday night was my first. It was Graves's card."

He chuckled. "Get used to it. Most of my cops are in here on a weekly basis bitching about it, but cooperation is up, especially if one of them is there at the scene. I won't say I agree that a total of four cops, a medical examiner, and an Outreach organizer runs the strip, but it is what it is."

"True. I checked out the set-up of the Outreach Saturday."

"Impressive, isn't it? Crime is down. There's been a decline in drug-related offenses and overdoses. I won't complain about less crime because I have a few do-gooders around."

"True."

"You've been here a while now. How are you settling in?"

"It's definitely different from Chicago, but not a bad thing. I missed my kid living several states away."

"Family is important. Okay, I'll let you get on with your day."

"That's all the talk was about?"

"Yeah. Were you expecting bad news? That happens with the door open. I yell to use you as an example. This was to make Stelman nervous. He's been watching the door since you walked in here. My husband will find this story hilarious when I get home."

"This department is filled with brats."

"We make life interesting. If you need anything, don't hesitate to ask. And as much as people don't like the Cold Case Unit, they're good ones to have on your side. Their combined experience and the respect they have on the streets is priceless."

"Thanks, Captain."

"You're welcome. Graves dropped off a report for you?"

"Yeah, our second victim wore a custom-tailored suit, and he found the name of the tailor who made it. I'm going to go show them pictures and see if they recognize it and know who ordered it. Also, I'm thinking our victim from Friday night might be connected, but I need to talk to Doc and see what he has to say."

"Well, keep me in the loop."

"Will do." I pushed up from the chair and exited his office. I went and grabbed the reports and names of the tailors and figured it would kill a few hours. Also, I needed to get out of the office and not think about Simon. With my coffee and the list in hand, I made my way back out to my vehicle. Luckily, the addresses I needed to go to were nowhere near the strip.

I could do with some distance, especially as my brain slowly started to accept that I was more than a little attracted to Simon. I'd attempted not to voice that or think it, but it wasn't working. Nothing was going to happen. I'd gotten pretty good at reading people in my line of work, and there wasn't an ounce of attraction on his part. I hadn't needed him to say I wouldn't be his type. Hell, he was straight. That should've warned me off right then, yet what had I done? I let my daughter strong arm me into going to the Outreach and see a side of him I couldn't ignore.

"Douglas," Remy yelled, and I turned to find him jogging my way.

"Remy, what's up?"

"Have you seen Graves today?"

"No, he left something on my desk for a case about an hour ago or so, but I didn't see him."

"Weird, he hasn't made it to the dungeon yet, and he's not

answering my calls or texts. If you see him, tell him to get his ass home."

"If I see him."

"Thanks."

"Not a problem."

"Baby, we gotta go," Robert yelled across the parking lot.

I grinned as Remy winked at me. "We've talked about that, Daddy."

"Just get your ass in the damn car. We're going to be late."

"It's a wonder I love him as much as I do." He turned and ran to Robert.

I got in the driver's seat and slammed the door, and before I started the engine, I sent Simon a text to see if he'd answer. I wasn't holding out much hope, but it was odd that he wouldn't make contact. If he hadn't answered by the time I was done with the interviews, I'd check in with Remy and go from there.

7

GRAVES

COLD CASE
UNIT

I didn't know why I did this shit to myself. I'd responded to my parents' less than polite summons for breakfast. I'd had a brief moment where I'd debated ignoring the call, but they'd have threatened me with something I didn't care about. Yet I'd pretend it was important simply to keep the peace. Each visit was the same as the one before.

"We're having a charity event on Saturday, and you're expected to attend." My mother glared at me over the rim of her delicate china cup.

"I have plans that night." I didn't tell them what the plans were but working the Outreach wouldn't exactly be acceptable for missing out on one of their events for the crème de la crème of society. They'd approved when they saw it as a publicity stunt, something for charity, but to lower myself to work there, they'd see it as another slap in their faces from me.

"Your mother didn't ask if you wanted to attend, Simon. You'll be escorting the daughter of one of our friends. You will arrive to pick her up on time and as planned." My father didn't care about anything other than work and appearances.

"Yes, sir, my apologies." I lowered my gaze to my plate with the egg-white omelet, fruit salad, and dry whole-grain toast that I choked down with unsweetened coffee.

"I made an appointment for you tomorrow evening to be fitted for a new suit. Your wardrobe is disgraceful since you started working with those people. You'll need a haircut as well. You will not embarrass us, Simon." My mother barely glanced at me as she warned me that I wouldn't disgrace them in front of their colleagues and friends.

I bit the inside of my cheek and refrained from tucking my curls behind my ears. My parents hadn't had me out of love but to make them look good on Christmas cards and in the papers for charity events. I was a six-two, one-hundred-ninety-pound, Ivy League-educated, handsome prop just like their showpiece of a home and expensive cars. That perfect thing in designer suits they bragged about in public and berated in private. They'd sent me off to live with a distant relative in England before I was shipped off to boarding school. Only summoned home when they deemed my presence worthy of the spotlight.

Mother was fucking her fourth personal trainer in as many years, and he was young enough to be her grandson. My father had no less than two extremely discreet mistresses that would no doubt lose their shine when twenty-five came around. And they pushed a friend or acquaintance's daughter at me at least once a month. They wanted perfect grandchildren to add to the Christmas cards and family values mailers that misrepresented them as the moral majority of the city's political landscape.

I wanted no part in any of that. I just wanted my work and the Outreach, but most people who saw me assumed I was the trust fund kid. And in some ways, I was, but most didn't know a good majority of my trust fund went to the Outreach monthly as an anonymous donor. I personally kept my programs going and a lot of Boss's funded. Yet I didn't want anyone to know, and I sure as hell didn't want the recognition.

"I'll email you the itinerary for the night and the

appointments I arranged. You should take better care of yourself, the wrinkles and the bags. I'll send you the number of my plastic surgeon, some *Botox* won't do much, but it's better than how you look now."

"Yes, Mother." I didn't flinch. I'd learned to avoid them smelling blood in the water when it came to hitting me below the belt long ago. My parents were physically flawless due to their surgeon, who they considered a yearly requirement to freshen things up in the guise of a vacation.

By the time we were done, and Mother handed me the doctor's card, I was just ready to go home and sleep the day away. On my way to my car, I tried to remember the last time I'd slept more than a few hours at a time. And as always, I couldn't remember. I tossed and turned and hoped for the best.

I unplugged my phone from the charger and groaned as it started to ping with missed calls and messages. The last one made me frown. It was from Douglas asking if we could get together to go over the case. Suspicion sitting heavy in my chest at the thought of him wanting to share the case or even ask my opinion. I knew what he felt about my investigative technique. It was probably an empty courtesy, and I wouldn't fall for his games. I'd had enough of that for the day.

Instead of answering him, I replied to Remy and Robert to get them off my back. I snorted as I received a selfie of my friends glaring at me with their heads pressed together. I stowed my phone and turned the key to make my way back to the precinct.

I wouldn't admit it to anyone, let alone my friends, but I was envious. At its core, I didn't comprehend what they had, Remy and Robert, Stevenson and Doc, even Vega and Cash, none of them should work. Although, they did. I saw the love and affection clearly when the couples were together. I wanted that connection but didn't understand or need the physical aspect of their relationships.

For years, I'd witnessed non-kink couples and others in the

lifestyle. I'd studied them and analyzed what made them a unit. There were a few times in my teens and early twenties where I'd asked myself if I just worked hard enough could I like someone like my friends had. The making out and the sex, but both left me cold as I imagined being that casual and vulnerable.

I kept trying to talk my way down from the Asexual label. I'd masturbated, and I liked it, but there were no fantasies. It was just something I did several times a year. I'd watched porn, but nothing. I'd even learned about Demisexuals who had to form an emotional connection with someone. All of it seemed so messy and complicated when I wasn't missing anything by not having sexual relationships. Why torture myself when I wasn't interested?

The thought brought up the arranged date. The last one they'd set up for me had tried to invite me up to her place, and she'd seemed shocked and offended when I'd said no. If I did try to push past the barrier and have sex, it wouldn't be someone I just met, who I barely liked, and I was fine with that.

My phone ringing pulled me out of my thoughts, and I hit the speaker button.

"Graves."

"Can't deign to send me a return message, Simon?"

I'd usually fight him on the use of my first name. I just didn't have the mental energy to deal with him and his refusal to call me Graves.

"I would've if I thought you actually cared about my opinion."

"Do I seem the type to placate you?"

I remained silent as time drew out, and he suddenly laughed, the first time I'd caused that in the asshole of a man.

"Don't be a brat. You know the players in question. I don't. What would be the logical course of action?"

"Fine, what do you want?"

"What about dinner at my place, and we go over the files and some of my theories? I've missed dinner with Savannah too much. You can share a meal, put up with her incessant questions, and then we can work while she hides in her room binging shows probably inappropriate for a thirteen-year-old."

"Free food I don't have to cook? It's tempting. I just ate an egg-white omelet, and I require real food."

"Isn't that something you'd normally eat? Except for your coffee and your diner addiction, you look like a health nut."

"I was made to eat unbuttered toast, Douglas, and fruit salad, feta cheese, and spinach. Make spending time with you worth it."

"My daughter's favorite meatloaf with cheesy mashed potatoes and chocolate cake for dessert."

"Text me an address and time."

"If I'd known food was all I'd need to get you to spend time with me, I would've tried it sooner."

"Smartass, don't make me regret this."

"You're having dinner with a man whose daughter is suddenly determined to get me a boyfriend. Prepare for one helluva pitch."

"I'll set her straight and save your ego."

"Much appreciated. Get to work. You slacked all morning."

"Asshole."

"Such sweet flattery, Simon."

I disconnected the call mid-laugh and made the turn into the parking lot. I didn't want to go back to Homicide, but I wanted in on this damn case, and I'd even deal with Douglas to do that. I put my parents and Saturday night out of my head as I entered the basement entrance with my code. As soon as I was in the office, I threw away the doctor's card. No one was around, so I settled in to get my own work done and to check some ideas I had for Douglas's case. Everything else could wait until the next day.

8

DOUGLAS

COLD CASE
UNIT

Savannah ran around cleaning our place like we never picked up. She'd gone into complete mania as soon as I came home with groceries and told her Simon was coming to dinner. She was too excited.

"He's coming by to work, and I'm making all of us dinner. It's not a date," I yelled from the kitchen as she cursed as I heard what sounded like shoes hitting the back of the closet beside the door. She'd have a panic attack before he even arrived.

I didn't understand why she was so determined Simon and I would make a great couple, but she was on a mission. I checked the meatloaf. I made it almost weekly because it was the first thing that I'd discovered she never complained about eating. Also, the extra cheesy potatoes—there was nothing better than cheese and carbs. At least I didn't have to deal with body image issues with her. She said she liked her food too much, but she was naturally thin because she hadn't hit puberty yet. I was waiting on the pad call, and I wasn't ready.

Everything was done, so I turned down the oven temperature and the burner under the potatoes to low. The cake had cooled, and I'd iced it while everything else cooked. I'd grabbed a bag of frozen peas and figured a few minutes in the microwave, and those would be good. Growing up, my chore was to make dinner for my dad and brothers, and I enjoyed cooking.

In recent years, I'd gotten out of the habit since it was just me. But when I'd moved into the apartment where she'd lived with Donna, I tried to have a home-cooked family dinner at least three nights a week together.

"He's late. What did you do?"

"He's two minutes late," I yelled back at her as she rolled her eyes at me, and then those same green eyes widened as a knock broke into our stare down, and she was gone.

She'd met him once, but she was in love. I had to admit he was an attractive guy, but I tried to ignore that. While she welcomed our guest, I left her to that and dished up dinner in serving bowls. I placed the baking dish in the middle of the table and then washed my hands. I smoothed my freshly trimmed beard and straightened my white button down shirt I wore with jeans.

I didn't get too fancy. I did invite him to go over the case with me, but I did want to make a good impression. I was a sad, middle-aged man, I whispered in my head as Savannah bounced into the room with a smiling Simon behind her. He had on a black, lightweight sweater that was perfect for the cool evenings, the sleeves pushed up his veiny forearms, and jeans that skimmed his leanly muscled legs. The man looked like a damn model, and beside him, I was a big, hulking brute.

"Hey, you're late." I accused, and Savannah, the traitor, mouthed *stop it*.

"Two minutes, Major was at work, Aria had a case of the sniffles, and I dropped medicine off to Saffy."

"That was just an excuse to see your favorite girl." I smirked at his haughty expression.

"I don't have favorites."

"I doubt that. Hope you're hungry."

"I spent my lunch hour in storage at the courthouse trying to find evidence that seems to have been destroyed. The clerk likes me less right now and I fear for my safety."

"That normally comes with a charge of premeditation."

He rolled his bright, emerald eyes at me. "I wouldn't put it past her. In her off time, she wears a lot of leather and has a very sadistic temperament."

"You have some very interesting friends." I grinned as his jaw ticked with his irritation. "What can I get you to drink? I have some beers. We have iced tea and iced coffee, Savannah's drink of choice, or water."

"Iced Tea would be great. I don't drink unless I go out with the crew."

"Have a seat, and I'll pour the drinks."

I caught Savannah showing him to his seat and motioning to it with flair. I glanced at Simon to see him watching her with a sense of indulgence, and they were both charmed by each other. Using my daughter as the peacekeeper apparently wasn't below me.

Once I had the table set with three tall glasses of iced tea, I took my seat. "Don't be shy. My daughter won't be."

And as I spoke, she started to load her plate down, and he rolled his lush lips between his teeth, but it didn't hide his smile. The normally grumpy and disagreeable man didn't fit the one at the Outreach or the one seated at my table. He was a mystery, and I'd always loved those. It was a big reason I'd become a cop when I left the Marines where I'd worked as an MP for most of my duty.

He waited for her to be done, and then I motioned to him to make his own plate. I watched him as I made mine. Studied his expression as he took his first bite, and damn, his eyes closed.

"Satisfactory?"

"I might help you just for the food alone."

"Thanks. If you weren't here to eat, what would you be doing?"

"Outreach to have dinner with some of the regulars or taste-testing something Bart was trying out, and then home." His answer didn't surprise me.

"You spend a lot of time there." He tensed a bit as if he prepared for me to make some sarcastic comment, but I respected his dedication to the Outreach, the people on the strip, and his job.

"I like being there. People have interesting life stories. Expectations are very basic there, respect and trust. You're not judged if you're not wearing the latest designer. Like I said, expectations are normal. What about you?"

"Savannah and I have scheduled sit-down dinners three times a week where I cook. This is one of them. She's a teenager and can't be bothered to stay home with her middle-aged dad on the weekends. So, we plan our quality time during the week."

"Dad's taking me to the boardwalk Friday."

"That's great. I haven't been down there in I don't know how long. I may have been in uniform the last time."

He easily smiled at her, and I couldn't help just taking him in. In our line of work, I relied on body language, and in the months since I was introduced to Detective Simon Graves, this was only the third time I'd seen him relaxed. The night in Bella Notte, at Outreach, and that night. I also remembered the way he'd defended what Carmine called his lowly profession and his tone as he mentioned expectations.

Other than knowing his parents were the city District Attorney and the State's Attorney who was rumored to want to be U.S. Attorney General, both from old money, I didn't know much about his personal life. I'd done my research on Simon when I'd taken over his cases. Seen his evolution from the stiff, grim-faced man in a suit with a buzzed head to the newest incarnation. Beautiful, curly-haired man in a sweater and jeans carrying on a conversation with my kid.

My kid kicked me under the table, and I realized I was staring and had barely touched my plate. I turned my focus back to eating and off Simon.

———

"NIGHT, honey, you go to bed. Your caffeine budget is going over." She gave me a hug and then waved at Simon.

"Goodnight, Savannah."

She made her way down the hall to her room. He lowered to sit on one end of my couch, and I went back to the kitchen to refill our glasses and bring them back out.

"So, what are these great theories?" He was rifling through papers and reorganizing my piles and timeline cards.

"Messing with my stuff now?" I asked as I sat down and put everything back where it was.

"You had it wrong." He stared straight at me as he rearranged them again with a defiant light in his green eyes.

"I don't think so."

"I can go home."

"No, you sat at my table, ate my food...I have bribed well for your time."

"Now, I see, bribery."

"Whatever works. Now show me how that illogical mind of yours processes."

"Fine. A case at its most basic level is a jigsaw puzzle without the box. Abstract pieces that eventually come together, but sometimes you think they fit because they appear to. And then you find a piece way over on the edge of the table, and they suddenly don't. Most criminals aren't logical, not even in the planning stages of a premeditated murder. No one can ever have all the pieces, Douglas."

"Marcel."

"What?" He narrowed his eyes at me.

"We had a friendly dinner with my kid, who I share with

almost no one. Most of the people I worked with didn't even know I had one. I think that warrants the use of my first name, Simon."

He gave me an eye roll before picking up the first image. "Marcel, you can look at this and say this is the exact way it is. Because you'll learn it's not. We had a first body drop, his fingertips burned off and teeth removed, reports show there were tool marks. Doc said, in his opinion, the victim was alive. They were tortured. Intent unknown."

"Did everything line up with the second exactly?" I scooted to the edge of the couch and grabbed the post-mortem report.

"Yes, tool mark evidence said the same pliers were used."

"Why don't I know this?"

"My partner is sleeping with the medical examiner, and I get perks."

"Y'all have a very weird friendship dynamic."

"Weirdness is what we have. My gut says Carmine is the intended target. We can talk to Seamus Finnegan, but I don't think he's in on it."

"Why? Show your work."

"Yes, teacher. Seamus has a very simple principle. This isn't his style. Seamus would make them kneel in front of Carmine and take the shot and then walk away. This isn't his work."

"Then, if we mark Seamus off the list, who's left?" I smiled as he listed names, one after another, without taking a single breath. "Okay, okay, who would you pick?"

"Dekland Mancini. Up and coming, wants to make a name for himself. Getting extremely active since Carmine started taking steps back to focus on his husband and children. Dek is, how should I say this? He's homophobic as fuck. Thinks men like Seamus and Carmine are ruining the image of the Families. Yet he also has an extreme temper, and his men aren't any better. He could be coming into his own, maybe finding a more level-headed partner."

"But I sense you're not sure."

"You see, over the years we've"—he glanced at me, and I arched my brow—"had a cease-fire arranged on the strip. Seamus and Carmine, Mancini very reluctantly, and several other gangs, all agreed that the areas surrounding the Outreach were essentially demilitarized zones. It's a well-kept secret of the truce. Could be one of the gangs lower on the hierarchy have decided to start a war. Yet they just don't know how to do it. What about the suit?"

"Didn't pan out. I know who purchased the suit, but it was arranged by a family who's loved one's last wish was to be buried in a two grand hand-stitched suit. That was about a year, year and a half ago." I didn't trust the slow smirk that lifted one corner of his full lips.

"You're going to love me."

"And why is that?"

"Because the fraud division busted a funeral home selling off clothes, jewelry, and reselling coffins about a year ago."

"I don't love you yet."

"Patience. No wonder you suck at your job."

"That was a low blow, brat."

"Broadus Merryweather. Got caught after an exhumation exposed a pine box instead of the three grand, top of the line coffin the family paid for. District attorney's office threw everything at him since he screwed up a case. They had to let a convicted murderer free since they couldn't prove their case by a reexamination of the body and evidence."

"Still not overwhelmed with love yet."

"The evidence locker has a ledger of all the sales and to whom because Merryweather was one step away from filling a kiddie swimming pool with money and wallowing in it naked."

I returned Simon's bratty smirk and shook my head. "Okay, you may have convinced me, but I have to see the ledger first."

"Suspicious."

"With you, always."

"Ouch, and to think I was nice enough to come here and help you."

"You came here for free food with fat content. It had nothing to do with me. Also, you want in on this case so badly you can taste it."

"Maybe I don't want it at all. Maybe I just want to see you crash and burn."

"You're going to hurt my feelings, Simon."

"I'll need to try harder, Marcel."

I caught his gaze and wouldn't let go, and his phone vibrating on the table broke the moment. And he picked it and groaned.

"Someone showed up with your card again?"

"Yes. Thanks for dinner."

"We can do this some other time. What about Saturday? My kid is abandoning me." He seemed about to agree, and then he grimaced and shook his head.

"No, I have something I can't get out of. We'll arrange something another time." He stood up and headed for the door. I followed and waited as he put on his jacket.

"Be careful, Simon."

"I'll be fine. Some uniforms are hassling one of our kids. I just have to straighten it out. Goodnight, Detective."

"Goodnight, Simon."

"We're not friends. You can call me Graves."

"I don't know about that. You've been almost sweet tonight, Simon. This could work for you."

He opened the door. "Don't get used to it, Marcel. I'm having a weak moment." He backed out and closed the door in my face.

"Such a sad, sad man, Dad." I spun to find her giving me a pitying look that only a teenager could give their poor, pathetic parent. "Not even a goodnight kiss on the cheek, something?"

"This wasn't a date. How many times do I have to tell you that? And aren't you supposed to be in bed...asleep?"

"I was hoping you'd act right, and you'd need to be supervised." She turned and walked down the hall.

I returned to the couch and fell back on it, bringing my hands up to scrub them over my face. There was no way I was meant for this shit. I was a happily single, divorced dad of one pain in the ass kid; I didn't need the complication of an unrequited attraction to Simon Graves. Too old for this shit didn't even come close to it.

9

GRAVES

COLD CASE
UNIT

My face hurt from forcing a smile for hours, and I was beyond done with the woman who'd attached herself to me. I'd finally escaped with the excuse to use the bathroom. Instead, I headed in the opposite direction, and I slipped out onto the back patio off the ballroom. I fell back against the wall in the dark and took deep breaths.

"Don't you look exceptionally handsome, Simon. Should've let the pretty curls free, though."

I groaned. "I didn't think my night could get any worse." I turned my head to look at a smiling Douglas in a tailored suit. His beard was neatly trimmed like the night we'd shared dinner. When he'd suggested we get together Saturday, I nearly said yes until I remembered the date that if I skipped would've subjected me to great censure at Sunday dinner.

"What's wrong? Not having fun?" I studied his face in the dim spotlight, and he didn't appear as if he were making fun of me.

"I hate this. Everything about it." We weren't friends, so I wouldn't go into detail about why I was there or that my attendance was ordered so that I could become their usual prop.

He already had enough ammunition, and I wouldn't give him more.

"That lady has her claws pretty far into your arm. She wouldn't let you go for a second."

"I'm surprised she didn't ask to escort me to the bathroom so she could hold it while I took a piss."

He chuckled as he turned and pressed his shoulder to mine. "I can call in an emergency. It would only take a few minutes. I could even call it over the radio."

"It wouldn't work. The cost of paying for it isn't worth it. What are you doing here?"

"A threat of activists protesting this very pretentious dinner that the money could've been much better used to feed the people the charity is for."

"And I wouldn't disagree."

"They called for volunteers, and since I didn't have anything better to do, here I am."

I wanted to deflect from the shitshow my personal life was, and the best way I saw was to bring up Douglas's daughter. "Did Savannah have fun last night?"

"She had a blast, tried to get me to talk you into coming with us. You have a huge fan in my kid."

"She's amazing. She must take after her mother." I turned away to stare off at the harbor and tried to pretend I wasn't standing outside the ballroom of an event I didn't want to be at. I should've spent that night sitting in the new server's section or whichever one seemed to be having trouble, maybe get to see Aria and Amber. The toddler always loved spending time with me. I closed my eyes, and then I heard Marcel clear his throat, and I jerked my attention back to him.

As he spun to brace his hands on the brick beside my head, I straightened and pressed my back closer to the wall. "What are you doing? You're a forty-three-year-old man, an excellent cop, world-class pain in the ass. And as hot as you are in that suit, it doesn't fit you."

I ignored him calling me hot because I wasn't uninformed that I was attractive. "I'll have you know it's a spectacular fit."

"Brat." There was no censure in his voice, it almost seemed affectionate, but I'd never really been good at gauging those things.

"Were you making a point, Marcel?"

"First name, huh?" I pressed closer to the wall as he leaned in closer.

"Since you're crowding me, Marcel seemed appropriate."

His chuckle was deep and warm, and I could almost say it sounded comforting. "My point is this isn't your scene, and you're missing dinner at the Outreach."

"I know, but it's easier to keep the peace."

"You're not the type to just go with the flow. You don't want to be here, so let me help."

"I just have to make it through a few more hours, and then I can go home."

"Who's going to rescue Amber?" He whispered the question, and I swore he moved deeper into my personal space.

I smiled as I dropped my head forward until my forehead rested on his chin, and then I jerked back at the contact. "Doc will do it. We're the only two who can talk her out."

"Fine, but I'll be close by, just look for me in the crowd, nod, and I'll get you out." He dropped his arms and backed away.

The distance he put between us allowed me to breathe easier. I had to figure out why I allowed him to push into my boundaries. Why my usual caution with letting anyone physically close wasn't there with him. Being around my friends, I had no issues with finding another man attractive. Aesthetically, I could tell if someone was appealing or not, but again I didn't have that urge to approach. Something about Marcel drew me in even as I wanted to knock the smug smile off his face.

"You better get inside before someone comes looking for you."

I groaned, and he laughed at me again, and I eased from between him and the wall. I headed to the far exit so I could sneak in unnoticed.

"Marcel?"

"Yeah?"

"Thanks."

"You're welcome. I'm going to check the perimeter, but then I'll be in. Just one look, and you'll be home in no time. How about I take you out for a greasy burger and fries after you're free? You didn't eat any of the bland-ass dinner they served."

"I'd kill for a burger."

"Not exactly the thing to say to a man who works Homicide."

"You're losing points, Marcel, a lot of them." I couldn't delay my return any longer and slipped through the curtains and went in search of my parents and date.

Decades of pretending to be somewhere I hated made plastering the smile on my face easy. The rest of the evening, during networking and speeches, I unconsciously searched out Douglas. I was surprised he was always close, never out of line of sight with me. He'd arch one of his brows, and I'd shake my head when all I wanted to do was detach my date and go have that meal he offered.

I didn't know what the hell was going on with me. This restlessness began a long time ago. Yet the intensity of it couldn't be ignored. I wanted my second life. If I never walked into my parents' home again, it wouldn't hurt me at all. Actually, my life would be less painful without them in it.

I shouldn't complain. I was a rich man but lived off my own money. My townhouse was my only major expense in the last twenty years. My parents' mental and emotional abuse didn't compare to what Remy had gone through or the countless other people I'd met. Remy would tell me not to compare my pain to another's, that neglect could be just as traumatizing. The pain we felt was based on experiences.

My date—I couldn't even remember her name, and she'd just been *the date* since I picked her up—dragged me off to talk with her friends. I only went along because it took me in the opposite direction of the District Attorney and State's Attorney.

"Simon, what is it you do?" A Ken Doll whose name I didn't bother remembering either asked.

"I'm a detective with the Cold Case Unit. Before that, I worked Homicide and Organized Crime." The corners of my mouth twitched as the men snarled, not finding me working in a more respectable occupation like finance or some other profession good enough while the women seemed more interested. Badges were like magnets sometimes.

"Didn't you work that serial killer case? The one who killed those prostitutes?"

"Yes, and they were underaged boys, and the term would be sex workers, *Chad*." I heard a snort close by and didn't bother turning to see where Marcel was roaming.

"Charles." The douche corrected me like I gave a shit.

"What are you working on now?"

"I can't discuss active investigations. It compromises the case."

And so it went, so on and so forth until I was about to pull my hair out. But finally, it was time to leave. While my date used the little girl's room, and those were her words, I stood in the foyer with her wrap.

"I don't think you made friends with *Chad*. Call me after you drop her off and tell me where you want to go. I'll ditch as soon as you're clear." He told me and then walked off before I had time to reply. Her place was only fifteen minutes away, five minutes to hopefully politely tell her that I wouldn't be coming up, and then freedom. I could last that long, or I fucking hoped.

10

DOUGLAS

COLD CASE
UNIT

"You don't look right." I growled as I stretched my arm out to free his curls of their product prison, and he batted my hand away as he tried to take a bite of his burger that he dipped in barbecue sauce. I'd arrived at the same diner we came to that night of the second body dump, and Mama Sue had snarled at me again. Him, well, the perfect Simon got love and hugs, and I pretended not to be slightly jealous when he tucked his face against her neck. All his stress had visibly disappeared and I wanted to be his safe place. Yet that was too much to ask of the man who saw me as only an acquaintance and an annoying one at that.

"I should start shaving it again."

"That would be a crime. So, tell me the real reason you were at the charity event."

He sighed as he shoved a few fries in his mouth. "My parents ordered me to attend and escort the daughter of the man they probably want votes or promises from."

"Whoring you out for the political cause." I tried to joke to get rid of his frown. I'd gotten addicted to his small smiles.

"Story of my life." I frowned at his harsh laugh. "What about you, Marcel? Why here?"

"That's a long story."

"I got time."

"I met Donna, my ex-wife, just out of boot camp. We had similar backgrounds, single dads, all brothers, the military for her was a family tradition. Me, not even close. Growing up, I knew I'd end up at my dad's construction company, but senior year I ran into a recruiter. Enlisted and shipped off a month after I graduated. I disappointed the old man with that one. He wanted me to start right up with the company full-time."

I loved my family, my dad and brothers were all I had growing up, and my mom's death screwed my dad up so badly that he never let a woman close again. He'd thrown himself into his work, and in the process, made working for the company a requirement from the time I was fifteen with clean up and training. I hadn't minded all that, but my brothers were just like him, and I wasn't. Escaping had been my only goal.

"Can't see you as a construction worker, but okay."

"Brat. As I was saying, Donna and I were both nineteen and hot-headed. We got married right before I shipped off to Iraq. We spent so many years of our marriage separated, and we didn't see any problem with that. She was on her way to command, and I was just fine working as an MP. When I returned to the States, for the first time in probably our entire marriage, Donna and I were in the same place for an extended period of time."

"Got sick of you, didn't she?"

"God, you're just lovely tonight." I glared as he smirked. "No, she got sick. We both freaked out. She was losing weight, so we made an appointment, and when we went, surprise, at thirty-five and after sixteen years of marriage, we were going to have a kid. It was one of the things we'd agreed on. Neither of us wanted kids. But when we found out she was coming, we were ecstatic."

"That must have been a shock, but you did pretty good with that one."

"We did. She's the perfect blend of both of us, but we have no idea where she got her attitude from." He snorted and added more ketchup to his already drowning fries. Only sociopaths didn't dip. "As always, Donna and I were the perfect team. But three years after Savannah was born, I retired with my twenty and became a full-time dad, joined the police force, but as much as I loved my wife...ex-wife, it wasn't the same. We're still the dream team, co-parenting skills are gold medal-worthy, we agreed on a friendly divorce. A year later, she was transferred, and Savannah went with her. I turned into the summer and shared holiday parent, and I hated it." He focused on me as I spoke, nodded as he ate, and not one snarky comment slipped from his lips. It had to be a record. "A few years ago, I got a call. Donna was headed to Japan. It was her dream position, but our daughter had friends she didn't want to leave. A year out from high school. She was getting to that age where she didn't want to be dragged all over the world. So I put in a transfer, sold my house, and moved here."

"Big change, Chicago to here."

"It was. But I hadn't seen Savannah since the summer before except for video chats, and I show up, and my baby is grown. She's wearing makeup. She has a bra. I was traumatized." I grinned as he nearly choked on the bite of his burger he'd just taken.

"She's a good kid. She knows she's loved."

"We didn't do too badly. What about you?"

"Long story."

"Like you said, we got time."

"I was political capital. My parents' political leanings are right-wing, but they hide how vehemently they detest people who aren't like them. Shows bias, and they have approval ratings. Mother wants to be U.S. Attorney General. Their marriage was more like a business agreement. Both were from old money, founding families of the original town."

"They're always on the news. Weird to have them as parents, especially with the job you chose?"

"They hate it with a passion, which is weird because they're as cold as can be. Especially since their Harvard educated son shit on his law degree to do this."

"Law degree? You're a lawyer?" I pretended to be shocked, but with his mind and the way he loved to argue, it would've probably suited him more than being a cop.

"Didn't get my license to practice. Instead, I took that nice piece of parchment and applied to the police academy almost immediately." He finished off his food and pushed his plate aside. "I was raised by nannies until I was five, and they shipped me off."

"Where?"

"England, to an old family friend. And a year later, I was accepted to a prestigious and pretentious English boarding school. I was there until I was eighteen. I applied to Oxford just so I wouldn't have to come home, but Harvard or nothing."

"You're such the stereotype for the poor rich boy."

"Hey, I didn't like it. The only times I was allowed home was when they needed my face on campaign literature or to parade me around in front of cameras. Perfection is a painful trap."

It suddenly all made sense. "Is that what happened tonight?"

"My parents think it's past time that I marry and add perfect grandchildren to the photo ops. It's a nasty eugenics project. They're throwing the most supposedly genetically superior women at me."

"Aren't you interested?" I didn't know why, but I held my breath waiting for his answer. There was a lead weight in the pit of my stomach.

"No, not that I wouldn't be, but it's hard to explain."

"Expectations? You mentioned it before."

"I was born with expectations. There was this list, a timeline of when and how to make these accomplishments."

"Nothing happens on a timeline, baby, nothing."

"Graves, Simon, and now, baby?"

"I do what I want."

"I've kinda noticed that." He called Mama Sue over as I finished off my meal, and he ordered three different desserts.

She took the plates and said she'd be right back. "What's the deal with Mama Sue?"

"Her son was a cop back in the early eighties, killed in the line of duty. She adopts any of us that come in. He was gay, and his boyfriend at the time was all she had left. When he died, the boyfriend crumbled and went home, married his high school girlfriend, and had kids. Left her alone, so she takes care of us. She told me one night that I reminded her of him. She showed me a picture, and that man was a beast with a good fifty pounds on me and gorgeous, but she said we had the same temperament."

When she returned with the desserts, she placed all three in front of him and leaned down to kiss the top of his head. For a split second, I saw the longing and hurt, as if that simple affection gave him something he'd never had. And from what he'd told me, he probably hadn't.

"You going to share?"

"Should've ordered your own, Douglas." Even as he snarked at me, he pushed the plates to the center of the table. Friends, I could deal with just friends.

———

HOURS LATER, and probably another sleepless night, I laid in my bed staring at the ceiling. I couldn't get that night out of my head. I'd walked the edges of the ballroom, bored out of my mind, and then I'd spotted him. Simon was gorgeous in his suit and perfectly styled hair, but I knew what it looked like when the thick waves were set free. Anyone else probably wouldn't notice, but he'd barely concealed those eye rolls of his as he interacted with his parents, date, and anyone else he was forced to talk to.

My guilty pleasure of the night was when I'd trapped him between my larger frame and the wall. His head had fallen forward, and his hair had brushed my lips. The strands were silky, and until he'd pulled away, I'd almost rested my forehead on the top of his hair just to memorize the texture. He hadn't worn cologne, but whatever shampoo or body wash he used smelled so good, and I'd wanted more of him.

My impulsive invite for dinner slipped out, and I was shocked he'd accepted. In that diner on the strip, something about that area made him freer. All the tension he naturally carried disappeared when he crossed into the neighborhood.

I spread out my hand on my chest and stroked downward over the hard curve of my stomach. How long had it been since I wanted like this? I combed through the tight curls at the base of my cock and then ran my fingertips along the length where it rested to the left. My back arched slightly. I bet Simon would let me love on him, slow and gentle for hours.

I didn't miss orgasms. I could get those fine on my own, but I missed the warmth of someone in bed with me. Physical and emotional intimacy. Simon was touch starved. I could see it—feel it in my gut. And he'd be terrified or pissed off, maybe both, if he knew how badly I wanted to touch and kiss him. I moved my hand away from my dick. I wanted to savor the need and my partial erection.

Getting off was never my main goal when it came to sex. That release was fleeting at best, but the buildup, praising your lover... that was the best part. I swore I knew he'd be beautiful held on the edge. No more in a hurry than me to get it over with.

Donna and I had a great sex life, but there were things I loved that she hadn't. We'd compromised, but I still craved what I'd never had. I'd laid in my bed edging myself, chest heaving with the need to take a breath, but stopping right before I shot over my stomach. I'd do it for days until I ached enough that I'd firm my stroke until I bit the inside of my cheek to keep my shout hidden.

My dad, my brothers, and friends I had, I never understood when they talked about sex and quickies or rough sex. It wasn't my thing. How could that be more than momentarily satisfying? Pound one out, come, and then roll over and go to sleep. Where was the fun in that?

Through all the conversations and their so-called bragging, I'd just nod and feel sorry for their bed partners. No wonder my sisters-in-law were cranky all the damn time. I called Simon a brat but had no urge to be a Daddy. I didn't want to discipline or instruct someone, so being a Dominant wasn't my thing. I wasn't averse to playing in the bedroom, catering to my partner's needs, but all I wanted was a person who would understand that no matter what I looked like, all six-six and two-hundred-seventy pounds of me was just a man who wanted to cuddle and be gentle.

The dichotomy wasn't lost on me. I was a hard-assed retired Marine turned Homicide Detective. Most people wouldn't look at me and say that's a man who's affectionate with a kink for making love for hours without getting off, but I didn't care what people thought.

When I left work behind, I didn't want to pretend to be something I wasn't, especially when I came home to a partner and my kid. I wanted a relationship and everything that entailed, but I was almost fifty with a demanding job. I had no desire to date when I knew it wouldn't go anywhere. If someone had told me at sixteen that I was going to be a man who didn't think orgasms were that great, I'd have laughed in their faces.

My dad and brothers were all for pushing me to meet someone, the Pansexual thing wasn't fully acceptable to them, but they also hadn't disowned me for it. Me and my kid didn't fit with them, and they never really liked Donna. I snorted as I imagined if I ever brought someone like Simon, or actually Simon home for that matter. Model beautiful, white boy with a snarky attitude, they'd hate him, but Savannah would threaten them for even thinking anything bad about her newest favorite person.

I let out a rough, heavy sigh and didn't even know why I was thinking about Simon and my family. The man had made it clear that he was straight and not interested. I really needed to get that through my head. I wouldn't break my heart on him, and I thought that was going to be the hardest promise I ever had to keep.

11

GRAVES

COLD CASE
UNIT

"No more, no more," I threw myself to the floor and held my hands out in a stop motion. I was tired, I needed about weeks' worth of sleep, and it wasn't happening. I'd taken everything, herbal, nighttime meds, and nothing kept me passed out longer than my normal two hours. At this point, I wouldn't be surprised if I wasn't living in some deranged hallucination because Douglas was being downright nice and polite, and it wasn't normal.

"Is this one of your investigative techniques that you've failed to mention?" He smirked at me from where he'd taken a seat on my desk. For a homicide cop with his own spacious squad room, he was spending way too much time in the dungeon with us again.

"No, I'm having a moment."

"Did you break him, Douglas?"

Stevenson strolled in with Doc attached to his back, and it wasn't even strange. Stevenson's baby's feet rarely touched the ground. It was disturbingly sweet. That proved it. I need someone to knock me out. Some to force me into that sweet oblivion so I could at least get a nap.

"I don't think so, but he does appear to be having a tantrum."

"I'm not having a tantrum. I'm simply lying here to have a moment to think. A moment of reflection about what mistakes I made to get me here. Shush." I loudly quieted them and closed my eyes. How long could a relatively healthy forty-three-year-old man survive with little to no sleep? I think it was four years so far, but I didn't hold out much hope for my continued existence.

"Vega used her facial recognition software she coded on your victims. Told the higher-ups she needed to do a test run." Doc spoke up, but I didn't open my eyes. "She got hits on all three."

With that, my eyes flew open. "Who?"

"Vic one, Graham Shaughnessy. Vic two, Boyd Harker. Vic three, Nash Staitland. All low-level criminals with no violent offenses or connections to any gangs in the city." Stevenson pulled files out of his backpack and handed them to Douglas, and then lifted Doc onto his desk. He sat down and then scooted close until he could hug Doc's waist.

"Why try to disguise their identity by burning off their fingertips and pulling their teeth?" Seemed a bit overboard when they're not players.

"No connection doesn't mean there isn't one. You still thinking someone's trying to move in and start a war?" Douglas asked as he scanned the pages in the folders.

"I wouldn't be surprised. I mean, they can move into power in the ensuing chaos. How do you do a hostile takeover?"

"Several ways, but one is infiltration. Send someone in. They collect intel without you exposing yourself. Maybe the main player took them as a liability after they got what he needed." Douglas set the files aside and stretched out his neck and shoulders. I grimaced, hearing a loud crack.

"*He*, very sexist of you." I pointed out.

"Ha-ha, brat."

"Okay, say that they dressed the second guy up in the

expensive suit, sent him into mix with Carmine's people. Form some connections, but I don't get why they're only getting dumped at Carmine's place." Stevenson piped up, and that's the question that bothered me the most. It didn't make sense.

"What about our main player wanting to bring the heat down on Carmine? Keep him occupied and under suspicion. He's the Alpha around here. His family's been running things around here since the nineteen-twenties," Doc said as he laid his cheek on top of Stevenson's head. You needed a damn crowbar to get those two apart.

"True. Carmine is too careful. No one would believe he'd be careless enough to drop bodies behind his club. It does bring down the heat on him, though. Think about it. We're in and out of there, talking to him. We've upped patrols in that area. That's why the third body confuses me." I ran all the scenarios through my head, and every time I got to victim three, my brain froze.

"He'd already had the damage done. The torture had run its course. What's in that area that would make it a good dumping ground?"

My brain kept formulating theory after theory which went nowhere fast. "Not much, Douglas, warehouse space. Since the drop in crime in that area, they've started a revitalization program to bring business in. Converting warehouse space into offices and artist collectives. Gentrification, my good man, it's all bollocks."

"Your UK upbringing is coming out." Douglas chuckled, and I rolled my eyes.

I stretched my arms above my head and arched. I needed to take a run or something. Every muscle in my body was tight to the point of snapping.

"We have gangs and crime families losing territory. Carmine deals in more refined clientele so it wouldn't affect him all that much. Just more people to come to his clubs and his underground gaming puts more money in his pocket. Seamus owns a pub and runs a nice stable of sex workers. No drugs, though. His sister overdosed when he was in his teens so that's not his game. Dekland, that bastard would do just about anything. He'd feel threatened, but he'd also try to integrate. He's extremely money motivated. The guys that run the strip clubs and escort services would relish the influx of higher-paying clients."

"I don't think we're dealing with an up-and-coming mob boss. It's something else. Whoever *they* are, they're going through a lot of effort. Three men, tortured then murdered, dumped in the area around Bella Notte. It's a smokescreen, but why? That's the big question, and we're no closer to knowing."

"Throwing knives, some of them have to stick. Doc, how long do you think our victims were tortured?"

"A few hours to forty-eight hours, bruising would be indicative of an extended period of sustained damage as there were several overlapping bruises of different time frames. There was blood inside the clothes, so they were dressed afterward. I found restraint marks, probably rope. I sent all the fibers and hairs not consistent with our victims to trace. Your guess is as good as mine as to when they'll get attention. They're backlogged with Coleman using the lab only for the newer cases. He thinks resources are wasted on the cold cases. Carmine is involved, so you may get lucky."

"I need coffee." I grunted as I sat up and got to my feet.

"I'll walk with you." Douglas slipped off the desk, and we exited, leaving the moaning behind us. "Do they ever separate?" he asked with a cheerful laugh.

"No, they really don't. It's the same with Remy and Robert, and Vega and Cash." I exited the basement door and started the walk around the building. "It's nice, ya know, you don't have to assume if they're a loving couple. Most of my life, it was all about partnerships because someone had something you needed."

"Not the same for me. My brothers love their wives, but they've been together so long they don't put the effort in anymore. We all married early, seems to be a Douglas gene. I was still the youngest to get married at nineteen, though. Um, I wanted to talk to you about something."

"Sure."

"Savannah."

"What's she up to? Still playing matchmaker?"

"Of course, she never stops, and she's recruited Donna. So now I'm getting it from both the ladies in my life. No, Savannah wanted to see about volunteering after school and on weekends with you. She didn't know if she'd be able to because of her age."

"We have programs she could help with. It's not like she'll be working for a wage. There's no labor laws to worry about. We could always use the help. Why don't I pick her up tomorrow? I have some paperwork waiting for me on my desk, and we'll go through our programs and see what she's interested in doing."

"That's great, thanks. I'll give you her number so you can text her when you're on your way or with a time to be ready."

"She really is a great kid, Marcel."

"She is. I worry, though," he said as we turned the corner to the courtyard that separated us from caffeine.

"Why?"

"She's so grown up. I want her to be a regular teenager. Break curfew. Yell at us. Rebel. We've never had any of that from her. I mean, we're not very strict parents to begin with. We don't worry about bedtimes for the most part. It teaches consequences when she has to get up early for school after staying up most of the night. We don't police what she says, watches, or believes as long as it doesn't hurt anyone or break the law."

I couldn't help my sudden laugh. "You gave her nothing to rebel against. She has absolutely nothing to do to scream *damn the man*. Make some rules…she'll hate you in no time."

I stepped up to the coffee truck and ordered my usual, added a large, black coffee for Douglas. I owed him one since he bought one for me the other day. I was excited to spend time with his daughter and humbled that he'd trust me with her. Who knows, maybe I could do this *friends thing* after all.

DOUGLAS

COLD CASE
UNIT

Everything seemed to be going good with Simon and myself, I'd almost call us friends, but I'd definitely moved up from acquaintance. We'd put in a lot of hours during the evenings over the past few weeks, some at my place and others at the Outreach while he took care of work, and Savannah jumped around programs as she looked for the right fit.

This was the first night that we weren't getting together, but he said he had plans that he couldn't get out of. I'd asked, but he wouldn't say. Savannah was spending the whole weekend with her best friends. I didn't know what to do with myself, so I'd called Remy.

I knocked on the door and waited for him to answer. A dog barked inside, and there were loud giggles and then footsteps. I'd only met Roo, their daughter, on a few occasions, and she was scary for only being seven. Her personality was very much Remy. The door opened.

"Hey, come on in, we're just getting through the chaos of bath time."

"I remember those days. They'll play for hours once in, but until you can talk them into getting in the rub, it's like arguing with a mini defense attorney." I stepped inside and closed the door behind me. I didn't know why I'd called Remy to see what they were up to, but there had to be a reason my brain made me pick up my phone.

"You got it in one. Robert is taking care of it. She handles his calm presence better than mine. I'd let her run around until she was dizzy. He gets to be the bad parent. The thing is, we're working on showers instead of baths now, and she's not at all happy with us." I followed him to the back of the house and into a large kitchen. "Coffee, water, I have some beer."

"A beer would be great." I watched as he opened the fridge. "You have a nice home."

"It was Robert's, and when he asked where I wanted to live when I moved in with him, I said here. So, what brings you to me?" he asked as he set down the unopened beer. I noticed the change in him, it was subtle, but he went from his usually bratty self to straightening his shoulders, holding his head higher, even his voice changed. His tone was calming, and I could see his training as a psychologist coming through.

"I don't know. Simon had plans." I opened my beer and took a big swallow as I dragged the top around with my index finger.

"Simon, I still can't get over him letting you call him that."

"I didn't give him much of a choice, and it annoys him so that's a definite perk. Also, my daughter, Savannah, is spending the weekend with her best friends and abandoned me."

"How old? I don't think you mentioned a daughter before."

"She's thirteen. Normally I don't share that I have a kid since I go up against some dangerous people."

"Understandable. Still doesn't tell me why you're suddenly besties with the unit you thought did shoddy work. Even though you did butt in during the Gerrrickson case."

I chuckled at his bratty smirk. "My daughter has pointed it out more than once, I'm a perfectionist asshole. I just don't understand your investigative process even though it works. It drives me insane."

"We care."

"What?"

"We care about every case. There's a lot of good cops, don't get me wrong, I've met them, and they do this job with compassion and respect. Yet, there's a lot of rotten apples, too. Graves joining us was a bit of a surprise."

"In what way?"

"He's a perfectionist asshole." I nearly spewed beer from my nose as I took in his mischievous expression. "He's never deviated from the path. Everything had to line up, or so we thought until he started working with us. He's brilliant. Yes, he's an asshole, but I think it's more armor than actual personality. I've seen him at the Outreach. He cares. He's compassionate and respectful, he gives his time, sometimes more than he should, in my opinion, but it makes him feel needed. You got a thing for Graves?"

"Honestly?" I huffed. "I don't know. There's no attraction on his side for me, and I've spent enough time with him, I'd be able to see something. But nope. My daughter is positive he's perfect boyfriend material, and not a day goes by that she's not asking have I gotten my head out of my ass yet."

"I like your kid."

"I'm sure she'd love the entire Cold Case squad, and *that's* why you're never meeting her."

"That was mean. Graves is...I don't know...he's still a mystery to us. He's one of us but not. He hovers right on the edge, but we don't let him. It's not a secret to most everyone that his parents don't approve. They were parading him in front of the cameras when *he* broke the Fellows's case. They loved being able to say their son caught a serial killer, but they never once mentioned the victims or sent their condolences to the families. To them, they were just sex workers, and they got what they deserved.

Graves has a lot to live up to, and in my gut, I don't think he likes the person he's supposed to be."

"I get that." I took another swig and tried to get my thoughts together. "He's two people. One is a closed-off bastard but an excellent cop. The other, Simon." I sighed. "He's a man who climbs through kiddie play equipment to rescue a toddler who's scared. He walks around in a sling with a baby on his chest. He's snarky and fun, relaxed, but…"

"But what?"

"I saw him at a charity event. He had a woman on his arm all night. He was playing the perfect role, and I could see how much he hated it. I can't separate the two sides. Or that I like him, the straight man, and I feel I'm too damn old for all this."

"I don't even know if Graves knows who or what he is. I've known the man for years, and not once has he checked out another person. We take him to clubs, and he sits at the bar and talks to the bartenders or servers. By the time the night is over, he knows their entire life story, and he has a new friend."

"I noticed that at the second crime scene for our case. He knew the bartender. He's besties with a damn crime boss."

"Drives you insane, doesn't it?"

"So badly, because I want to demand his story and I get nothing. People talk about exes or what they do with their off time. And with him, there's nothing, just these vague bits and pieces." I didn't want to talk about the conversation we'd had after the charity event because it seemed like something just for me, and he'd trusted me with that information.

"He has no past relationships that I know of. But before he became one of us, work and home were separate. He wouldn't even talk about what he did over the weekend, or if he took a vacation, he didn't talk about the fun he had. I think being told what and who you are for so long, it just turns into programming. You don't know any different."

"That's why I'm so damn confused."

"Just be his friend. Yeah, I know you want to get him in bed so badly you can't stand it, but trust is a powerful thing. And I think you have to earn his to get as close as you want."

"It's not even about the sex. I just like him. I'm almost fifty, and I feel like I'm fourteen again with that crush on the unattainable person. I was married for twenty-one happy years. How the fuck do I start over after that?"

"You learn to adapt." I turned my head as Robert entered the kitchen. "She wants to say goodnight to Dad."

"Douglas, I'll be right back. Talk to Robert. I think he has better advice than I do." Remy quickly kissed his husband and strode out of the kitchen.

"Finally admitted you want Graves?"

I groaned at his question. "Does everyone notice?"

"Probably not. I do know people are noticing you should move your desk to Cold Case."

"Strangely, I work better in the basement. Tyson said that it wouldn't hurt his feelings if I seduce at least one of his best detectives up from the basement. The captain is looking nervous."

"Who wouldn't want to work with us? We're the fairy squad last time I heard."

"Stelman called you that, and I told him he was assuming I wasn't a fairy. Who even uses that one anymore?"

"Stelman Jr is no better than his dad. I worked with him about sixteen years ago. Worst year of my life. What's this about me giving better advice?"

"I mentioned being too old for crushes."

He laughed and leaned over to rest his forearms on the counter. "Never too old for those. I was married for over thirty years. I loved my wife, still do. I think she loves Remy more than me now, but I can understand why she does. I was a strait-laced Homicide Detective who was recently divorced, and Remy arrived. I instantly liked him. I let him into my family. He became my best friend for the two years we were just work partners. I didn't realize I'd fallen in love until he shut me out. Bisexual or whatever I am, I love my husband and our children more than anything in the world. I was fifty-five when I fell for him."

"He's not attracted to me, and I need to get over it." That's what I kept telling myself, and as much as I wanted him to have even a small amount of attraction for me, I had to accept that it wouldn't happen. He'd told me I wasn't his type.

"Graves is a tricky one. He's a lot like me. I had the expectations of a wife and family and making sure I had enough time for them. Which I never did. Then after the divorce, I was single-mindedly focused on work. I had nothing outside it until Remy and the people he introduced me to…his found family. Graves has his work and the Outreach. I think the real Graves is on the strip. He loses all the tension."

"Yeah, I noticed that."

"But be his friend and see what happens. He's not one to trust easily, and who knows, personal trust might lead to that attraction that you want."

"I don't know."

"You'll figure it out. You two have been working pretty close together the last month or so. He's willingly spending time with you. That's out of character."

I nodded. Maybe I subconsciously knew I needed advice, and the best people were Robert and Remy. They were opposites and yet seemed to make it work. I didn't know what I was supposed to do. I'd spent so many years focusing on my career and family that I never really thought about myself and what I wanted. It was like completely starting over.

"Donna and I just worked. I don't know if we even dated. We hung out, and it was a natural progression. Six months after we met, we're getting married by a judge. She never wanted the whole spectacle of a big wedding."

"Is that what you wanted?"

His question confused me. "What do you mean?"

"Did you want the whole thing, the dating, the parties, and the wedding?"

"Not really. I was nineteen and about to be shipped off overseas. We loved each other and wanted to get married. Maybe I wanted the romance, but do men really admit to that?"

"Toxic masculinity doesn't fly in this house. I take Remy out all the time. Buy him small gifts I know he's looked at, but he prefers to get stuff for Roo or the grandkids. We make time. I do special things that I know will make him happy. My husband, my baby, he needs those things because he never had them before, and I'm more than happy to provide him with whatever will keep him smiling. You've probably remembered the people you met and how Remy knew them."

"About Remy's past, yeah, those have come up a few times, and they just make him a better cop."

"He's not ashamed of that past, but he has a lot of trauma responses. Life wasn't kind to Remy, but he came out of it stronger. So, if he wants romance, he gets it. So maybe romance is the way to go. Be all sweet and shit."

"That would be out of character."

"Well, we adapt to what our person's needs are."

"Why did I come here?"

"Because you wanted advice but didn't want to admit it. Want another beer?"

"No, the one is good. That's usually my limit. One after I get off work to relax."

"Food then? We have leftovers."

"No, I grabbed a sandwich when I got home. My daughter abandoned me for studying this weekend."

"A daughter. I have two. Carol, I don't know if you've met her, and you know Roo."

"Your Roo is a little scary."

"I know. We made her that way." Robert smiled proudly. "She

had a horrific start in life, and we made sure she never had to experience that again."

I finished off my beer as Robert started making popcorn, and when Remy came back, I sat there to observe them. At the office and work, they didn't hide that they were married. Remy spent most of his time sitting on his husband's desk. In a profession like the military and law enforcement, it was hard to be out. I'd never announced to anyone other than Donna, Savannah, and my family that I was Pansexual. I also didn't hide it, and if I ever found my person, I'd proudly say so.

Yet looking back on my life, I'd repressed a lot of what I wanted for my career, for what others wanted. I was forty-eight, so maybe it was time to figure out what I really wanted.

13

GRAVES

COLD CASE
UNIT

I was in the Pit with Vega, and Doc was seated on her lap as her fingers flew over the keys, and I settled on a table away from the chaos. Apparently, Vega was babysitting Doc while Stevenson followed a lead on a case he was working. Since Doc's kidnapping and the attempted murder, Stevenson didn't like his boyfriend alone at home overnight. I didn't blame him. I'd seen how torn up Stevenson was when Doc had gone missing.

"Cash working the door upstairs again?"

"Always, my wife is very protective of her Mami."

I snorted. They had an odd dynamic. Vega was a strict Dominant, but Cash went out of her way to threaten anyone who looked at her Mami and Mistress sideways.

"Are you worried about the stiff?"

"Stop calling him that. We have to be nice."

"So protective. Something going on there?"

"No. We're stuck with him until this case is over with." Vega still wasn't sure about Douglas, and to be honest, neither was I. He was a good cop. Decent investigator, but he wasn't bad to work with. We'd even made strides to get along. I still didn't think we were at the friend stage, but it was better than nothing, I guess.

"I don't think you mind being stuck with him."

"Just do your thing and leave my nonexistent love life alone."

"What if one of our jobs entails helping with your pitiful lack of a love life?" Doc asked as he peeked over Vega's shoulder.

"Not everything in life is about getting laid. We've talked about this." Doc and Vega were the only ones I'd talked to about Asexuality, and surprisingly they hadn't made fun or whatever.

"We didn't say anything about your sex life, just your love life, and Vega and myself, think you need some loving."

"Doc doesn't speak for me. Asexuality is a spectrum, Graves. We've seen you checking out his ass," Vega announced.

"I have in no way, shape, or form checked out Douglas's ass." To be honest, I hadn't paid much attention to Douglas other than he annoyed the hell out of me most of the time.

"I call bullshit," Doc announced loudly.

"Does Cash have a badge because I've never been frisked so thoroughly in my damn life?" Douglas muttered all the way down the stairs, and we all laughed.

"Call it a Cash Special. Daddy wanted to file charges for assaulting a police officer the first time he was here," Doc said as he shifted to straddle Vega's lap.

"Is Vega a supervillain?" Douglas whispered to me as he leaned back on the table next to me.

"I think it's one of her life's goals."

"Why was I summoned to the lair?"

"Douglas, you were summoned to bask in my brilliance."

"Your ego is astonishing, Vega."

"Thank you."

I grinned as I crossed my legs and leaned forward to rest my elbows on the inside of my knees, and cupped my chin as I waited for Vega to get around to what she wanted us there for.

She might be way out there, her and Doc, but a lot of our cases had found resolution with her help.

"Your three victims have no criminal associations or ties to Bianchi. Which I know isn't a surprise, but they're all from the neighborhood. All single. All have no immediate family. No significant others or children. In essence, they're throwaways."

"Throwaways?" Douglas asked as Vega spun in her chair, patting Doc's back.

"No one will miss them. No one to file missing persons' reports. They rented month to month. Searches of their apartments found the bare minimum. A few suits in the closet. A few changes of clothes. Which I found suspicious as hell, but none of my searches pinged any of the federal databases, and let me tell you, I searched and noisily, hoping the Feds would come looking."

"So, we have bodies that had their teeth removed and their fingertips burned. Was that just a cover of some sort?" I asked, and it didn't make sense. Nothing about this case lined up.

"Not that we know of. I mean they were nobodies. Which would make them the perfect victims. There are no employment filings, assistance, or any legal income. All their offenses were mainly misdemeanor charges. The most time they served was a few months in county."

"Still not helpful." I snorted as I caught Douglas's eye roll.

"I'm not here to do your job for you. I'm just here for the assist."

"So, we have three unknowns, tortured, identifying characteristics removed, and all dumped outside or near a club where the owner is a mob boss who has no idea who they are. Nothing about this case is moving forward. None of the victims make sense. It's too random."

"Maybe that's the point, Douglas. They don't want the victims connected in any way. Victimology establishes motive and a pattern, but they're so random that it *is* a pattern."

"Vega, you exhaust me, and is Doc asleep?" he asked as he leaned to the side.

"Very. Don't wake him up. I'll have Cash carry him up soon."

"You have a bunch of victims who, if they disappear, won't cause a stir, but the locations of the body drops are calculated. Is it a deflection technique? A cover-up for something else? Cold Case's involvement wasn't planned. Douglas is too new to have made enemies." I was sure I had more than a few—inside and outside the department. Organized Crime was rife with megalomaniacal personalities, cops, and criminals. "I don't know what the point would be. No taskforce is going to be formed. The Feds aren't coming in unless it suits them. Organized Crime squad isn't interested because there really isn't anything compelling. Carmine didn't commit the murders, and other than location, there wasn't anything that would call it Mafia-related. We need more on the victims. When did they show up on anyone's radar? When were the apartments rented? Was it strictly cash?"

"I'll do some more digging. Like I said, I tried to see if running them would throw up alarms at any federal agencies. I called in some favors but haven't heard anything back yet."

"Want me to carry him up?" Douglas asked.

"Really?" Vega's surprise was evident as she asked.

"Yeah, he looks to be dead weight." He straightened, and I watched as he crossed the room and easily lifted Doc into his arms as if it were something instinctual. Being a dad, it probably was.

I shook my head as Doc cuddled into Douglas as he made his way up the steps. Doc had a need for affection and cuddles, and he was cute in the way it just made him happy. I didn't understand it. I'd never craved something as simple as human contact. Maybe that's why Remy and Robert, Doc and Stevenson, and Vega and Cash fascinated me so much.

"He has Daddy potential."

"Vega, I have no need for a Daddy. It works for my friends, but it's not for me." I loved my friends, and on most days, that realization shocked me. But I didn't feel a need for that power exchange or have some Daddy to care for me. There were plenty of Asexual Kink participants. Yet I knew myself enough, or at least I thought so that I was sure it wasn't for me.

"I was just stating he has potential. I didn't say he was or that you wanted one. You're bratty but nowhere near Little material."

"I'd say thank you, but I feel I was insulted."

She giggled and shook her head at me. "It wasn't meant to be an insult. I still think for a stiff, he's not a bad guy. I'm still dubious about his investigative skills."

"He's more linear and logical than we are in his process."

"True. No one is perfect like us. You doing okay, Simon? You're looking more exhausted than normal."

"I have about four years of sleep to catch up on, but I'm good."

"Something you want to talk about, just between us?"

"Really, just us?"

"Yeah."

"I've been restless lately, and I don't know what's causing it. I'd think it was a mid-life crisis, but I think I'm too young for one. Although, I also feel like I'm too old to make any changes."

"Honey, you're never too old to make changes in your life. Our lives aren't supposed to stagnate. We're supposed to always be moving forward, and if you're feeling restless, maybe your brain is trying to tell you that you need a new direction."

"I love my life, my work, what I do at the Outreach. It's just sometimes it feels like something's missing."

"You'll figure it out. Must be driving you insane, though. You loathe the unknown. This case must be fucking with you, too."

"It is. Like Douglas said, nothing lines up. None of the victims or evidence make sense. Why do this production if the victims won't give away the killers?"

"We have to remember something. Not all killers have a

motivation other than killing. Their motivation is taking someone's life and nothing more. Yet, I think it's more than that. There's something about these victims, along with the locations. I just don't know what it is."

"Nice nursery," Douglas commented as he jogged down the steps.

"My babygirl and Doc put it to good use. I'm a very willing platonic caregiver."

"What did I miss?"

"Nothing much other than we might just be dealing with a killer who just drops his victims away from his location. Could Carmine's club just be nearby?" Vega asked.

"There's a lot better places to dispose of our victims. There's the harbor. Landfill. A state park an hour's drive away. Could stow it in a shipping container at the shipyard, and no one would notice until the container was offloaded. Hell, there's a nice acid bath option." There were countless ways to get rid of a body that you didn't want to be found.

"It's all just circles. We keep coming back around to the fact we don't know shit." Douglas checked his watch. "Shit, I gotta get home. My kid is expecting dinner."

"Say hi to Savannah for me."

"Will do. You still picking her up to help you tomorrow?"

"Yeah, we're short on daycare workers for the evening kids."

"Nice seeing you again, Vega. Simon, call me if you two figure anything out."

I nodded as Douglas jogged up the steps to head home, and I leaned back against the stone wall.

"You're hanging out with his kid?"

"Don't get any thoughts in that head of yours. She wanted to see about volunteering and goes with me to the Outreach any night I do. She's a great kid. Extremely smart and motivated." I didn't want to admit spending time with Douglas's kid made me think about how much I'd wanted a family. Years had passed since I'd seriously considered it as an option. Being single and my job, it was unfair. That could easily be an excuse to keep myself from breaking my own heart.

"Why didn't you ever have kids?"

"Vega, it takes a partner to have kids, and I'm not exactly in a position to have one of those or to do anything to make said kids."

"There's adoption. Remy and Robert adopted Roo."

"But they're married. There were special circumstances when it came to Roo. My job would mean I'd have to have a partner who'd be active in their life. I've thought about adoption in the past, but it wouldn't be fair to a partner or child."

"A kid would be lucky to have you as a dad. Get home and actually sleep, Simon. You look like shit."

"I'm feeling the love, Vega." I slipped off the table and headed for the stairs.

"Simon?"

"Yeah?"

"You're a great guy. You need more than us and the damn job. Asexual persons can be in relationships. Not everyone requires sex."

"I know, but I just don't know if I have it in me to try."

Thankfully, she didn't say anything else, and as I ascended the steps, my legs seemed to weigh a ton. I took a minute to say bye to Cash, who was making dinner, and I exited the house. I'd go home, feed my antisocial cat. Maybe for once, I'd be exhausted enough to sleep. My tank was beyond empty—I wasn't even working on fumes anymore.

14

DOUGLAS

COLD CASE
UNIT

The Outreach was utter chaos, and I sidestepped children and adults alike as they ran around. My mouth twitched at the corners as I headed for Simon's office and found it empty, and then I was off to the daycare area. Since Savannah had decided Simon was her new bestie, this had turned into a nightly routine after I finished at the precinct at the end of the day.

"Detective Douglas, you're becoming a regular the last month," Boss said, calling out from down the hall behind me. I turned to find the compact wall of muscle jogging towards me. Boss was odd because he wasn't attractive, but he also wasn't unattractive. He was personable, but you wouldn't want to come up on him in a dark alley. I hadn't yet gotten a read on him.

"That would be Savannah."

"A badass young lady you got there. If you're looking for her, she won't be in daycare today. Well, she's working with that program, but it's our weekly extreme hide and seek challenge. Her and Amber are paired up, but it's almost coming up on the bell. It signals the game is over. Whoever isn't found gets ice cream. And right now, all our teams are getting ice cream. I think they all conspire not to be found."

I chuckled at his amusement at their deceptiveness. The level of selflessness that went into a program like the one Boss had still shocked me even after all I'd seen and learned. The first time I'd met the Cold Case squad, I just thought they were an odd group of people who were ostracized by most law enforcement. After I saw them in action, my perception of them changed, but the confusion was still there.

"You've got one helluva program. They don't have something this scale even in major cities." Even after weeks of visiting there, the enormity of what Boss and his team did still amazed me. After meeting everyone, it shouldn't have. I'd learned with the Cold Case squad and the people at the Outreach, what you saw was what you got with them.

"Thanks. I grew up here. This was my turf. Out and proud gay man in the seventies, I was looking at getting my ass kicked just walking down the street. I fell in love with a sex worker back in the day. He was a beautiful young man. We used to talk after he'd be done at night, and he talked about this magical place where everyone could get help and were accepted. He was beaten to death by a very rich trick. This was my gift to him. A way to still have a connection to him."

"He'd be proud of it and you."

A moment of nostalgia seemed to soften his harsh features. "I like to think so. We were watching our friends die. The start of the AIDS epidemic and Reagan, no one cared. It was God's punishment for our deviant behavior. We were all terrified with nowhere to truly go. I was thirty, a few years after Juan died, when I secured funding for the first storefront. Back then, it was mainly a food pantry and a free clinic with volunteer doctors and nurses. The lesbians went above and beyond. Our community was a lot smaller back then but no less passionate."

"But how did it get to this point?" I turned to lean my back on the wall.

"Chaos theory. Random and unpredictable. At first, this was

for the gay community, clinics, safe sex classes, mobile soup kitchens where we set up in abandoned parking lots where sex workers and the homeless could come to get a hot meal. Then other needs came to light. Single mothers who couldn't find jobs because daycare was unaffordable. A growing problem with addiction. And so on and so forth. Every year I added new programs, pushed for better public and city funding, donations, and thirty years later, the empire was complete-ish."

"It's never-ending."

"Unfortunately, human decency is in short supply. We have to take up the cause where we can."

"But you love it?"

"I do, as much as it exhausts me, and I sometimes don't know where all the funding is coming from. We have one anonymous donor who practically keeps us running on a monthly basis. Enough about business. How are you finding our city?"

"It's good, an adjustment. Pretty much hit the ground running and haven't stopped since. But my daughter had friends here, and her mother was transferred to her own command. So I moved here so Savannah wouldn't have to leave."

"They do get to the age where friends and fun are more important than the pitiful woes of their parents."

"Exactly. But she's a great kid, and I missed her. I was her only full-time parent for a long time while her mother was deployed, and then Donna was transferred here, and I became the holiday parent, the one Savannah only saw during a month in the summer. I'm glad to have my kid back even if my job doesn't make parenting easy."

"Parenting is never easy. I've been around long enough to know that."

"I have to know, what's this extreme hide and seek challenge?"

"Older kids are paired with the younger kids, mainly to keep them inside the containment area. Volunteers and staff are the seekers. Simon is a seeker today. I made him get out of his office.

I told him his two favorite humans, Savannah and Amber were paired up today."

I'd remembered Amber from our dinner, and the relationship between her and Simon was close. You could see they adored each other. "What's the story with Amber?"

"Her parents died about a year and a half ago, murder-suicide. Fran is one of our volunteer social workers and Fran alerts me to special cases, and we offered Janice, her foster mother, a bit of support."

"Fran and I sort of met when Major and Saffy had the baby. She came to the hospital."

"She's been an amazing help around here. She's up for retirement in a few years, and I've already had her agree to come work with us. She was a massive help when Remy wanted to foster and adopt Roo. Amber was in a similar situation. At least she was at her babysitter's when the incident happened. Her babysitter called the cops when her parents failed to pick her up, and they did a welfare check. They died maybe an hour after the mother dropped Amber off. She was in protective custody until cause of death could be determined and then was moved to a foster home. Janice does the best she can, but her husband's hours make her a full-time single parent. Janice comes here three nights a week, and it allows her to have some help, and the kids get to play."

"Why hasn't she been adopted yet?" She was an adorable, petite biracial little girl with curls that surrounded her face.

"Amber has some behavioral issues. Attachment disorder. Remy explains it better than me. She was too young to understand why she never saw her parents again, but subconsciously she has some issues stemming from the sudden abandonment. She'll need therapy and one-on-one attention that makes it a requirement that she needs a specialized home."

I was about to ask what he meant by a specialized home when a buzzer blared. "End of the game?"

"Yep, come on, everyone heads to the cafeteria to meet up and do a roll call."

I followed him through the maze of hallways until we reached the massive open space of the cafeteria. Laughter rang off the walls as Bart set up an ice cream bar, and I searched the crowd for Savannah and Simon. They were off to the side, and she was tucked under his arm with Amber seated on Simon's hip as he smiled and talked to both.

The difference between Detective Graves and Simon was still so contradictory that it was too hard to accept. On the one hand, I respected Graves as a cop, but Simon drew me like no one before. During our time working together and nights like these where I saw him outside the needs of the case, I'd learned to accept my attraction to him.

I skirted the edge of the crowd to reach Simon and the two girls. He gave me a smile as he spotted me.

"I see the seekers lost today," I said with a smile and winked at Amber as she shyly waved at me.

"We lose every time. I agree with Boss that the teams conspire so everyone gets the reward."

"They're vicious. This is the first time I got paired for the hunt. Amber can be so quiet." Savannah held out her arms and Amber practically jumped into them. "We're getting our reward. Do we have time, Dad?"

"Plenty of time. Go have fun." I shooed them away and was left there with Simon. "Is it really that hard to find them?"

"It really is, which is embarrassing for a detective." I chuckled at his almost bratty grin. "Any news on our case?"

"Vega said she might have something for us, but she needs to check a few more things to corroborate the information before passing it on. She's thorough."

"She is. She's a bit out there, but she knows what she's doing." He pushed his fingers through his loose wavy curls, and I hated when he came to work all primped and his hair tamed in a professional style.

"I think that entire squad of yours is the best of the best."

"Thanks. Most of the time, we're just the ghouls in the basement."

"I did my research, and y'all are way more than that." I turned away so he wouldn't catch me watching him. I knew he wouldn't take offense, but I didn't want him to see my attraction. Wanting someone who didn't want you back—it was an ego and pride killer.

"Are we still getting together tomorrow night to work on the case more? Savannah said she was spending the night with a friend after a dance. Is she going with someone? She's too young to date."

I softly chuckled at his belief that she was too young. "She's going with a group of girls. They're having some spa-type day. Hair, nails, the friend's mom is taking them to the salon. You should've gone dress shopping with her and saved me the trauma. I'm not ready for all this."

"You don't have a choice, Douglas. It's inevitable, but she's a great kid. You're really lucky to have her."

"No kids in your future?"

"To me, as a single man with a dangerous and demanding job, bringing a child into that would be unfair to them."

I didn't miss the pain and regret in his tone, but I could sympathize with him. Even with Donna, it was still hard to raise a well-adjusted and confident kid. We'd lucked out with Savannah. I still regretted that she didn't get enough of our undivided attention.

"I understand that. I'm always worried she doesn't get enough of my time, but as the kid of active military and law enforcement, she doesn't know any different. It's been that way since birth, and all her friends were the same until she moved here. They developed their own little club."

"But you have your ex-wife who's still a big part of your life... your friend. I don't have that. If I did, I might have thought about adoption. But again, I have to think about what's best for a child, and I'm not it."

I wanted to argue, but I wouldn't disregard his feelings on the matter. I caught his face brightening, and I followed his gaze to find his attention locked on Savannah and Amber. There was adoration and care. The man deserved so much, but he didn't think he was worthy. I wanted to know why he had such a low opinion of himself, but we weren't close enough for a heart-to-heart on that level. I'd make him trust me, and to do that, I knew I had a battle on my hands. If I was good at anything, I excelled at fighting for what I wanted and needed.

15

GRAVES

COLD CASE
UNIT

I dropped the doors that led down to the steam tunnel, and spring had finally taken the chill out of the evening air, but I'd still made sure that Savannah had worn a light jacket. Douglas had called me saying he was stuck in an interrogation for another case, and Savannah didn't want to hang out with friends or the neighbor lady, so I told him she could run errands with me. We weren't friends but friendlier, and I loved spending time with his daughter. He'd earned a few points there. She'd started doing some of my volunteer work with me, and he hadn't argued.

We both needed a break from the case. I did this, and who knows what Douglas was up to when not pouring over endless confusing details. We hadn't come across any suspects yet, and every day that passed, we figured the case would be bumped down to the basement any day. There were suspects, but none fit. The pattern had been a body a week, and we hadn't had a new one in over a month. Part of me thought that Davian almost catching them that they'd wanted the heat to die down. We were at the point where we were just throwing ideas around and going in circles.

"Thanks, Simon." Savannah tucked herself under my arm as

we walked back to my car after delivering meals and some non-perishable items to the underground homeless community.

"You're welcome but thank your dad for letting me take you with me." I glanced over my shoulder as I heard footsteps, not the typical soft-soled shoes that were usually worn down there or the click of high heels. I kept a normal pace, and just as we broke the mouth of the alley, shots rang out.

Automatically, I grabbed Savannah up and hugged her to my chest. I had my off-duty weapon but didn't bother wearing my vest. I'd left it in the cargo area of my vehicle. I cursed myself for not wearing it so that I could protect her.

My brain mapped the area, and I was on the move to a warehouse a few minutes away. I knew this place as well as I did my own neighborhood on the other side of the city.

"Honey, I need you to be really quiet." I kicked the door and rushed inside. The steps behind me quickened, and whoever was back there was breathing heavy. Out of shape or lack of cardio, either way, that worked in my favor. I had to come up with a plan. I needed her safe.

I softened my steps as I crouched down to sneak around the large crates until I found one in the packing area with the top off. I lifted her slight weight and put her inside. As long as she listened and kept her head down, I could get them to follow me and lead them as far from her as I could get.

"Honey, I want you to tuck down really tight, okay? Don't make a sound." She'd left her phone plugged into the charger in my car. "Do you know how to use this?" I removed my gun, and she nodded. "Okay, I don't care who comes at you. You see them, you shoot. I'm going to make a run for it."

"Simon, no." As she reached for me, I caught her arms and urged her back into the box.

"Honey, I know you're scared, but I can't protect us both at a full run. So you wait here, and when you hear someone say butterfly, that's our code word, you do not come out until then. Promise me."

"Promise."

"It's gonna be cramped, and it's gonna be dark, but you'll be safe. Just be quiet." I handed her my weapon and flipped off the safety. I put the lid on the crate and stood up. Then I yelled, "*Police*," to identify myself and to draw attention.

I searched for the nearest exit making as much noise as possible. This was going to hurt. I slammed my shoulder into the door and pulled out my phone as I escaped into the night with my unknown pursuers behind me.

"Honey, what's up?"

I quickly cut in his greeting because I had a few seconds at most. "Carmine, I need you and a team at a warehouse on fourth." I gave him the exact address. "I need you to pick up a package for me. The package will only respond to butterfly. Repeat it for me."

"Butterfly."

"Make sure the package doesn't have a mark on it. I'm unarmed with two, maybe three men behind me. I'm not going to be able to outrun them, but you make sure the package gets where it needs to go."

"On it. You better stay alive, Simon."

"I'm not making any promises." I barely got my phone back into my pocket as I kept up a pace that wouldn't outrun them, but they damn sure wouldn't catch me right away. I avoided public areas to save on casualties and drew them as far from the warehouse as I could get.

The shots were hitting walls so close to me I could feel the way the air displaced. I needed to start running in the mornings again. My lungs ached, and my chest tightened as I reached a fence. I scaled it and fell on the other side. I scrambled to my feet and pushed hard to make up the lead I'd lost.

The fence exploded behind me as another gunshot told me they blew the lock. I was near the docks. If I could just make it, there was plenty of cover. I ducked down as I slipped between two shipping containers and listened for footsteps over the sound of blood rushing in my ears and my own labored breathing. We were miles away. Carmine would get to Savannah, and everything would be okay.

"Come out, Detective Graves. Where's Douglas's brat?"

Someone demanded, and I hit the side of the container on purpose as I headed for the cover between two more. The place was several miles worth of freighters and containers. If I was hit, they wouldn't find me for days, and I'd made the choice I wouldn't leave the shipyard that night.

"It's just me and y'all. I got nothing for you." Maybe both of us were the target. It was dark enough, and I'd kept ahead of them so they probably didn't see I'd stashed Savannah. At least I hoped so, but if not, please let her stay hidden like I told her.

"You and that detective are ruining all of our plans. If we can't have her, maybe you'll be enough of a warning."

Shit, the speaker's voice was closer. The sound of footsteps in different directions informed me they'd separated. I started to back out of the space only to jump forward when a bullet connected only a few feet above my head. I bit back a shout as it ricocheted and hit just above my right shoulder blade. I spun in the dirt and pressed my back to the cold steel. Shadows blocked my escape, I was trapped on both sides by four men, and I wasn't making it out of this shipyard.

I pretended to reach for my weapon, and a cheap, leather shoe stomped down on my hand. In the event I did survive, I cataloged everything from body size, if the voices were deep or nasally, what they wore, and every detail I could.

"Gonna add cop killer to your list?" I was defiant. *Make them mad, keep the focus on me,* I repeated in my head.

"Where is she?"

"I'm not giving her to you, might as well shoot me now."

"We're not gonna make it that easy." The leader motioned to one of the men on my left, and they knelt beside me.

With a jerk, they broke my little finger, and I refused to yell.

"Where is she?"

"I said kill me now."

They asked repeatedly until each finger, and the thumb on my left hand were bent at odd angles, the pain radiating upward into my arm.

"We do the other hand next."

I only had one chance, and I wasn't going to be able to take down all four, but if they were going to kill me, I wanted it over with. With my vision dimming at the edges from pain and the wound to my back, I lunged forward, grabbing the leader around his waist.

With my uninjured dominant hand, I went for the kidneys, punching as they battered at my back until I couldn't hold up under the assault of four men. They were determined to kick me to death when I was hoping for a quicker one. My ears rang as a stomp connected with my head, and I went limp. I inhaled and held it as I pretended to be dead. Hopefully, they were too stupid to check.

"The boss isn't going to be happy."

"Doesn't matter. He's dead." The speaker's voice preceded a shot, and fire moved across the side of my head, and it took everything in me to stay silent.

Footsteps retreated, and I laid on the ground that turned wet under my head as pain and nausea warred with my attempts to stay conscious. I dug out my phone with shaking hands and swiped the emergency call option. The operator picked up as I called in my approximate location with the officer down code. That was as far as I got as my eyelids got heavy, but I fought it until there was nothing left but the beating of my heart and blackness.

16

DOUGLAS

"What the fuck happened?" I yelled at Captain Tyson as I tried to get information on Simon and my daughter.

"We don't know. An hour ago, an officer down code was called through nine-one-one. We immediately triangulated the call with the approximate location Graves gave us in the shipyard. When we arrived, paramedics went to work on him. He was shot twice, shallow wound to the right shoulder blade and another graze to the left side of his head. All the fingers and thumb on his left hand were broken."

"Captain, my daughter was with him." I saw the professional face crumble as soon as I said my daughter could be a victim. "Was there any sign of her?" I demanded.

"Detective Douglas, we have a package for you and a vicious one she is." I spun at the sound of Bianchi's voice, and he stepped to the side to expose my crying daughter with a protective wall of muscle behind her. "Simon called in a favor."

I barely caught my daughter as she threw herself at me. "God, are you okay?" Relief nearly took me out at the knees, but we still didn't have any information on Simon.

She nodded. "Simon put me in a crate and told me not to

come out until someone said butterfly. Then he made a lot of noise."

"Detective, if you'd like to secure Simon's weapon, it's in the rear of one of our vehicles. He left it with the sharpshooter in training. One of my men is being tended to for an injured shoulder." He seemed amused as he looked at my daughter.

"He drew fire without being armed?" I hugged Savannah to my stomach as my heart sank.

"He told me to point and shoot."

"It's fine, honey."

"Is he…" Her voice broke, and she sounded so much younger. Like the little girl who'd told me about the first monster hiding under her bed.

"He's fine. They're just checking him over." I looked at Bianchi. "Where did you pick her up at?"

"Warehouse on fourth, it was recently reopened. Two exits were broken. It appears he found a crate in the packing section still open and hid her inside with his off-duty weapon."

"Savannah, I know you're scared, but just focus a little longer. I need you to tell me what happened?" I knelt in front of her. "Did you see anyone? Hear something?"

"No. We'd just left the camp where we'd dropped off a hot dinner and some other stuff. He was leading me back to the car, and he was going to take me home." She sobbed, and I rubbed the tears away as fast as they fell. "As we stepped out of the alley, someone shot at us. He grabbed me and put me in front of him and just took off running."

"Carmine, did he tell you anything?"

"Just told me that there was a package I needed to pick up. Only referred to her as it. I think he was trying to keep anyone from hearing."

"He was found miles away from where he left her, but he kept to deserted parts of the city on his route," Tyson commented from behind me.

"He didn't want anyone else to get hurt. He said he wasn't going to outrun them, but to take care of her and get her where she needed to be."

"Dad, can I see him?"

"Honey, that's—"

"Please, just really quick."

"I'll clear it with the doctor." Tyson disappeared, and I checked Savannah over.

"Are you hurt anywhere?"

"No, he kept me in front of him as he ran and then just put me in the crate."

"Detective, if you need me to, I can take her home with me. She'll have her own security detail. Sylvia will keep her company."

"I don't—"

"Let her see Simon, and afterward, you can make a choice. We'll wait here, but you have my numbers if you need to call me. She can stay with us for a few days until you figure out what happened."

"Douglas, he's stable. She can go back and see him. They're going to move him to a room soon."

"Come on, honey, let's see Simon." I stood and wrapped my arm around her, and she held tight to my hand with hers as they shook.

I didn't know what we'd see, but she wanted to check on him, and I couldn't deny her that. When a nurse led us into a room past the curtain draped in front of the door, for the second time, my legs threatened to collapse. He'd taken a beating. His head was wrapped. The beeping of the heart monitor was too loud in the quiet. Simon was never silent or still, and he'd put his life on the line for my kid. I know he would've done it for anyone, but it was Savannah, and he'd called in a favor to give her an entire security detail. He'd drawn fire without thought of a weapon or vest.

"Are you his family?" a doctor in a slightly wrinkled white coat asked.

"Yes." Savannah spoke up as she pulled away from me to walk toward the bed.

"I'm sorry your dad is hurt, but he should be fine. He's going to be miserable for a while after he wakes up. We're waiting on x-rays to see how bad the breaks are and if we need to fix them with surgery. Although, the captain said your dad was right-handed."

"But the head wound?"

"Your husband sustained a superficial graze, and head wounds always bleed badly. But he does have a bad concussion that we're going to monitor until he wakes up. We can leave her to visit. Can I speak with you outside?" The doctor asked, and I nodded as I told her I'd be right outside the door.

"Is something wrong you didn't want to say in front of her?" I asked as I crossed my arms over my chest and stared down at the shorter man.

"No, she doesn't need to hear the details unless you choose to tell her. As you can tell he took a significant beating. We put in a catheter, and he has some blood in his urine so we're going to monitor his kidneys and bladder. Your husband is in excellent physical shape. With time, he should fully recover. Although, his hand is going to take weeks to heal, that's if he doesn't require surgery. The bullet wound to his back appears to have been made by a ricochet. It had lost significant power before impact."

"So, he'll be fine? He'll wake up?"

"Yes. Head wounds are tricky, but right now, we don't see any significant swelling or bleeding. Once he's awake and ready to be released, he'll need plenty of rest. Physical therapy will be arranged before his discharge."

"You don't know Simon well, but he's going to hate being taken care of."

"Cops normally do. Worst patients I have in here are first

responders. I'll let you get back to visiting. We're arranging a room to transfer him into soon."

"Thanks, doctor."

"Douglas, what happened?" Remy yelled as the entire Cold Case Unit, including Doc, skidded to a stop.

I relayed the story or everything I knew until Simon woke up. Every one of them cursed and peeked around the curtain. My daughter was seated on the bed with her head gently resting on Simon's chest. I could see tears still filling her eyes.

"We can take Savannah. Robert and Remy have Roo to think about." Stevenson offered.

"No, I already have arrangements made, but thanks." Until I knew which one was the target, Simon or Savannah, I went with Simon's choice to protect her. Carmine had run in without a second thought to take care of her.

"Douglas, we're headed out, or should I stay?" Carmine asked from a short distance away.

"Could you stay? I think Savannah should spend a couple days with you. It's going to take that long to get her mother home, if we can skip delays in emergency leave."

"Of course, I'll phone Stephen to prepare a room for her. She'll be perfectly safe."

"Simon trusted you to take care of her, don't betray him."

"You just find out who attacked him and why. Let me worry about the newest member of our family. I'll be in the waiting room until she's ready."

I nodded at Carmine. Him and his people left almost as a cohesive unit. Even in the hospital, his security team guarded him.

"Are you sure about that, Douglas?" Robert asked.

"He was the one Simon called first. I'll go with his judgment even though he left his weapon and drew fire without it."

"Detective Douglas, I'm Tony. I'm in charge of your daughter's security detail." A big man with a bloody shirt came to stand beside me.

"Are you up to it?"

"She's brave and not afraid to aim and shoot. It would be my honor." Tony actually smirked as if he wasn't sporting what looked like a pretty painfully wound.

"I swear my life is getting weirder by the moment. He's going to be moved upstairs soon if you want to look in on him." I scrubbed my beard with my left hand as I took in the worry and anger on every face of the Cold Case Unit. I understood exactly how they felt. Someone had tried to take Simon and Savannah from me.

"We're going to, and then we're hitting the streets. Roo's with her babysitter, and Mrs. Walton will get her ready for school," Remy said and then ducked into the room with Stevenson and Doc behind him.

"This is going to cause a war," Robert whispered.

"What?"

"They attacked one of us, and I'm not talking about a cop. He's part of their community. They'll tear down the strip to find out who's behind this. Prepare to get really busy." Robert patted my shoulder and went to join the rest of the family.

"Do you know what exactly was said when Simon called?" I asked Tony, and he pulled out his phone, tapped the screen several times, and held it out.

"Honey, what's up?" Carmine answered the phone, and I held my breath, hearing Simon labored breathing as he ran. A picture formed in my mind of him moving through alleys and the dark leading men away from Savannah.

"Carmine, I need you and a team at a warehouse on fourth." He relayed the address. *"I need you to pick up a package for me. The package will only respond to butterfly. Repeat it for me."*

"Butterfly."

"Make sure the package doesn't have a mark on it. I'm unarmed

with two, maybe three, men behind me. I'm not going to be able to outrun them, but you make sure the package gets where it needs to go."

"On it. You better stay alive, Simon."

"I'm not making any promises."

I fell back against the wall as the recording ended. He was ready to die, probably told them to kill him when he was finally caught. It was there in his last sentence. He wasn't making promises. How did you repay a man for sacrificing himself for your kid? I'd already fallen hard for him over the last month of working closely with him, and he still showed no attraction, but he loved my kid. She loved him. I had to keep telling her that Simon and I weren't meant to be, but she was so determined.

"Why did he do it?"

"It's not my place to say," Tony answered matter-of-factly.

"Tell me."

"I've seen him with your daughter. He loves her like she's his own. It's there in his eyes when he looks at her. I've known him a long time. He was prepared to lay down his life for her, and he won't have had a single regret. I'll be out front when you're ready for me to escort her to Mr. Bianchi's."

"Thanks."

"Like I said, it will be an honor. She's vicious. She didn't even hesitate."

"Sorry she shot you."

He chuckled. "I should've said the code word louder. She was coming out of the box when I turned the corner out of nowhere. It was instinct, can't blame her for that."

He walked away, and I turned to reenter the room. Savannah still hadn't moved, and I anticipated that I was going to have a fight on my hands to get her to go.

"We're here to see our son, Detective Graves."

"He's in there. He has his husband and daughter with him."

"Husband?" I peeked out to find two people dressed as if they were going to a black-tie event with their noses snarled. They pushed into the room and froze, staring at the bed. We should've come up with another cover. Simon was going to be mad when he woke up.

"Who's that child?" State's Attorney Graves asked with a hiss.

"That's my daughter," I said, and her and her husband turned to me. "She's saying goodnight before I send her home, and she'll have all the time she needs." At that moment, I didn't care who they were, or the thought of their son being gay was disgusting to them. They wouldn't say anything in front of my child.

"What is his condition?"

"He'll be fine, but he has a concussion and isn't awake yet. They're moving him up to a room soon."

"Please inform him to phone us when he's home. We have an event to return to," District Attorney Graves announced in a clipped and unemotional voice. If he showed any emotion, it was being inconvenienced.

I stared at them, shocked as they turned and left without even approaching the bed or asking to see the doctor.

"Don't let it get to you. He's a commodity. They only had him to look good in campaign flyers. He was at boarding school until he was eighteen," Doc whispered from beside me. "When he gets particularly pissed or sleepy, his British accent comes out. It's kinda sexy." I shook my head as he winked at me.

"You're all trouble. I should pack up my daughter and move back to Chicago."

"And miss out on all this fun? We'll leave you alone with Simon and your daughter. We have work to do," Remy said.

"Keep me updated."

"You'll be added to the group text. Prepare yourself, Douglas. You're about to see real crazy." Robert looked almost remorseful on my behalf.

I groaned as Doc gathered everyone up, and they all said bye to me before disappearing through the curtain. Once we were alone, I approached the bed.

"You okay?"

"He's really going to be okay?"

"Yes, I promise, he's going to be fine. You're going to stay with Bianchi for a few days until I can get Simon to our place. Is that okay?"

"Yeah, but you're bringing him home, right?"

"Whether he likes it or not, he'll be staying with us," I said, reassuring her.

"He would've died for me, Dad. Why would he do that?"

"He must love you very much."

"You'll take care of him." That wasn't a question she gave me an order pure and simple.

"I won't leave him until he wakes up."

I let her cuddle with him a few more minutes, and then I led her from the room and out to where Bianchi and his men waited. They all stood.

"I'll come out with you to retrieve his weapon before you take Savannah home."

"We'll take excellent care of her, Douglas. You have my word, just like she was my own because that's what Simon would want."

I hugged her several times before I let her get in the middle car with Carmine and Tony in the back with her. The other men got in the lead and follow-car, ready to protect her in case of ambush. I got Simon's gun, secured it in the safe in the back of my SUV, and returned inside to wait for Simon to wake up. He was the only one who could give us the entire story about the men who tried to kill him and my daughter.

GRAVES

COLD CASE
UNIT

The death metal band playing in my head meant I'd survived, but as the pain in my body was head to toe, maybe it would've been better if I hadn't. I groaned as I forced my eyes open and was thankful the lights were low.

"Easy, baby, don't move too much." I turned my head and instantly regretted my decision. "What did I say?" I snarled but didn't know if I was pulling it off when Marcel's face hovered above mine. "Still with the land of the living, huh?"

"That's debatable." The argument over him using endearments would wait until a later date when I had full use of a painless body.

"As much pain as you're in, I'd say you're alive. I just hit the call button for your nurse." His voice was so deep and gentle that I thought I could just close my eyes and slip back to sleep.

Then it all hit me, where was my girl? "Savannah!" I panicked and tried to get up. Despite the agony I was in I fought him, but he kept his weight braced over me, his arms still positioned on the pillow on either side of my head.

"Baby, please, just be still. She's fine. She's spending time with

Carmine and has her own personal detail, the leader of which she shot."

I let out a shocked chuckle and moaned as the pain in my ribs and chest. "She doesn't have a mark on her?"

"Not one. She didn't come out until Carmine yelled butterfly. Just like you told her to."

"Good, good." I finally took time to calm my breathing, and I'd think about my near-death experience later when I could process past the pain.

"Baby, we're going to have a long talk when you're better about provoking men while unarmed and not wearing a vest." He stroked my cheeks with his thumbs, and I closed my eyes. Savannah was safe. I was better than I'd planned to be. Everything was good.

"She needed it."

"I think Tony would disagree." I opened my heavy lids again to see his smirk.

"I'll straighten him out when I get out of here," I said in warning. Back during my Organized Crime days, we'd gone at it a few times, and he apparently forgot he lost every fight.

"I think he's taking it as a badge of honor to get shot by Graves's kid," he whispered as I felt lips brush my forehead, and he chuckled.

"Don't make me laugh."

"Simon." I frowned at the break in his voice. "Thank you."

"Mr. Graves, I see your husband kept you calm." I barely paid attention to the nurse as I stared at Marcel, and he mouthed *later*, and I nodded. She did the usual checks, told me a doctor would be by on rounds soon, but gave me another dose of painkillers to ease some of the death-would-be-preferable-level of pain.

"I wanna talk to her," I demanded as I reached out as if looking for a phone.

"Don't trust me she's okay?" he asked as he brushed his

thumbs across my lashes where they laid over what I knew were horrifying bags and probably bruises.

"Wanna know if she still has the gun and tell her Tony's weak spot." My words slurred, and he shook his head.

"I think he's a bit too in awe of her to care."

"She's thirteen. I'll kill him if he tries some old-world betrothal, arranged marriage bullshit."

"You need to go back to sleep."

"Let me talk to her." I pouted because I wanted, needed to make sure she was fine.

"Sleep, baby. I'll have Carmine bring her by so you can see for yourself, but first rest. You did so good, baby. You just have to rest a little longer."

My eyes closed as the world started to fade, but I swore full, firm lips pushed to mine. Sleep—maybe ending up in the hospital would be good for something. I needed all the sleep I could get.

"You really couldn't take down only like two men?" I hissed at Savannah as she cuddled up to my right side. "Thought you had more skills than that." Carmine chuckled from the corner of the room with Tony beside him.

"Wow, when did she develop your personality, Douglas?"

"I think that's more your personality than mine."

"And it was four, sweetie, four, three, no problem, four…my limit." I hid my smile as she huffed and turned slightly away from me, but she never moved. She'd plastered herself to me since she'd arrived with Carmine and Tony.

"What happened?"

"Shit, a lot of it's fuzzy as hell. The doctor said it's the head injury."

"What do you remember, baby?" Thankfully, no one

commented, but I didn't miss the rise of a perfectly groomed brow nearly hitting Carmine's hairline.

"We'd just come up from the steam tunnels after visiting the camp. We stayed about an hour longer than I planned. Savannah was talking to a lady that was doing braids on her daughter, and they seemed to be having fun, so I talked with a few of the men in charge about anything they may need when someone comes next time. When we came up, I dropped the doors, and Savannah was under my arm. We were talking, and I noticed steps...the shoes clicked on the pavement. It was different from the soft-soled boots and sneakers most everyone wears. As we reached the mouth of the alley, someone started shooting. In hindsight, I don't think they were aiming to kill, more wound, but I just snatched her up, placed her in front of me, and kept moving." I held her close as she turned to lay her head on my chest and tried to soothe her the best I could.

"Is that it?" Douglas asked from the chair he sat in, leaning over with his forearms braced on his knees as he looked to be taking notes.

"No, no, sorry. I mentally mapped the area. I know the entire strip. I know they had a warehouse reopen as an industrial shipping company. I knew it would be deserted but places for her to hide. It still had the old wooden doors because the metal ones I wouldn't have had a chance. I kicked it in, lightened my steps, and found a crate to hide Savannah in. I asked her could she shoot, but with Marine parents, I figured she could. I clicked off the safety and told her to shoot at anything that came near her unless she heard the codeword."

"Why did you give her a codeword?"

Savannah spoke up before I could. "We do it at the Outreach. Each day has a new codeword. The kids are told to run if someone can't give them the right one. Yesterdays was butterfly."

"And I made as much noise as possible. I didn't know who was following. So I went with who I trusted, Carmine. You were in an interrogation earlier yesterday, and you forget to turn your ringer back on sometimes. I ran fast enough to stay ahead but not enough to lose them. They were breathing heavily. I thought they were pure muscle, no cardio. Ask Tony."

"Don't even bring me into this, you little shit. Your girl shot me."

"Wouldn't be the first girl to shoot you, probably brought back memories." I snarked, and as Tony flipped me off, Savannah giggled.

"Children, behave." Carmine tried to settle the room.

"Why the shipyard?" Douglas asked.

"Lots of places to get lost. Badly lit. Plenty of shadows. Last thing I really remember is taking a round to the back, and then it's just pieces." I closed my eyes and rested my head back, searching for everything missing. "They were asking for Douglas's brat, and I told them they weren't getting her and to shoot me."

"Simon." Savannah broke down.

I grabbed her face the best I could with splinted fingers that luckily were mostly dislocated. "Hey, honey, you were the only thing that mattered to me, okay? I could take it, and I'm fine. A little laziness and weeks of being in a cast was all worth it. Tell me you understand that? Savannah, tell me."

"I understand." She went back to resting her head on my chest, and I used my uninjured hand to stroke her hair.

I shot a glance at Marcel to find him staring at his notes but didn't seem to be reading them. I was fine. No one would've mourned me beyond what was publicly acceptable. My parents would've used my death as some political stunt. Sadly, I was okay with that. I understood because that was all I'd ever known, but Savannah had so much, she had her friends, her parents, and she was an amazing kid.

"Savannah, could you do me a favor?"

"Yeah."

"Could you find me the largest caramel coffee in this damn building? They tried to give me tea disguised as coffee when I woke up." I nodded toward her dad, and she gave me a smile and ordered Tony and Carmine to follow her.

"Give that girl of yours power, and she's trying to take over." Carmine mouthed for me to take all the time I needed and then left.

I waited for the door to close, but Marcel never looked up. "What's going on in your head?"

"They tried to kill my baby."

"Savannah will be fine. What other kid gets a full security detail of mob muscle? She's probably becoming corrupted by the power of it."

"Don't joke about this. You dared them to kill you."

"I didn't dare them. I ordered them to."

"That's unacceptable, Graves." He used my last name, and for some reason, it felt like a slap. "You gave up your weapon and led an unknown number of armed assailants into a shipyard without a fucking vest."

"My parents would've gotten a nice, folded flag out of it."

"Simon." He rumbled my name, but he may as well have roared with the rage that was in those two syllables.

"I don't have a death wish, I'm notoriously anti-getting-shot, but she's a baby, Marcel. She's sweet and compassionate, and the world needed her. You and her mother needed her. Who the fuck needs me? I was okay with my life ending in that shipyard. I'd already accepted it when I realized what I'd have to do. Every time I slowed down. Every hit to a container or heavier steps. I knew, and I was completely fine with it."

While I waited for him to fight me, he shocked me instead as he turned and stormed out of the room. The door slammed against the wall with the force of the jerk. I laid my head back and wondered what the fuck I said wrong.

DOUGLAS

COLD CASE
UNIT

Who the fuck needs me? His words still repeated in my head, and I didn't know how to handle them. This man I'd fallen for, who had ordered armed men to kill him to save my daughter, and he wondered who the fuck needed him?

We did, his friends, and found family, because fuck his biological one. When he'd awakened, I felt so much relief, and then one of his first conscious thoughts besides the pain was if Savannah was okay. Then he demanded to see her, and I could see how much he had to prove to himself he'd kept her safe without a scratch on her. If I hadn't assumed it before, I would have in that moment—he loved my kid like she was his own.

It was there in everything he'd done since I'd introduced them, and when the three of us had dinner. He spoke to her every day, and he video chatted with her over schoolwork when I was clueless. I thought I was a pretty smart man, but math was ridiculous, and he always answered.

"Are you okay, Dad?"

I threw my arm across her shoulders and hugged her to my side. "Yeah, yeah, it's just all hitting me now. What about you?"

"I'm fine. Tony's in the waiting room ready for orders to take me back to Carmine's. Is Simon okay?"

"He'll be fine, I promise."

"You left really mad earlier. We saw you storming down the hall before the elevator doors closed."

"He just said some things that I didn't know how to process, and I had to go before I said or did something I couldn't take back."

"You can't be mad at him."

"I *am* mad at him, but not in the way you think. He purposely put his life on the line."

"He did it for me. Wouldn't you do the same?"

"But I'm your dad."

"He loves me, he makes time, he helps with homework, and lets me interrogate him at the Outreach."

"But he doesn't love me." *Fuck!* I let my head fall back against the wall. "And I'm having a hard time trying to get over that, okay? This is nothing for you to worry about. I just need some sleep. I think we all do. And I shouldn't even be thinking about this right now. We have a case, and someone is trying to kill the most important parts of my family, you and Simon."

"Is Mom coming home?"

"Soon. She put in a request for leave. She explained to the general what was going on and should be on a transport in about a week."

"Simon is still coming home with us, right?"

"Of course. Who else is going to make him behave?"

"Um, Dad, I don't think you making him behave is actually possible."

"I could make him act right if I wanted to."

"Uh-huh."

"Savannah," Carmine called her name, and I turned to watch him approach with Tony slightly behind him. "Stephen is about to start dinner and was wondering if he should set our new girl a place."

"Can I?"

"Of course. Go say bye to Simon, and we'll come get you when it's time to go." She gave me a tight hug and then ran back to Simon's room, Tony close on her heels. "Carmine, thanks for this."

"Think nothing of it. Simon trusted me to protect her. Once you have her mother home, Tony will still be staying close by. He's yours until you know who attacked your daughter and Simon."

"What's the word on the street?"

"Word is, Boss is working damage control in the wake of the Cold Case squad. No concrete evidence yet, but I don't think it'll be long before the tips start coming in."

"Any bodies?"

"None that seem to be connected to this. Graves's parents are on the news playing the hero son angle. They're just waiting for a way to use this to their advantage. Your captain is making appeals on the news for any information leading to information on the attack of his detective."

"What about Savannah?"

"Nothing about her. I think he wanted to keep her name out of it. Until Simon said something, I think most people were saying he was the target. As far as anyone knows, she was never at the scene."

"Thanks."

"Are you okay?"

"He planned to die, Carmine, and I'm not sure how to handle that."

"I know. When he made me no promises, I knew. Saving her was all he cared about, Douglas. That she got home to you without a scratch. Don't take that for granted."

"I don't. He's my friend."

"But you want so much more. Patience is key, but until then, I'll protect your daughter. You just keep Simon alive and try to make him understand that we'd mourn him even if he doesn't think so."

I nodded, and Carmine turned to head back to Simon's room, but I remained, leaning against the wall several rooms down from his. When I'd stormed away, I hadn't gone farther than the waiting room, but then I wandered back to be in eyesight of his room. I'd try to explain my feelings away as gratitude at what he'd done, but they were there before. Every new smile or joke, the way he'd started to relax.

We'd gone on high alert when they'd announced the officer down call and the entire force was being mobilized. My world had imploded around me when Captain Tyson had a uniform officer tell me I needed to come to the hospital but wouldn't give me any details. On the way there, I'd called Simon and Savannah's phones repeatedly, but no one answered. I'd known I was about to mourn one or the both of them.

And I instantly regretted that I'd never told him how I felt, even if he didn't return the feelings. Simon couldn't comprehend someone cared about him beyond what he could do for them. If I had, maybe he wouldn't have acted so quickly, thinking he wasn't worth existing. Almost losing him and Savannah was too much for me. I didn't understand why it had to happen at that moment, and I was too wrung out to deal with the revelation.

All I could do was get him home to heal and then get this case solved. After that, I'd decide what to do. Would I confess or leave what we had the way it was? I knew he still didn't want me, but that was my issue, not his. I let out a deep sigh, inhaled and exhaled until I brought myself under control and returned to his room.

When I walked inside, I froze just inside the door.

"Honey, I'm fine. Look at me."

"You look like shit."

He softly laughed as he swept her curls out of her eyes with his right hand. "I'm feeling the love."

"Dad said you're coming home with us."

"No. I can take care of myself. It's probably safer if I go back to my house."

"You gotta come home. If you love me, you'll come home."

"Emotional blackmail, really, Savvy? You're gonna play that card with me?"

Seeing my daughter and Simon together showed me just how close they'd become and if I made my move and confessed my feelings, I could hurt him and her if it didn't work out. I'd stick with being friends, no matter how badly that hurt. I focused on them and their conversation.

"I am."

"Fine, I'll think about it."

"Not good enough. I'll make Tony drag you home for me."

"He knows better. I already shot him once."

"I did, too." She squealed.

I covered my mouth with my hand to hide my grin as Tony groaned and Carmine chuckled. I wanted that story more than anything. Also, it was probably inappropriate that Simon was encouraging my daughter's crimefighter streak.

"Go home, so Stephen can make you dinner. You've been here most of the day."

"Okay, I love you, Simon."

"Love you, too, honey. Go on, and behave. They said I'd probably get out of here tomorrow after they put on my cast."

I stood back and let everyone say goodbye, and then I was left alone with Simon.

"What did I say?"

"When?"

"To make you mad."

"I think it was a culmination of all of it, the way you were so ready to die and then had the nerve to ask who needed you. My daughter does. You think she would've recovered from thinking that you died for her. She's thirteen, Simon. She considers you a member of her family."

"I'm sorry. I'm not used to all that, Marcel. I'm not…all of this is weird for me. I have an attorney in charge of all my affairs. Everything's being sold and-or given to the Outreach or charity. My body is going to be buried in an unmarked grave, no funeral. That's my life, that's how it's always been, and I don't see it changing."

"You're coming home with us. Until we figure out what's going on, you won't be out of my sight for any period of time."

"You're not kicking me off this case."

"You're as hands-on as you can be. You have to take care of that hand, though. That's why you're taking a few days to heal up, and you'll work from my couch. We'll go by your place on the way to my apartment to get anything you need."

"Do you like cats?"

"Why?"

"Moriarty is one of my things I need."

"You have a cat?" I didn't understand why that shocked me. He didn't seem like the pet type, but I would've thought he'd be more a fish person. Maybe he had a low-maintenance cat.

"He doesn't require a lot of care, put out food, give him catnip, we get along just fine."

"Why Moriarty?"

"Because he has a psychopathic personality, and it seemed to fit."

"So you want to bring a psycho cat into my apartment?"

"He's very antisocial, too. I got him a year ago as a rescue. They were going to put him down. He kept getting returned for behavioral issues. Put his cave in a corner, and you'll never see him."

"Fine, for you, I'll put up with your cat. He seems to have the same personality as you."

"You're not funny."

"I'm hilarious. Get used to it."

"Are we okay?"

"We're fine. I think we just need sleep and to get back to work. Everything will be back to normal."

I hope he didn't see my lies. I stepped away from the door as there was a knock, and it opened, showing the daytime nurse coming in.

"Detective Graves, it's time to change your dressing on your back."

"Okay," he muttered and leaned forward, pulling the hospital gown down in front.

Damn, he exposed thick hair across his lean, flat pecs that thinned to a line down the center of his flat belly, but the sheet and blanket bunched around his waist didn't let me see if it fanned out beneath his outie belly button. As I watched as she tended to him, I saw a thin, faded scar on his left side between his ribs and hip. There was a peppering of what looked like pellet wounds to his right shoulder. Other than that, he was flawless.

He'd kept himself covered since he woke up, and they'd always asked me to leave whenever they removed his gown in the ER and then after they'd moved him to a room. I still had to explain the husband and daughter lie we'd played into, but that could wait. Who knew if he even remembered after he'd awakened in so much pain?

We'd go back to my apartment the next day, and I'd work my ass off to solve this case. I was ready to move on with my life, whether that included Simon or not. Even though losing him didn't feel like an option for me.

19

GRAVES

COLD CASE
UNIT

"You're going to owe me big time for this," Marcel said as he snarled and held the cat carrier at arms' length while my cat had a psychotic break inside. I'd spent the hour he took to wrangle Moriarty laughing as he used a couch cushion as a shield as he tried to herd the beast into the crate.

All ten pounds of hairless cat had almost taken the big, bad detective out. Hell, it was barely more than a kitten. He was only a few months old when I got him. I sat on the couch watching him as I adjusted my arm in the sling.

"You didn't say I needed hazard pay."

"He weighs ten pounds."

"He might as well weigh two hundred. He has the personality of a rabid lion."

"You're so dramatic. Once he's free, he'll be happy." I didn't mention that said cat needed a bath weekly and he wasn't fond of them. Douglas was going to be thrilled with that chore since I only had one hand, I couldn't do it.

"There is no happiness, only evil." He placed the crate on the carpet in the center of the living room.

"You might want to put his cave in a corner first," I suggested and earned a glare. But I took a page from Doc, Remy, and Roo's handbook and batted my lashes. "I warned you."

"You're having way too much fun."

I shrugged as he backed away from the carrier, set everything up, and put the extra litter box in the laundry room before he made his way to open the door. He stood behind it, pinched the closure, and swung it open. Just as I'd told him, Moriarty was on the move until he spotted his dome hideaway and darted into it.

"See, I told you."

"I'm sleeping with my door locked, or I'll wake up with my throat ripped out." He warily stared at the hideaway Moriarty disappeared into, and I studied him.

He seemed a lot more relaxed in the recent weeks. He smiled, and he joked. He was still sarcastic, but I chalked that up to a personality quirk. He wore a t-shirt that barely contained his muscular upper body. I'd never paid attention to how a person was built. To me, bodies were bodies. They were built large or small, thin or muscular or fat. I could tell people of all kinds were attractive. Yet I'd never noticed the play of muscles beneath the skin or the way clothes highlighted a person's form. He confused me, always had, and I still couldn't figure out why.

"When is Savvy coming home?"

"Carmine is going to bring her by after dinner. Stephen's making some dessert she wanted to try."

"Stephen is very domestic. He drives the house staff crazy."

"Have you been there?"

"I have."

"How is it you became besties with Carmine? It had to be more than about you showing him respect." Marcel crossed the room and fell back onto the couch.

"Organized Crime squad is a bit feral. You have to learn to adapt. Carmine has the usual ego of the man who would do anything to keep his position. When we met, he hadn't gotten married yet. It was my first assignment after I earned my detective's shield. He had dossiers on everyone in the unit. Knew who my parents were. The first time we went to his club, he was polite and personable. In my gut, I knew it wasn't an act. It was well-known that he'd gotten rid of some of his father's business interests when he took over. After a while, I noticed changes in him, and I got suspicious. He was harder to find, and a few months later, I found out about Stephen."

"He said Stephen was a single, divorced dad."

"Yeah, kinda weird, but after Stephen found out who he was, he cut off all contact with Carmine. For a few years he spiraled so badly. I won't say he's on the completely legal path now, but a lot changed when he realized he couldn't live without Stephen and the kids." I turned my head to see if he was disgusted by my friendship with Carmine, but I only saw amusement. "Internal Affairs hounded my every step. They still keep a pretty close eye on me."

"What's the story behind you shooting Tony?"

I smirked. "He shot me first."

"The shotgun blast to your shoulder?"

"Pretty close range so he wasn't aiming to kill. Come to find out, Carmine ordered me to be off-limits. They could maim but not kill. Now, Tony has to tell any women he's with why he was shot in the ass."

"You didn't?"

"He shot me in the shoulder. I peppered his backside. Still won't forgive me for that, especially since I love telling the story."

He let out a heavy sigh and scrubbed his hands over his face. I could tell he needed some major sleep, but it wasn't my place to tell him to take a nap. I wouldn't let him order me to do that.

"What do you want for dinner since we're on our own?"

"I'm not picky."

"You need a pill?" he asked.

We'd stopped on the way to my house to pick up my

prescriptions and the non-stick bandages for my shoulder. I'd get the stitches out in about a week.

"Not right now, maybe after I eat."

"You'll be taking my room. Donna is going to bunk in the guest room. I'll take the couch."

"I can take the couch. I don't sleep all that much anyway."

"I can tell. You always have a lot of baggage." He crossed his left arm over his chest and stroked along the skin under my eye. He was gentle so as not to push on the bruises, and I made myself not frown at me allowing him to touch me. Other than Savvy or Amber, the kids at the Outreach, I avoided letting people into my personal space.

"No wonder you're single. Your flattery sucks."

"Probably. I had a lot of fun in my teens, and then I married. To the complete dismay of my kid and my ex, I haven't really looked since the divorce."

"Why not?"

"I don't know." He dropped his hand to his thigh and looked away from me. I wondered what he was keeping from me. "I have a certain...there's things I need in a relationship, and I just haven't found them yet."

"If you need a Little, Doc, Remy, and even Vega could help. They go to Xanadu regularly." After it was out, I didn't like the thought of him there.

He laughed loudly. "No, I'm not a Daddy or a Dominant. I don't have the urge to be called Daddy or Sir, or any of that. Consenting adults are allowed to have whatever kink makes them happy, but it's not my thing. What about you? I've heard you're a regular at Xanadu."

"A regular is a big stretch. They drag me along."

"No girlfriend?"

"No, or boyfriend for that matter. I just don't..." I laid my head back on the cushion. "I just haven't met anyone who makes me want to give up my solitary ways. Yet most people think I'm bi or gay by association, though. All my friends are."

"I'm Pansexual, everyone I've been with is a cis-woman, and then I was married for over twenty years, and I think I'm just not ready to start over with anyone."

"Being a cop and single dad can't be good for the dating life."

"That's an understatement. Last date I went on, I got called in the middle of dinner. They were not impressed with me."

"I think the right one will be."

"Maybe. Let me go see if I have anything to cook for dinner. Tonight, we relax, and then tomorrow it's back to work."

"This is going to sound weird, but I've really missed work."

"I'm sure. I have all the files and drives. Someone's going to bring whatever they found on your attack tomorrow." He pushed up from the couch, but I didn't lift my head.

I closed my eyes for a few minutes and enjoyed the peacefulness of his apartment. Almost three days of being poked and prodded, I was in the mood to decompress. As much as I wanted to ask him to get me the files, my brain just wasn't in it. Pain and the meds were making everything muddled, and my fascination with the way Marcel looked was a side effect of the stress I didn't need.

There were already too many changes in my life that I hadn't planned or prepared myself for. I'd spent most of my life being alone except for the past few years. Before the Cold Case squad, I'd thought I was content, maybe not happy, but I was good with where my life was. Then I met Marcel, and I hated to admit it, but I loved fighting with him, and then he'd introduced me to his daughter.

They made me question my choices and everything I was positive I understood about my life—about myself. I was too old to change. I didn't want to, or at least I hadn't thought so.

"Baby, did you fall asleep?" The softly whispered question made me open my eyes to find Marcel smiling down at me.

"No, just thinking."

"About what?"

"Nothing important."

"Is Chinese good for dinner? I really need to go shopping. My fridge and freezer are pretty empty."

"That's fine. Like I said, I'm not picky." He handed me a menu.

"Pick what you want while I call Savannah and see if she wants anything. She's constantly hungry, and she'll eat cold leftovers for breakfast. I'm an excellent dad just in case you're questioning my competency."

"I wasn't." I focused on the menu as he went back to the kitchen. I could survive this. Everything would be back to normal soon, and all the stupid shit in my head would disappear—like Marcel was an attractive man, and my heart was sure I loved Savvy like she was my own. I couldn't have any of that, and I'd do well to remember that. None of this was permanent. Once I was healed it was back to my place and we'd work the case. Everything would be back to normal just the way I needed it.

20

DOUGLAS

COLD CASE
UNIT

I leaned my shoulder against the doorframe of my bedroom as I watched Simon sleep. His nightly dose of painkillers had knocked him out. I should've fallen asleep hours ago, but all I'd done was lie on the couch and think about him in my bed. I'd pictured him there for months. Although, in my dreams, I'd curled around him and held him close.

How did I fall in love with him and not know it until I'd thought I'd lost him and Savannah? I hadn't imagined he'd be the one to make me want to change my life. The front door opening drew my attention, and I reached for my weapon I'd clipped back on my hip when I got up. I released the grip of my gun when Donna appeared at the entrance of the hall.

"Hey."

"Hey." She approached with a smile. She hadn't changed since I'd seen her last, maybe a bit happier, but exhausted from her trip.

"I thought I was coming to pick you up."

"I got in earlier than I thought and didn't want to wake you or Savannah. Is that him?" she asked as she leaned the front of her shoulder on the jamb and stared into the room.

"Yeah."

"Pretty."

I chuckled at her. "Please don't tell him he's pretty. I don't think he'd appreciate it."

"Doesn't change the fact he is. That's what you get for falling for a man gorgeous enough to be a damn model."

"Who said I've fallen for him?"

She snorted at me to show me what she thought of my question. That's one thing about Donna. She knew me better than anyone else. We'd been husband and wife, best friends, and if we hadn't decided on the divorce for our own happiness, I could see us still married. Same routine, but neither of us could continue like we'd done for over twenty years. We both deserved a present partner.

"I know you, Marcel. We spent two decades together. You're in love whether you want to be or not. And who's the bouncer at the door checking IDs?"

"That's Tony. He's the head of our daughter's security detail."

"He's very enthusiastic. I was waiting for a pat-down. He's hot enough I may have let him."

I snarled my nose and fervently shook my head. "Please, no mob enforcer boyfriends."

"Mob enforcer? What?"

"He works for Carmine Bianchi, a local ex-ish mob boss. Simon trusted him to come in for the rescue, and she's been under his protection since."

"What the hell happened? You didn't tell me everything."

"Come on to the kitchen. We'll have a beer."

"God, I could use one."

I led her to the kitchen. This had been her apartment, and I'd just taken it over when she moved. I opened the fridge and pulled out the last two beers, and reminded myself I needed to make a grocery run. Opening both, I handed her one and leaned back against the counter. She hoisted herself onto the counter beside me.

"Simon took Savvy—" I stopped as she snorted. "Simon's nickname for her and she loves it. As I was saying, he took her to drop off food and non-perishable items to an underground homeless community. When they left, he heard footsteps and got suspicious. As they reached the opening of the alley, shots were fired. He found her a place to hide, gave her his weapon, and led an unknown number of men away from her without a weapon or vest."

"Did you have a talk with him about that?"

"Not yet. He made a call to Carmine to pick up a package and make sure it didn't have a mark on it. When they caught up to him miles away, they asked where Douglas's brat was, and he told them to shoot him because they weren't getting her."

"He told them that?"

"Yes, another thing to have a talk with him about."

"Have you figured out why they wanted her?"

"Probably a warning. Maybe they think I'm getting too close? We really don't have anything. Hate to say it, we need another body."

"Is our daughter okay?"

"She's good. She's ordering around a mob boss and his enforcer, the enforcer that she shot."

She laughed. "That's our girl."

"He said something similar. His first thought when he woke up in pain, and he only wanted to know she was okay. He would've died for our daughter and I..." Every time I thought about it, that panic hit me in the center of my chest.

"You're thinking what-ifs, Marcel. He's alive." She leaned her chin on my shoulder.

"But he was willing to sacrifice himself."

"And he would've done it for our daughter, and if he hadn't, we'd have lost them both."

"We got a...oh, hi."

Donna and I jerked our gazes to the door to find Simon in the doorway in low-slung pajama pants. His thick black pubes peeking over the waistband. *Shit.*

"Damn," she whispered.

"No."

"If you're not, I definitely am." I nudged her with my elbow.

"What do we have?"

"Another body, near Seamus's bar. Doc says the same missing teeth and burned fingertips."

"Torture?" Donna asked.

"Yeah, from what Doc said, this is the worst one yet. He already sent pictures off to Vega to run facial recognition but they're not holding out much hope. I got the address."

"Get dressed." He nodded and turned to head back to my bedroom.

"Marcel, my oldest friend and former husband, if you don't get him, I'm making him mine."

"Back off. Give me a chance at least."

"He's going to need help with doing up his jeans, I'm going to offer…" I barred her from jumping off the counter.

"Stay right where you are." I handed her my beer I hadn't even had a chance to take a sip of and went to find Simon. When I stopped outside my door, I heard his curses. He'd gotten his jeans up, but he wasn't having any luck zipping them and securing the button. "Need help?"

"Yes." He hissed. "I'm not going to the crime scene in sweats. Especially not around Seamus."

"I finally get to meet the infamous Seamus."

"Don't get too excited."

He kept his eyes on me as I crossed the room, I tugged the jeans higher onto his hips, and he held his breath as I slipped the button through the hole, and then zipped up his fly. I was careful not to touch him any more than necessary, but his thick, treasure trail teased the backs of my fingers. I'd never wanted to pet a man so much in my life.

"Need help with your shirt?"

"No, I think I can get that one on my own. Thanks."

"You're welcome."

"Was that Donna?"

"Yeah, she's a few days early. Let's get going." I went to my dresser and pulled out jeans and a t-shirt. I dropped my sweats, pulled on my own clothes without turning around.

I glanced over my shoulder to see him slipping his feet into his boots and then bending over to pull up the zippers on the inside. He was grunting and groaning as his body protested.

"You sure you want to come along?"

"I'm fine, Marcel. Keep Seamus away from my ass. I might shoot him if he even thinks about spanking me." He grumped as he clipped his holster and shield to his waistband.

"What is it with you and mob bosses?"

"Let's face it, even at my advanced age, I'm still pretty."

"Advanced? Try being almost fifty."

"Um, you're not pretty, Marcel. You're delusional."

"Ouch, get your ass in gear, pretty man." I chuckled as he left the bedroom.

"Marcel, I require caffeine," he called out, and I shook my head.

What the hell had I gotten myself into? I was going to be trapped in the apartment with my daughter, ex-wife, and the man I wanted, not to mention the psycho cat. That was four against one, and I wasn't liking those odds. I put on my own boots and walked out of my bedroom, and took a minute to write a note for Savannah.

I never left while she was sleeping without leaving a note to at least say I loved her. Our jobs were dangerous. We wanted her to always know we loved her. Before I left her room, I leaned down to brush a kiss to her forehead and tucked the blankets tighter around her.

"When did you get a house goblin?" Donna asked as I entered the kitchen to find Moriarty seated in the center of the table.

"That's not mine. That's Simon's. I am *not* claiming that one."

Simon tossed a few cat treats onto the table from a safe distance. "He roams at night."

"Of course, he does. No wonder I couldn't sleep." I snarked, and he rolled his eyes. "Donna, meet Simon and Moriarty, Simon, meet Donna. Are you two being polite?"

"Why wouldn't we be polite? I have so many stories to share."

"She promised to tell me all your embarrassing ones."

"I'll pay for you to stay in a hotel, Donna."

"Not a chance. He seems nice, Marcel. You've been calling him a pain in the ass for months. I think half-ass cop a few times."

"Oh, is that right, Douglas?" He left the kitchen glaring at me the entire way.

"Did you really have to do that?"

"Oh, yes, yes, I did. I'm getting you a boyfriend before I leave again, and Simon is going to be said boyfriend."

"You're aiming too high there. He's in no way attracted to me."

"We'll see. Get to work."

Ten minutes later, after telling Tony what was going on, he just nodded and settled into the chair he'd set up beside the door, and we were headed off to the crime scene. Carmine and now Seamus, what the hell was going on?

21

GRAVES

On the way to the crime scene, I tipped my head back and took a quick nap. Those damn painkillers were kicking my ass. I hated medicine of any kind. For the first time in four years, I'd had a dreamless sleep with no tossing and turning, that was until the phone rang. When the SUV lurched to a stop, I lifted my head and opened my eyes as we parked outside Seamus's pub. I tried to avoid this area as much as possible.

"Do you need to stay in here?"

"No, Marcel, I'll be fine. I need to get back to work."

"I know you do, but you're hurting."

"I know my limits. Let me do this." I pulled the handle and got out without looking at him again. I slipped under the crime scene tape and spotted Doc with his clipboard. Stevenson was nowhere to be seen, but I knew he was around. That man wouldn't let Doc out of his sight

"Look at you, practicing for the eventual downfall of society where Zombies take over." Doc batted his silver lashes at hyperspeed, and I flipped him off.

"Your Daddy needs to stop letting you watch horror movies."

"Daddy likes how I cuddle during those horror movies."

"You two behave. What do you have for us, Doc?" Marcel asked as he crouched down beside the body.

From what I could see, the beating was much more severe. His face was swollen and was almost unrecognizable, so Vega has her work cut out for her. I checked the crowd for any familiar faces, saw several, but no one who was going to talk. Even with our free passes, a lot of people didn't want to be seen talking to the cops.

"Looks to be the same, I'll need to compare tool marks, but the type of torture was kept out of the press. I'll open him up once I get him back to the office. He looks to be about mid-thirties. Physically fit. What I can see of the nails and cuticles, they're clean and manicured, but he has some thick callouses. I checked and there's blood inside the clothes."

"Seamus recognize him?" I asked.

"Seamus isn't talking. The uniforms are getting nothing. He was told the assigned detectives were on their way."

"I'm not going in there," I said as I backed away.

"If I have to go, you're going. I'll make sure he doesn't get one hand on your ass."

"I don't trust you." Suspicious of his amusement, he'd probably let Seamus smack my ass just to be able to laugh at me.

"Aw, come on, baby."

"Well, this is a new development." Doc giggled.

"You're learning bad habits from Stevenson," I said accusingly.

"And I enjoy every one of those bad habits. I'll call you when I start the autopsy."

"Thanks, Doc," Marcel said as he stood back up.

I reluctantly followed Marcel into the pub and found Seamus behind the bar with a pint. His eyes instantly lit up, and I groaned. He ducked out from behind the bar. He was a big Irish bastard, all muscle and not many brain cells.

"Simon, what an unexpected and very sexy surprise. How you been, baby?"

"I'll shoot you with a smile on my face." I made sure to keep him away from my back as he moved.

"Foreplay, I can deal with that."

Marcel cleared his throat obviously to cover a laugh. "I'm Detective Douglas. What do you know about the body in your alley?"

"Like I told the uniformed officers, I don't know shit. Can I get y'all a drink?"

"No, we're just here to ask questions." I leaned back against the wall and crossed my arms the best I could.

"I didn't survive this long on the streets, and as a successful business owner"—I rolled my eyes at Seamus—"would I leave a body outside my pub?"

"Anything weird happening lately, Seamus?" I asked.

"No."

"Any new players in town?"

"No. You know we're pretty territorial, baby. You've been around here long enough."

"Who would want to bring down heat on you and Bianchi?" Marcel asked, shifting a bit until he was between me and Seamus, as the bigger man made a few more steps towards me.

"Again, no damn idea. We mind our own business. You're respectful, then we're respectful."

"Did you recognize the victim?" I asked.

"Nope, but he wasn't looking his best. Listen, Simon, you know me. If I want to handle business, I make sure someone knows who the message is coming from. This ain't my style."

"Detective Graves already vouched for you."

"Knew you loved me, baby."

"I'd rather date Dekland."

Seamus let out a big booming laugh. "You're going right for the kill shot, aren't you?"

"Whatever works." I kept my expression neutral. I didn't mind Seamus. He was too handsy for my liking, but I knew he wouldn't bullshit us. I just didn't believe he was telling us everything. "Cut the shit, Seamus, you know something."

"I don't know anything. All that we've heard is there's bodies being dumped at Bianchi's place. We all assumed he was the target. Bring down heat on him…take it from somewhere else."

"Who do you know who would have it out for me or Douglas?"

"You? There's a damn long list, but you're on a no-touch list. Bianchi, and me, Boss, you're untouchable…we made sure of that. The less well-known guys don't have the clout or balls to go against us. Douglas, never heard of you before this." He barely bared Marcel a glance.

"Why is Simon protected?"

"What you see is what you get with him. He's relentless but fair. He doesn't pull that bullshit all the other cops do when it comes to us. Also, he's a part of the Outreach, and we've always respected what Boss and his people do. Have you talked to Boss?"

"Why would we talk to Boss?" Marcel asked.

"They're hitting the areas right on the border of the demilitarized zone."

"They are, aren't they? You heard rumors about someone targeting Boss?" I asked and tried to remember any threats but couldn't think of anything. If someone really wanted to mess with the Outreach and us, those bodies would've been dropped closer. Drama like that would cause trouble with our funding.

"No, baby. Boss wields a lot of power around here, more than even we do. Power creates enemies."

"But taking Boss down, we haven't heard anything around the Outreach."

"I'm just saying, doesn't mean it has anything to do with the Outreach. We done here? The cop cars are fucking with my business."

"Might as well close down for the night. Those lights are going to be flashing until dawn." I smirked

He closed the distance between us and leaned into my space. "Why won't you admit it? You want me, baby. How long are you going to be able to ignore it, huh?"

"Seamus, you'll be the next to turn up on one of Doc's tables, and I could get away with it."

His bearded cheek brushed against mine. "Dump the stiff. You can go home with me. Salvage my night."

I made sure he could hear as I released the snap. "I'll ruin every night for you. Try me."

"You know the more vicious you are, the sexier you get."

"Simon, let's go." Marcel pulled me from between the wall and Seamus. He handed Seamus his card and followed me out of the pub. "What is it with you and mobsters?"

"I warned you." I growled over my shoulder and flipped him off as he smirked.

"It's fucking amazing."

"I was starting to like you, and you're losing a lot of points again."

He stepped up beside me. "You know this would be easier if you made an infographic for this so-called points system I'm supposed to adhere to."

"That would make it too easy for you to game the system. We need a free wall when we get home...back to your apartment. I need a visual board. Will Savvy be okay with that?"

"Savvy shot someone." I smiled. "You and Donna could be a little less happy about her turning bloodthirsty."

"She's the daughter of a Marine and a Homicide Detective. She's already corrupted."

"True. I'll have Doc send us his notes and all the witness reports. Do you think this has something to do with the Outreach?"

"My gut says no, but we can't afford to ignore any line of inquiry. We haven't received any threats. No threats of reduced funding which is usually our main concern. All-hands-on-deck when the committees start calling. Like I said, crime is down. No gang or drug activity. The city looks at us as if we're revitalizing the community."

"But what if that's an issue?" Marcel asked as he opened my door. "Gentrification of an area brings up housing prices. There's been a lot of new industry and business lately."

"I'll talk to someone at the permit office when they open and see if one single company has been requesting permits for new construction or renovation stuff."

"Let's get you home, you didn't sleep enough, and I hadn't slept at all." He closed the door, and I watched as he circled the front of the vehicle. Then he'd settled into the driver's seat.

"I thought you went to bed the same time as me."

"I have a lot on my mind right now, and then Donna came in, and then the call came. It's still early enough for us to get a bit of sleep."

I nodded as he backed out onto the main road and headed back toward his building. "I can sleep on the couch, Marcel."

"No, you'll be comfortable in my bed. The couch is fine for me. I bought the damn thing because it was comfortable to stretch out on."

I turned my head to study his profile. "If I'm too much trouble, you'll tell me, right?"

"Simon, you'll never be too much trouble, and Savannah would make me drag you back home if you even tried to go back to your place."

"I adore your kid. You know that, right?"

"Feeling is definitely mutual."

I turned my attention to the scenery flying by, the bright lights of bars and twenty-four-hour businesses. I was exhausted, and I hurt, and I just wanted to go back to bed. The dead-end case was driving me insane. Most people watched TV and those true crime shows and thought everything could be solved in a few days. It was sometimes months of investigation before the case made it to some box that would just collect dust. And if it was solved, there was still the process in court that could take years.

I just wasn't ready to have four bodies with no answers. I needed to solve this one, and I needed to solve it quickly because I wanted my life back. One where I wasn't having weird feelings about my damn temporary partner or that I checked him out when he'd changed in front of me. Or even the fact that my brain wasn't protesting the endearments from him when I wanted to gut anyone else who used them. Four decades of disinterest, and I didn't want to find out what came next—I didn't know if I was prepared to feel something.

22

DOUGLAS

COLD CASE
UNIT

We'd gotten home after attending the autopsy of our newest yet unnamed victim. I'd picked up all the witness and forensic reports that were available. Simon needed to get more rest, and I knew he was hurting, but he didn't want anyone to see especially Savvy.

I was learning quite a bit about him. For one, Simon constantly ate as I handed him his second bag of popcorn that afternoon. I didn't even want to talk about his lethal ingestion of caffeine with mind-boggling levels of caramel syrup. He barely looked at me, and he muttered a thanks but hadn't taken his eyes off the wall where we'd tacked all our photos and timeline cards. His brain never shut down, and it shocked me his body hadn't just collapsed from lack of sleep.

A weird chirping sound drew my attention to the cat's cave, and Simon threw a treat. I barely saw the cat pounce before he was back inside. That thing hid all day and roamed all night. It was a creepy wrinkled mass of dark gray skin. It looked like something from nightmares, but Savvy and Donna were determined to make friends with the thing. I should've known they were delusional.

"You know your animal is creepy, right?"

"He's adorable. He has a certain charm. Don't hate on him." He fussed at me as he bumped my shoulder with his.

I was about to argue with him when his phone rang, and he instantly answered. A sweet voice over the speaker made Simon smile as he placed his phone on his thigh.

"Hey, Miss Flo. Been behaving yourself?"

"You're not around so, yes."

Another one, why am I not surprised? How is the man single when he had more admirers than a dozen people would have in their lifetimes? He was a gorgeous man, and I understood the appeal. I was more than tempted.

"I don't think I could keep up with you."

"I'm sure you could, honey."

He laughed. "What about that young man I got you a date with? Perfect cougar bait."

"Couldn't keep up. You'd think a man in his thirties could rock my sixty-year-old—" He cleared his throat, and she giggled. "So, what do I owe for the pleasure of hearing your voice?"

"Anyone been buying up property around the strip? Maybe a company filing too many permits?" he asked as he tried to get his legal pad to take notes. I took it from him and grabbed a pen. He mouthed *thanks,* and I nodded.

"Nothing suspicious. Just the usual construction and remodeling projects. No new companies that I know of, and you know we love our gossip around here."

"Any rumors about revitalizing the strip area?"

"No. Boss pretty much has a monopoly down there. No one is going to succeed unless they approach the area and people with respect. You know he's all for new businesses to increase employment and better housing."

There was another mention of Boss and how he ran that area, and as much as Simon said his gut told him it had nothing to do with his friend or the Outreach, we needed to schedule a sit-down with Boss.

"Nothing to spark concern?"

"No. This about the body dumps?"

"What have you heard?"

"Nothing much. News isn't really saying more than bodies were found. No statements were made, or the public being urged to call in tips. Seems suspicious."

He snorted. "You still going to your Murder Mystery Nights?"

"Yes, the new host is hot as fuck, honey, a little older than my usual type, but I may make an exception."

"Of course, you will. Men over forty aren't out to pasture, Miss Flo."

She clucked her tongue and huffed as if he'd caused her the greatest of offenses. I didn't know why but I was picturing an unassuming grandmotherly looking woman at work and probably running a club like Xanadu as her Queendom at night.

"If you'd take me up on my offer, I'd know for sure."

"I am more than sure that I wouldn't be able to keep up with you." I gave Simon a double take as his voice dipped until it was low and sultry. Where the hell did that come from? "I'm old and exhausted."

"You just need some good loving, Simon. You have my number."

"I've got it. Get back to work, Miss Flo. If you hear anything, you call me."

"You'll be the first one I do."

"Thanks." They said their goodbyes, and he disconnected the call and then tossed the phone aside. "Another bust."

"You have way too many admirers."

"I'm surrounded by flirty people." He smirked, and I loved that little quirk of the corner of his mouth.

"Simon, I know what your gut says, but we really should sit

down with Boss and pick his brain. If we asked the right questions, maybe it'll spark a memory."

He sighed and ate a few pieces of popcorn. "Boss is the only one who's completely hands-on with the Outreach. I'd like to say that he'd tell us if he were receiving threats, but he doesn't like any drama. He prefers to take care of all that on his own."

"Can't hurt to have a conversation."

"True. Where did Donna take Savvy?"

"Dinner with Savvy's security detail, of course. I think Donna's paying way too much attention to Tony."

"Tell her to ask about his scars."

I loudly laughed as he scooted down the couch and kept staring at the wall. "What are you thinking?"

"It's like chess," he said, then picked at his snack.

"What?" The man made me dizzy with his subject changes. I think he was worse than his friends. I'd learned his process, and while I didn't get how he worked it out, he did.

"Pawns are typically sacrificed in play because they hold no power. One or two moves, back or forward."

"So now we're looking at this case like a game of chess?"

"I hope not because it was never really my game. I hated playing at school."

I liked when he let things slip. Little details about his life because even as much as we hung out, he wasn't always forthcoming. I just wanted him to open up to me.

"So, if we view our murdered unknowns as pawns, they're being sacrificed for a greater movement. What are they covers for?" I asked.

"Could be a power play. Carmine, Seamus, and Dekland are the biggest dogs in the fight. Someone planning a coup would need to take those three out. Again, an assassination plot is the better option. Kill shot, take it. Seamus has no one with enough brains or power to ascend. Carmine made sure his sons wouldn't want to follow in his footsteps. He's been clear that when his reign ends that the Bianchi family is no more."

"What about Dekland?"

"Mancini likes to talk big, but he doesn't have the backing or financial means to take over Seamus or Carmine's territories. He doesn't have the allies he needs either, unless he's partnering with the smaller gangs. Again, he doesn't have the backing. He's pretty much floundering now."

"Floundering?"

"He doesn't have the respect that Seamus and Carmine have. Honor among crime bosses. They're not friends, but they respect each other. Dekland has approached them on several occasions to form an alliance. Seamus laughed in his face, and Carmine doesn't mess with drugs or sex trafficking. Those are Dekland's main sources of income, and let's just say business has been bad. He's been getting a bit more heat from the Organized Crime squad the last year or so."

"Hurt pride is a huge motivator."

"Yeah, especially for him." He shifted and grimaced.

"Do you need a pill?"

"Later, I'd like to stay conscious a bit longer. As much as I like catching up on sleep, I'm not exactly used to being lazy."

"You have a right to be lazy, baby. You took a beating just days ago. You've been shot. That would warrant some downtime."

"I know, I get that, but I'm just not the type to let myself give in."

"I won't freeze you out of this case, but I need you to take up residence on this couch to work it. I'll take you to all the scenes, the coroner's office, wherever, but promise me you'll let yourself heal for me."

"I'll try."

"Not good enough."

"Well, it's the best you're getting. Keep trying to order me around, and I'll leave Moriarty treats on you while you sleep and let you fend for yourself."

I gasped at his cruelty, and he grinned. "I'm liking you a little less. You're losing points now."

"You say that like it'll break my heart, Marcel."

"Brat."

"You talk so sweetly, Detective." He turned away and went back to his study of the wall.

I shifted to lean back against the arm of the couch, and I studied him. He was so focused that nothing else existed for him except the photos and note cards. He reached for the stack of cards, but I got to them first and handed him those along with the pen.

Was it pathetic how much I wanted to be the subject of his focus? I dropped my gaze to his mouth and wondered what those curves would feel like under mine. And not just that quick one I'd taken at the hospital. I just didn't know what it would take to get his attention or if I even had anything that appealed to him. I rubbed my hand over my shaved head, felt the stubble where my receding hairline started. I was a big man, and I was still muscular, but my belly was getting a curve to it. We only had a five-year age gap, but he carried his so much better than me.

I bit off a deep sigh and got off the couch. It was too early to think about dinner, but I needed a distraction. I was close to doing something stupid, and backing off was my only option. Staring at the beautiful man just drove me closer to the edge.

23

GRAVES

I stumbled into the kitchen, rubbing my hand over my curls in search of coffee. The apartment was quiet, but I'd heard Marcel softly snoring on the couch. The guest bedroom door was closed, but the hallway bathroom shower was running. It was a school day, and Savvy must have been getting ready. My left hand was pretty much useless, but it had been a week, so the bruises were fading. They'd started turning that sickly jaundiced color that stood out on my pale skin. The bullet graze over my ear wasn't as bad as it could've been. The scar would be minimal.

A lot of that night was still a blur after I entered the shipyard. As hard as I tried to remember, the memories seemed to get farther away. I'd known I told myself to catalog everything, but the details weren't there other than the pain and me ordering them to kill me. They'd wanted Savvy. That's why I was beating myself up so much because it was her, and I needed to protect her.

I started a pot of coffee as quietly as I could and started searching the fridge for something to make for breakfast. I needed to start learning to do things for myself. More than anything, I needed to go home soon. At least I was decent in the kitchen. I hadn't needed those skills in a long time. Cooking just for myself was depressing on a good day. I remembered pre-Cold Case squad vegan and gluten-free, no fat Simon Graves. My former diet went the way of my buzzed head.

The new unit meant a chance at a do-over with my life. Summons by my parents was the only time I ate anything I hated. I cursed as I struggled opening packages but worked it out when I found a pair of kitchen scissors. By the time I sensed I wasn't alone in the kitchen, I had bacon in the oven to keep warm, eggs ready to scramble, and toast started. That task turned into a bit of a nightmare.

"Why aren't you still asleep?" Marcel asked as he passed close behind me and patted my hip as he went to pour himself coffee. I frowned at the affectionate touch.

"I slept all night." His answering grunt amused me.

One thing I'd learned above all else—midnight to two AM, and Marcel was ready to go, seven AM, and he was unbearable. I dropped butter into the pan, dumped in the eggs, and instantly started stirring.

"Savvy sounded like she was getting ready for school."

"This is about that time," he muttered as he refilled my mug and poured one for Savvy as I heard steps coming down the hall.

"Am I in an alternate universe? Breakfast that's not leftovers or microwaved?" I heard her backpack hitting the floor, and I glanced over my shoulder.

"Good morning to you too. Thank Simon, because this wasn't my doing."

"I know. Morning is fending for myself."

I chuckled as Marcel growled, and she hugged my waist. I dropped a kiss to her soft hair. "Make your coffee and then butter the toast for me, please. That's not working for me one-handed." I'd tried it and ate the three pieces I'd broken the first slice into.

"Got it."

"You're awfully agreeable at this early hour."

"Simon made me food."

"Can't I go even a few days without being awakened at the taint of dawn?" Donna's annoyed voice made Marcel's morning attitude seem cheerful.

"You signed up for early mornings." She snarled at Marcel as I carried the pan to the table.

I thanked Marcel as he quickly finished setting the table, and we all sat down after Donna poured the last of the coffee and started another pot.

"What's everyone's plans for the day?" Savvy asked.

"I'm taking the early riser to work to see about getting the rest of the forensic reports."

"Good luck getting those from Coleman before the next century," I said snarkily as I made my plate after Savvy piled food onto hers.

"I'm going to meet up with some friends that I let know I was back in the city. I'll be back by the time she gets off school."

I tensed as a big hand squeezed my thigh. "Thanks for cooking," Marcel said before he went back to eating.

Conversation went on around me as I tried to dissect why him touching me made me feel odd. Did the concussion and head wound mess up my usual calm and caution when it came to physical contact? I'd never liked it before, but with Marcel, I didn't feel overwhelmed or annoyed by the touches and teasing.

Savvy jumped up, gave out hugs, and headed for the door yelling bye. I snorted as she ordered Tony to get his ass in gear.

"She's going to be completely lost without enforcers to bully." I joked.

"This is all your fault. She didn't need any more encouragement to be assertive, and now she'll want to plot world domination."

"She'll excel." Donna and I said in unison, and Marcel shook his head.

"My home life has turned into four against one, and I'm not happy about it."

"Four? It's just me, Simon, and our daughter."

"That damn cat."

I nearly choked on my coffee. "He's ten pounds. You act like he's an apex predator ready to take you out while you're asleep."

"Exactly."

"You're ridiculous." I finished off my breakfast and stood to head to the sink.

"Baby, you actually think you're doing dishes one-handed?"

"I cooked, didn't I?"

"I don't care. Go get ready. We also have to see about getting your stitches out."

"Doc said he'd remove them for me and to just come by the morgue when I was ready."

"Then we'll hit the morgue on the way to work." He got up from the table and picked up his plate. He approached me. I stepped out of the way before he was close enough to touch. I couldn't keep allowing him to invade my personal space. "Um, I'll help you get dressed after you shower." He turned his back to me, and I noticed Donna staring at us.

Because it seemed like my only option, I escaped to his bedroom and quickly made the bed. With the plastic bags and rubber bands he kept in the bathroom for me, I wrapped my casted hand, and I was growing tired of the hard plaster that went to the middle of my forearm. I'd finally been able to stop taking the painkillers except at night and just used over-the-counter meds for the last few days.

I turned on the shower to heat as I stripped down and missed my large walk-in shower with the multiple showerheads. I needed to go home, but anytime I mentioned it, Marcel and I had an argument. I wanted to be surrounded by my things—the quiet that helped with my irritation.

I stepped into the tub, lifting my arm to rest my wrist on the shower rod to keep it from getting wet even with the bag. The water beat down on the back of my neck and the stiff muscles of my back. I carefully washed my hair and body. I couldn't wait to take a real shower or bath.

Before I lingered too long, I turned off the water and got out because Marcel still needed to take a shower. I dried, removed the bag, and brushed my teeth. I did the best I could with my curls with just finger combing them and using a bit of product to control any frizz. The steam of the shower hid my reflection. I couldn't recall the last time I'd looked at myself for longer than it took to get ready. People told me I was an attractive man. Some even claimed I was gorgeous, but I didn't see it.

It wasn't that I saw myself as an unattractive man or didn't take pride in my appearance, I just didn't always see the big deal in studying myself too much. I opened the bathroom door and stepped out into the bedroom. Found clothes and put them on, even tried zipping and buttoning my jeans so Marcel wouldn't feel obligated to help.

A knock sounded on the door, and I knew it was Marcel and told him to come in. "Did you put medicine on the graze?"

"I was waiting to get dressed first."

He didn't speak as he went to the bathroom and came back a few seconds later with the tube of antibacterial ointment. His big body crossed the room, took the cap off and put the medicine on his fingers, and then tossed the tube aside. He lifted my hair and carefully applied it.

"You don't have to keep taking care of me."

"I know I don't." He glanced at me and finished smoothing the thick medicine on.

"Just because of what I did for Savvy, you don't owe..."

"Simon, I do owe you for saving my daughter, but even if you hadn't, I'd still want to help with this, okay?" He buttoned my pants and slid the zipper closed. He didn't linger or try to touch me any more than necessary. "Are you okay? Need help with anything else?"

As I shook my head, he walked to his dresser, and I took in his profile. He had a strong, handsome face. He was a lot broader than my lean, slender frame and was built more like Remy. Tall, husky with a slight belly. My fast metabolism made it where I had to eat often but still didn't gain weight. I'd even tried lifting weights to bulk up and had lost several pounds instead.

"I'll take a quick shower and be ready to go."

"I'll fix a few travel mugs to go." I stepped into my unzipped tactical boots and bent at the waist to do them up.

"Thanks, baby, I appreciate it."

When I exited the bedroom, Donna was walking toward me.

"Thanks for breakfast, Simon."

"You're welcome."

"Can I talk to you for a minute?"

"Sure."

"What you did for Marcel and our kid, there's no thanking a person for that."

"I told him thanks wasn't needed."

"It is needed. But don't do anything like it again. Unarmed without body armor? Do I make myself clear? Marcel wouldn't have been able to live with you ending up dead no matter how expendable you think you are."

She didn't wait for me to answer, and I turned my head to watch her until she disappeared into the guest room. I'd always been expendable, and that wouldn't change. I shook my head, went to make our coffee to go, and filled my cat's bowls with water and food. I made him a small pile of treats he could pick from throughout the day. He never took more than one at a time as if he worried that he wouldn't get fed.

He'd been underweight and neglected when I got him, and

instead of eating fast, he'd always savored his food. We were both broken from some form of neglect. I thought he'd be all I needed when I found him at the shelter. I hadn't anticipated Savvy or Marcel, no more than I had my friends. I needed a break, but I didn't see one coming my way until we solved the case and I could get back to my life as normal.

24

DOUGLAS

COLD CASE
UNIT

He told me I didn't have to take care of him, but that's all I'd wanted for months. We'd gone to have Doc remove his stitches, picked up the reports, and headed to the basement. Tyson kept side-eyeing me every time I showed up in Homicide and then disappeared. I thought my new temporary office made him nervous. I flopped into Simon's chair as he sat on the edge of his desk and sat cross-legged.

"Toxicology is showing traces of a tranquilizer in all our victims," I said as I read over the new reports.

"Understandable, all four of our vics are well-built men. But they were also found with rope burns, which is one of the reasons Doc assumed they were held for a period of time."

"Did he find any stress injuries to the shoulders as if they were suspended?" I asked even as I went back to the ME reports.

"Not that he could find. The joints weren't dislocated. The tox reports and restraints open up the possibility that we're not looking for a male assailant."

"I'm getting more frustrated by the day." I sighed as we just kept throwing shit out there, and nothing was coming full circle in the way of evidence or getting us closer to a suspect. Simon wasn't bothered by it. What we were doing was his process. I respected the way he got the job done. Yet that didn't mean I was having an easy time of it.

"Join the club, Marcel."

"Although, tool mark analysis said it looks like the same pliers were used on all our victims. There was no degeneration of bone, no gum disease, or bad oral health. Someone would need some strength to remove the teeth." I scanned more of the paperwork. "What if we're looking for a woman who wants to take over? The drugs in the system. The way they were undressed and re-dressed after the murder. It's all too clean for a man, and I'm not stereotyping."

He stilled as if he'd had a thought. "We do have Jackie Darner. Her deceased husband ran the west side for probably twenty years before he came up missing, and his body was found a few weeks later in the landfill. Rumors are, she or their children took him out. It was well-known he ruled his crew and family with the same brutality. After his death, there was a big shakedown in the west side precinct by Internal Affairs, several uniformed cops and detectives were charged in a corruption sting, and there were a lot of transfers. Money laundering. Narcotics. Those cops became a one-stop-shop. Ms. Darner wasn't connected to the criminal side of her husband's business, but that doesn't mean she didn't take over."

"Do you think she's capable?"

"I wouldn't put it past her. Greed is a huge motivator, but for all intents and purposes, she's been living quite well off a life insurance policy and the proceeds of his company which her sons still operate. At least that's what I last heard."

"Was he connected to Seamus and Carmine?"

"Carmine, yes. Darner did business with him, but they fell out when he witnessed Darner strike his wife because she interrupted negotiations. Seamus...he wasn't big enough back then to cater to Darner's ego. Seamus had just taken over after his boss died from a heart attack. Thing is though, Darner wasn't part of the crowd."

"In what way?"

"You see, Donnie Darner was old money. You ask anyone, and they'd say he was a brilliant businessman, country club, tee times with the who's who of politics and big business. Ran a multimillion-dollar investment firm. They didn't think he worked his way up. He bought his way into the game with money and favors. Doing your time in the trenches is extremely important to Carmine, Seamus, and even Dekland."

"You think we can talk to Darner?"

"Yeah, let me make some calls."

"What about Dekland?"

"We're probably going to have to make a surprise visit. He won't go out of his way to be cooperative in any way. But his place is pretty much a compound, and I'd prefer to have our meeting...public. He has his own army. I can say he's slightly paranoid." He hopped off the desk and leaned over to reach his keyboard. He muttered to himself as he had to type with one finger.

I watched as he did a search for contact information on Jackie Darner, but I moved my attention away from the screen onto the man. I should be completely focused on the case, on all my cases just like I'd always been. Nothing and no one except Savannah had ever come between me and my work. Although having him in my home and working with him twenty-four-seven was fucking with my single-mindedness when it came to my goals and closing my investigations.

He picked up the receiver on his desk phone and punched in the number. I relaxed back to listen to his side of the conversation. My gaze moved over his lean body, and I wanted to hold him more than anything. Our mornings and helping him dress were completely fucking with my head.

"This is Detective Simon Graves. I'm trying to reach Ms.

Darner." He paused. "No, sir, this is just a request for an interview. My partner and I can meet with her at her home or at the Southside Precinct at her earliest convenience...Yes, I'll hold thank you." He covered the mouthpiece. "Keep your fingers crossed."

"Do you think she'll meet us?"

"I don't see why not. If she doesn't, we'll just have a reason to look closer...Yes, yes, Ms. Darner, as I told the gentleman who answered, I'm a detective, and my partner and I would like to meet with you. Unofficially, we just want to ask a few questions."

The corner of my mouth tugged upward at his bratty eye roll at whatever the lady was saying. I wanted to listen in, but I'd have to wait until he filled me in.

"Yes, you're not being investigated for any wrongdoing. We have a few cases, and we've spoken to some of your husband's business associates...I understand he's been dead for nearly a decade, but we'd just like to inquire about his...Yes, ma'am, if you could just give us a few minutes, we'll come to you if that would make you more comfortable."

An interview on her turf may help her relax enough to let us question her. He was a brilliant man. He was the entire package that I had no chance of getting.

"You're more than welcome to have your attorney or your sons there with you. As I said, this isn't official. Just working on clearing up some theories...the Cold Case Unit, ma'am... Tomorrow at ten would be perfect, thank you, ma'am. Have a good day." He hung up and turned to smile at me. "We'll have one chance."

"It's all we'll need if we ask the right questions."

"And do you know what those right questions are?"

"Don't be so defeatist." I smirked as he glared at me.

"Well, another couple getting cozy in the early mornings. Stay out of our corner, though. Third row in the right is Doc and Stevenson's spot, so you'll have to find your own." Remy warned.

I narrowed my eyes at him when Simon straightened and turned his back to me. The first time Simon wasn't rushing to get out of my personal space, and Remy had to be his normally bratty self. As Remy went to take a sip of his coffee, I flipped him off, and he proceeded to choke. Just what he deserved.

"You think we have time to stop by Dekland's?" I asked.

"Not a bad idea. Make sure you have your vest on."

"I'm not the one who forgets, baby." I fussed at him as I stood and headed for the door right behind him.

"I was off work. I didn't need it."

"It appeared that you did."

"I don't want to be in listening distance when those two give in to all that sexual tension," Remy said behind me, and I threw a pen at him as I passed Stevenson's desk.

"You really want to stay down here, Simon?"

"Um, who has recently been spending all his time down here?"

"I was told Tyson wouldn't be mad if I seduced someone up from the basement." I stepped up beside him as we exited to the parking lot and headed toward my vehicle.

"You're out of luck, everyone else is paired off, and I'm Asexual. You've already failed at that assignment." He grinned at me, and I nearly stumbled at his revelation.

I knew Asexual people. Some had sex, some were indifferent, but I'd never really thought that was an option with him. One friend I had was sex-repulsed, and they didn't even like thinking about it. I was in love with a man that wouldn't ever let me love him or love me back. It was like a punch to the gut, but my choice to just be friends didn't change. His Asexuality didn't matter because I already knew we'd never have a romantic relationship, but that didn't change the fact that my heart was breaking a bit at the news.

"You work with a lot of sexual people."

"Sex positivity doesn't bother me. I don't have any issues with sex. I've just never been interested. I'd never really thought about it until after I talked with Doc and Vega one night while they were having one of their debates." He paused at the front of the SUV. "It's why I hate when my parents try to set me up because I know they only do it with the intention that I marry and give them grandchildren."

"Your wishes should be respected."

"You'd think so, but it doesn't. Let's go talk to Dekland, and afterward, we'll discuss strategy on how to approach the interview with Darner."

"Sounds like a plan. Do we have to stop and pick you up food? It's been a few hours."

"You're not funny, but, yeah, let's hit a drive-thru."

I chuckled as he hurried to get in the passenger side, and I shook my head. I was going to need to start keeping snacks in the vehicle. Then I realized once this case was over, I was back to Homicide, and he was back to his cold cases. Our time was running out, and that was another thing I didn't know how to process.

GRAVES

COLD CASE
UNIT

I called an older partner of mine who still worked Organized Crime and got the whereabouts of Dekland. Why was meeting him always like a bad gangster movie? The restaurant we'd arrived at was closed for him. Guards littered the room, and he was having lunch.

There was one thing I'd learned I hated most about my job, and his name was Dekland Mancini. He was as bigoted and old school as they came. He learned being a mobster from *Scarface* and *The Godfather*. I was ready to hear him talk like *Brando* or *Pacino*. I just wanted to punch him and get it over with. As most people said, can't get much more demoted than the dungeon.

I drank my espresso and tried not to glare; Marcel's badly concealed amusement wasn't helping my mood. My hand was killing me on top of everything. I should've taken half a pill before I left the house.

"Enjoying your lunch there, Dekland?" I asked.

"I was until about ten minutes ago. You're no longer in Organized Crime or Homicide. What did I do for you to fuck up part of my day?"

"Maybe I just wanted to fuck up your entire day."

"I wouldn't put it past you, Graves. So, ask what you want to, and we can end this visit."

"What do you know about the bodies being dumped around Bianchi and Finnegan's places?"

"Couldn't happen to a nicer two men."

"Cut the shit, just tell me."

"Listen, Graves. I don't know shit."

"Show him the pictures," I told Marcel, and the man pulled out the photos and laid them out one by one. "Four men, all clean slates and ready to be erased with not even a blip on the radar. Do you recognize them? I'm not fucking asking you to confess to some crime. I just want to know do you recognize them."

He studied each one as he wiped his mouth, and I waited for him to say something. "Seen them around. They work for some construction company." He snapped his fingers, and I gritted my teeth. "They hung out over on Frederick Ave, where foremen pick up day labor."

"And how would you know that?"

"My old man had a remodeling business. Most of his labor came from them so he didn't have to pay anyone on the books. I didn't always have this." He waved around the room.

"Shoving little girls into shipping containers must be very lucrative for you." I smirked as his face turned red. Probably wasn't the best idea to provoke the guy. He'd rubbed me the wrong way since he came on the scene. I could excuse some drug running or a beat down or two, but he sold girls to whoever would pay him the highest price. Thing was, all we had were rumors. We'd never caught him in the act, but I'd give anything to take his ass down.

"Disgraceful business that, I have five sisters. Couldn't imagine…"

"Don't even try that *I have sisters* bullshit with me. I've known your ass way too long." I glanced at Marcel as he picked up the photos from the table and slid them back in the envelope.

"Believe what you want, Graves. You and your lot are no better than me. You run the entire strip."

"We offer support and give respect to anyone on the strip. You heard about any trouble coming our way?"

"You, Remy and Boss, if you weren't considered untouchable, you'd have targets right between your eyes." He paused, and the corner of his thin lips pulled up into a nasty grin. "Seems someone didn't listen to the word on the street. Heard someone tried to kill you."

"Wasn't you, was it?"

"If it was me, you wouldn't be sitting there. There's something you gotta learn, Graves. Power is all we have around here. In this city, the biggest and baddest rule. Yet when you have a very small group of supposed do-gooders who run the biggest territory, someone's going to try to take you out."

"Is that a threat I heard, Dekland?" I was a bit paranoid after the attack on Savvy and me, but I wouldn't put anything past Dekland. We'd never been the friendliest rivals.

"No threat, Detective. All I'm saying is someone may be gunning for you all. We all have enemies. Is this conversation over with?"

"Thank you for your time." I stood at the same time as Marcel and was amazed he'd stayed quiet most of the exchange. He preferred to take the lead. We exited the restaurant into the late afternoon sun and headed for the SUV. "You were awful quiet."

"You had it handled. I don't think he did it, though. Although, I would like to knock that smug expression off his face."

I snorted. "He gets that a lot. I thought about it the entire time I was talking to him." I opened the passenger door and got in. I buckled up as Marcel got in. "Another dead end?"

"Maybe not. Want to check out the address he gave us?"

"Sure, nothing planned for the afternoon."

"What are your thoughts on Darner tomorrow?"

"I don't know. Outside the events where I met her and Mr.

Darner, nothing much to remember. Quiet. Very much a cultured lady. We talked a bit about boarding school life." She'd seemed conditioned to her status in life. She'd hid a bit of humor under her cool exterior. Her husband had never been one of my favorite people to interact with at functions. It wasn't hard to notice the way she tensed when he'd approached or placed his hand on the small of her back or grabbed her elbow to guide her where he wanted her to go. My cool politeness hadn't missed his attention either and hadn't cared all that much.

"Sounds exciting."

"It was a blast." I threw a bunched-up napkin at him as he chuckled at my expense. "All I wanted was to have a normal life."

"What would you consider a normal life?"

I flinched at the question and tried to remember what I'd assumed a regular, boring life would be like. Before I answered, I thought over how much I wanted to give away, and in the end, I said fuck it and answered honestly. "I don't know, never had one. I wanted friends instead of adversaries. I wanted to be a little less hunted by the popular guys because I was an uptight American. Go home at night, over the weekends, or at holidays."

"So, you were just flown in for the requisite photo op." There wasn't any amusement in his voice when he spoke.

"Yep, that's unless they had a layover between flights to some tropical paradise. What about you? You said you had a dad and brothers, sisters-in-law?"

"My mother passed away from an embolism a few months after the birth of my baby brother. I was seven. I don't remember much about her other than the stories my dad and older brothers told. Dad worked, we took care of ourselves, and then when we got old enough, we started working at the family construction company. First site clean-up. Yet one of my big chores was cooking for everyone."

"Really? Those cooking skills of yours are more than a little rusty."

"Hey, you said my food was worth putting up with me."

"It had fat and flavor. I would've given you any compliment."

"I'm not feeling the love, baby. After all the devotion and care I've bestowed upon you…it's disappointing and ungrateful."

"I'm going home."

"No, you're not, not before we find out who's trying to kill you and our kid."

As my chest tightened at him calling Savvy ours, I jerked my gaze to him to see if he was making fun of me. "Our kid?" I gave myself a mental slap on the back as the question came out steady.

"She claimed you, so, yes, our kid."

I didn't have a chance to answer as he pulled into the parking lot and parked along the front of the lot where trucks were pulling up with men sitting in the back. There were a few familiar faces. I unbuckled and got out.

"Hey, Chance," I called out, and the tired guy turned, a smile tilting his mouth. Even knowing he was Cash's brother, I couldn't see them as siblings.

"Graves, what brings you out here?" He approached but slowed down when he spotted Marcel.

"This is my new partner, Detective Douglas. We got a few pictures for you to look at. You got a minute?"

"For you, all the time in the world."

Marcel pulled out the same images we'd shown Dekland and handed them to Chance. "Do you recognize them?"

He cycled through the four images. We still weren't holding out much hope with the fourth victim. The attack had pulverized his nose, jaw and displaced his orbital sockets, but Vega was still working on reconstructing them the old-fashioned way.

"Shaughnessy, he'd been around the past six months or so, got picked up and never came back. Figured he'd gotten lucky and scored a full-time gig." He handed the photo back to Marcel. "Boyd, mean motherfucker. Got kicked off job sites until word got around, and no one wanted him, not even if they were desperate." He studied the third. "Staitland, asshole, always smelled of alcohol no matter how early it was, but he did whatever job he was offered." Chance checked out the fourth one.

"We haven't gotten an ID on him yet, you'd make Vega happy, but I think she's having too much fun gluing his skull back together."

Chance choked on a laugh. "She would. My sister has that twisted little computer geek wrapped around her finger."

"You're Cash's brother?" Marcel asked.

"She's the oldest and got all the height in the family. Playing music doesn't always pay the bills. This helps when studio or bar gigs are slow." He brought his attention back to the image. "Could be Kerouac, not his real name, and don't think he ever gave it. Always had some Beat Lit book in the back pocket of his coveralls. Pretty smart and interesting guy. He went missing several weeks back."

"Did they all get picked up by a common guy?" Marcel inquired as he took the last photo and put them back in the envelope.

"Not that I remember. Weren't ever on a crew with me."

"Did this Kerouac guy maybe ever mention where he lived or anything?"

"Some flophouse on the strip. I think Ticket owns the building. Kerouac mentioned his name. Graves, you know Ticket isn't too discerning in his tenants as long as they pay their rent every Friday and don't have the cops come to his buildings. He rents to everyone."

"Thanks, Chance. If you notice someone else going missing, you let me know, okay?"

"Not a problem, Graves. I gotta get going, need a shower and a cold beer."

"See you later." I returned his wave as he jogged off to get in his car.

"Is any of that information going to help us?" Marcel leaned back against the grille of his vehicle.

"I don't know. None of these companies give names, and they all pay cash. This seems to be the common denominator, though. These guys are out here just for the cash jobs. Promise of that, and most of them would do whatever was asked. We can go talk to Ticket, but he won't be very helpful. Like Chance said, he's not too particular about his tenants if they pay. Although, if this guy is the one we're looking for, Ticket might still have something he couldn't sell. People get kicked out, and he pawns what he can."

"Better than what we had a few hours ago."

"I'll give Vega a call and tell her what we know about the possible fourth victim. She'd probably have more luck with Ticket than us."

"Information is information, no matter how we get it, and Vega is pretty scary."

"Why is everyone so scared of her?"

"Have you met her?"

"Yeah, but she's good at her job."

"Did you get the pat-down?"

"I thought I was going to have to tase her. That was more action than I ever wanted to have." I flipped Marcel off as he loudly laughed. "Let's get back. We still have to talk about how to approach Ms. Darner and what questions to ask. Like I said, we have one chance at this, and it's best we don't offend her."

"I'll let you question her. You have a history with her and her former husband. Maybe that will help us out."

I could only hope he was right, I was running out of knives to throw, but we didn't have time. We just needed to find some suspects because I didn't want to rely on another body to move our case forward.

DOUGLAS

COLD CASE
UNIT

I t was odd being back in my suits, I'd gone more casual since working with Simon, but I wouldn't complain about being able to see how he filled out a hand-tailored suit. I was a big man and always had my suits custom-made, but next to him, I looked shabby. We'd been silent since we'd left the precinct. We'd practiced our approach until the early hours of the morning.

I'd made sure he understood I wanted him to take the lead. They had a common background and had spoken in the past, so maybe that would ease the sting of any of our questions. We exited our vehicle and made our way toward a stately manor. The home was in Hylen Estates, the most affluent part of the city. As we stood on the stoop, I glanced at him. Took in the lift of his chin, the strong set of his shoulders, and he looked like he belonged there.

"You okay?"

"Yeah, yeah, I'm fine. We just have to make sure we get this right."

"You'll be perfect, baby. You're a familiar face."

"But that was years ago. Let's just hope she has a long

memory," he said as he pushed the button of the doorbell and a loud chime sounded inside.

A few minutes later, the door opened, and a petite woman in a maid's uniform answered. "Good morning, gentlemen. How may I help you today?"

"Yes, good morning, I'm Detective Graves, and this is Detective Douglas. Ms. Darner is expecting us."

"Of course, please, come in. I'll show you to the sitting room and let Mrs. Darner know you've arrived."

I motioned him to precede me and then I followed him inside. The sound of my dress shoes echoed too loudly off the expensive tile floors. We walked into a large room with two sofas positioned in front of the massive fireplace. The lady motioned to one of the couches, and we took a seat as she exited. I felt so out of place, but I tried to relax the sudden stiffness of my body. If I was tense, then they'd notice.

The soft click of heels made us stand, and then a woman, maybe in her seventies, entered in a bright, red pantsuit. Her completely silver hair twisted into a flawless up-do.

"Simon, it's a pleasure to see you again." She greeted Simon with a friendly smile, and she held out her hand.

He gently took it and shook as he gave her an award-winning smile. "You, too, Ms. Darner. I was wondering if you'd remember me."

"You were the highlight of those boring functions."

"As were you."

"I doubt that, but you were always a gentleman. And you must be Detective Douglas." She shook my hand, but it was less friendly and shorter than the one she'd given Simon.

"Yes, ma'am. Thank you so much for meeting us this morning."

"Of course, I don't know what I can do to help." She motioned, and we retook our seats.

"We just have a few questions, Ms. Darner." Simon's serene

tone belied his nervousness before we'd entered and this was probably more his turf than mine. Surrounded by opulence and a sophistication only money could produce.

"Please, call me Jackie. I'm not particularly attached to that name."

"Of course, Jackie."

"Marta is bringing us coffee and some pastries." She sat down and gracefully crossed her legs. "While those are being prepared, maybe enlighten me."

"Of course. Did you want to have one of your sons or your attorney sit in?" Simon asked, and I knew what he was doing. If she or her sons had something to hide, they'd want to be there to get a read on what information we had.

"No, Simon, I'm a capable woman to handle my own affairs."

"Yes, you are, but I wanted to make sure just for your comfort." He was about to speak as Marta returned with a tray, quickly set us up with coffee, and excused herself. "As I said on the phone yesterday, we just wanted to ask some questions about your former husband."

"Distasteful business that man was, but I'm sure you're well aware of that, Simon." She delicately added sugar and cream to her coffee and then lifted the delicate cup to her lips.

"I am. There's been four homicides. Three of them have been dumped outside or in the vicinity of Bianchi's club and one outside Finnegan's. We haven't had any around Mancini's territory yet. Your husband was well-known as a successful and respectable businessman, but as you're aware, he had interests outside his legitimate businesses." His voice sounded so cultured, and if I wasn't mistaken, there was a hint of a British accent. I lifted my own black coffee to my mouth to hide my smile.

"I always liked Carmine, he had integrity, and I respected him greatly for the way he stood up for me. Mancini...nasty piece of work. Wanted to do business with Darner, but wasn't... how should I say…classy enough. Finnegan was just considered a brute, but he was amusing."

"Seamus has his moments. The reason we're contacting you is we just wanted to see how far back our case may go. And since Darner ran the more affluent faction, we have to ask. This isn't an interrogation, we—" She held up her hand.

"Simon, as much as I appreciate your politeness. I spent thirty years with Darner. He was a despicable man, and despite the rumors, neither I nor my sons did away with him. My sons have taken over his firm and made it twenty times more successful than he ever came close to doing. As you can see, my sons take exceptional care of their mother. You can have whatever you want from me, Simon, but I assure you I have no knowledge of the murdered men."

"Do you remember any enemies Darner may have had?"

"Bianchi, but that was more a case of Carmine's superior morality as odd as that may sound. A morality my former husband didn't possess. Finnegan wouldn't give him the time of day. I know he had several run-ins with Mancini, though. Mancini is strictly blue-collar with delusions of being some old school gangster."

"We visited him at lunch yesterday, and it was very *Godfather-*esque."

She softly laughed at Simon's description. "So that hasn't changed. Darner kept me out of the business, but I assure you that wasn't out of some protective instinct. We married out of a sense of duty, two powerful families uniting through marriage. The firm was originally run by my father, but as I wasn't a son, he needed me to be married off. There was no love between Darner and I. To be honest, I was glad when he found outside interests, mainly several mistresses he kept very well and who I gave a nice chunk of money to for putting up with him. I knew what it was like to be married to him."

"Do you remember any of their names?" I asked as Simon

took a sip of the dark brew and took a pastry. It had been a few hours since I fed him.

"I can write you a list."

"That would be appreciated. Do you remember any odd behavior on his part before his disappearance and subsequent murder?" I took over the questioning so he could eat, and I caught Ms. Darner's small smile.

"Nothing out of the ordinary. He was always absent a lot before a big deal, legal or illegal. Although, he did appear to be rather nervous in the weeks leading up to the night he disappeared. I'd overheard a conversation or two where he seemed to be preparing for a rather large shipment."

"Do you know what the shipment may have been?" Simon asked.

"Unfortunately, no, he'd gotten deeper into drugs and sex trafficking."

I schooled my features, that was Mancini's stock in trade. Had Darner got into bed with Mancini and crossed the wrong person? That was another reason to take another look at Dekland. As much as my gut said he wasn't connected enough, that didn't mean he wasn't trying to make a play for more power.

"Were there any odd things in his financials?"

"Not that I could tell, but I'll contact my sons and our accountant to see if they noticed anything. I didn't have any knowledge of our finances during our marriage. He transferred money into my account monthly for me to do with as I saw fit. The main accounts were completely under his control. I'll have any records we can find sent to you."

"We appreciate that, Jackie. Do you have any idea who murdered Darner?" Simon asked after finishing his pastry.

"That is a long list. Investment Banking and Trading isn't always a profession that endears you to others when money is lost that a client couldn't afford to lose. Again, I'll check into any threats and send those along as well."

"Anything you can send us would be appreciated. We're unsure if Darner has anything to do with our cases, but we're looking into the major families, and as you know, Darner became a focus of an Organized Crime inquiry when I was in that unit."

"Anything I can do to help, Simon. I spent a lot of time with you at events, and I enjoyed your company. It was a kindness that I'd never experienced before, and I'd like to repay the debt."

"You don't owe me anything, Jackie. I always enjoyed our conversations. I want to thank you for your time and the refreshments."

"I remember you were constantly eating."

"That hasn't changed," I commented, and she smiled affectionately at Simon.

"Well, I will contact everyone I need to and will call you when I have gathered the information you need."

"Here is my card. Also, call me if you remember anything at all." He handed her his card, and I offered mine as well.

"Are you going to the Smythe's function at the end of the month?"

"I'd planned to skip it, but for you, I'll plan to attend."

"I will be thankful for the company."

We said our goodbyes, and Jackie showed us to the door. I stood back as she offered her cheek, and Simon brushed a kiss to her flawless skin, and then she patted his cheek. When the door closed behind us, I chuckled and shook my head.

"For a prickly bastard, you've charmed a lot of people."

"Being a gentleman was ingrained in me. It's a hard habit to break."

"You do know that you have a bit of an accent."

"I sound all posh. I don't know why it happens. I worked really hard to get rid of it when I returned to the States."

"It's kinda sexy."

He huffed at me. "I'm still hungry. Feed me."

"How do you not gain a pound?" I shook my head at him as I opened his door.

"One day, my metabolism will catch up with my age. Until then, I'm going to eat when and how I want."

"Then let me feed you before you get all hangry. I see it coming."

As he started to buckle himself in, I slammed the door and walked around the front of the vehicle to get into the driver's seat. I needed to find the nearest drive-thru. If there was one thing I'd learned about Simon, he got cranky when he wasn't near food at all times.

GRAVES

"Graves." I'd answered my phone with my eyes still closed, and for a minute, I tried to remember where I was. The pattern had started the first time I woke up in Marcel's apartment.

"Simon, it's Remy. We have an issue." The tone in his voice put me on edge. I hadn't heard it since the Fellows's case, and all my sluggishness disappeared.

"What is it?" I tightened my abs and sat up, throwing my legs over the side of the bed.

"Amber Ellis was found wandering the strip with a note clipped to her pajamas with your name on it and our precinct. Cree was out and about. Someone found Amber and brought her straight to Cree. Amber has no idea how she got there. She was taken to our precinct."

"Is she okay? What about Janice and her husband?" The panic started to set in. If Amber was away from Janice, was there a crime scene? I surged to my feet and grabbed clothes off the top of the pile Marcel had washed the night previous.

"Paramedics say she's unharmed, just really scared and asking for you. We had a cruiser go to the address. They didn't even know she was gone. The screen was cut, forensics is on the scene, and the initial report says it looked like the lock was opened with a knife. Whoever they were entered and took her right from her bed. The twins were still asleep."

"But she's..." My voice broke as I stumbled around trying to get dressed with the phone held between my shoulder and ear.

"Simon, you need to stay calm for me. I woke up Fran. She's on her way there now."

"I'll be there, don't let Fran take her anywhere."

"She's already been told that Amber doesn't leave until it's cleared with you first. Wake up Douglas and get down there. We'll work everything out."

I disconnected the call as I awkwardly held up my jeans and jogged to the living room. "Marcel."

He sat up and stared at me. "We got another crime scene?" he asked and was already on his feet.

"Someone broke into Janice's place, grabbed Amber, and let her out on the strip. She had a note on her addressed to me. I don't know what it says but..."

"We'll get there." He was fixing my clothes even as he spoke. "Give me a few minutes to dress, and we're out of here. Baby, don't freak out on me yet, okay?" He leaned in and gently kissed me and then rested his forehead on mine.

I nodded because there was no way I was going to be able to answer with the fear like a rock stuck in my throat. I followed behind him to sit on the side of the bed to put my shoes on.

"This place is busier than I need right now." Donna stood in the doorway in a t-shirt and briefs.

"A kid from the Outreach was grabbed and dropped off in the middle of the night. We have to go."

"Go, I got Savvy covered." She instantly left us to finish getting dressed.

When we left the apartment, Tony's nighttime replacement was given a short report on what was going on, and we were on our way to the precinct. I was trying to hold my shit together, but first, they went after Savvy, and then they grabbed Amber. Anyone who saw me around the Outreach knew I had a soft spot for that little girl—for both of them. This was my fault.

The blare of the siren pulled me from my thoughts as we hit a traffic jam of Last Call at all the bars. Marcel easily worked his way through the vehicles. I was glad he hadn't said anything, but I was also losing my cool. Marcel barely parked before I was out and running. As I entered, I saw a tiny form flying across the lobby and dropped to my knees to grab her up. Pain shot through my hand, but I didn't care.

"Hey, honey, are you okay?" I applauded myself for my voice not betraying my panic. She was dressed in a small yellow ducky onesie, and she didn't appear to have a mark on her.

"She's fine, Simon. The paramedics and I checked her over. She's just scared." Fran said from my right, and I looked up to find her watching us.

"She's coming home with me," I said with a forced smile as I wiped the tears from her face.

"Of course, I already put in for an emergency protective placement on my way over. One of the uniforms on the scene had Janice pack a bag at my request, and it arrived a few minutes ago."

"Have units been assigned there to protect Janice and the twins?"

"Yes, everything has been arranged. Captain Tyson is the lead supervisor on this, and he's waiting to talk to you upstairs."

I nodded as I stood, and Amber wrapped her arms around my neck. She held on tightly as if I planned on leaving her. As I straightened and shifted her to my good side, I sensed Marcel's presence behind me.

"Hey, honey, remember me?" Marcel asked, and I felt her little nod. "Could I hold you? Simon has a hurt hand, but after I carry you upstairs, I'll give you right back to him."

She hesitated but finally loosened her grip, and I passed her over to him. He winked at me and gave me a gentle nudge toward the elevator. We entered the car with Fran.

"Did forensics find anything on the note?"

"Not that I know of. They had a tech pick it up, but someone took photos so you can read it. Tyson said that it was top priority right now. He wanted answers by the end of the day, or he'd come get them himself. I think Coleman was ordered out of bed by several detectives."

I would've loved to have seen his face when he answered that knock on his door. The man needed to lose his job, but it hadn't yet happened. We stepped out onto the chaos of the squad floor, and I turned instantly to check on Amber. She had Marcel in a death grip, but he was rubbing her back in soothing circles.

"Graves, my office," Tyson called out, and I made my way through the desks with Fran beside me and Marcel still comforting Amber.

I took a seat on one of the chairs in his office and held my arms out for Amber. She was back in my arms as Tyson handed me the tablet with the image of the note.

Detective Graves. We can get to those you love. How willing are you to let this little girl die? Next time you'll find her body instead of wandering around the streets in the middle of the night. Back off, and we won't make you pay. Detective Marcel, is he as willing as you to sacrifice everything for your badge?

The block letters gave nothing away, and my chest tightened as I saw mine and Marcel's addresses, along with that of my parents, at the bottom of the plain printer paper. "What's being done?" I held her close and tried to soothe us both.

"The lab is working on trace evidence. Scanning the original note for any underlying writing that may give us a clue. Are you close to naming a suspect?" Tyson asked.

"No. That's the thing. We don't have any evidence to suggest who may be behind the bodies. All we know is that it's the same killer or a pack."

"Someone has to feel you're getting too close."

"We did visit Darner, and then suddenly Amber is found wandering." Marcel spoke from behind me.

"It's too easy. They're hoping in our panic that's the lead we'll jump on. Darner was always in control unless his authority was questioned. All the information we have is his operation died when he did. I can't be sure that Darner's sons didn't do something stupid, but they have a lot more to lose, especially since most of them are conservative Republicans, and they barely turned the company around when their father's shady business dealings came to light."

"Well, Fran and I talked. For the time being, Amber is in your and Marcel's custody. Units have already been dispatched to your parents until we know this isn't a credible threat. You're still at Marcel's, right?"

"Yes, he's holding me hostage." I rolled my eyes at Tyson, and he shook his head. "I have a guard on the door of the apartment around the clock, but I want marked cruisers outside the building, too."

"Done. Until further notice, you'll be working from home. We'll provide everything you need, I've already been contacted by your squad and Vega, which I could've done without, and this is their only case for now."

"Remy and Robert have Roo to think about." I protested.

"They already know the risks. They're moving to an undisclosed location on the strip for a while."

As soon as he spoke, I knew where they'd go. When shit went down, everyone ran to Boss and the series of safe houses he ran. We needed to have a talk with him soon to check if he'd heard any weird rumblings through the neighborhood. I didn't care how big or small, I needed to know.

"Simon, I have some papers for you to sign so you can take

temporary custody of Amber. I have her bag and a car seat for you to use."

I nodded as I realized Amber had gone completely limp against my chest and was happy she felt safe with me. We talked a bit more as I filled out the forms and when Fran leaned down to hug me. "This is my last case. Start the process for adoption."

"First thing in the morning, but think before you give up your job." She kissed my cheek. "I've been waiting for this day, though." She gave me a knowing smile as she straightened.

I'd talked to Fran on several occasions about adopting Amber. I'd even qualified as an emergency foster dad, but I never felt I was the right parent for her. It wasn't as if I couldn't change careers by getting my license to practice, but it also worked if I retired. I had more than enough to care for us as a full-time parent. I loved my job, but I wanted a family, and this was my only option. I could keep her safe.

Marcel picked Amber up and cradled her to his chest as I stood. Fran and I followed him back to our vehicle to install the car seat. I wasn't equipped to handle it. By the time we were loaded up and on our way home, the stress hit me, and I collapsed in the seat.

"I'll get us home, we'll get her settled into Savvy's room on the trundle bed, and we can get more sleep. We'll work everything out when we're not stressed and exhausted, okay?"

"Yeah, your apartment is getting crowded. If we're in the way—"

"Baby, you and her won't be in the way. We'll make it work. I lived in a three-bedroom house with my dad and six brothers and was in the military. I can adapt. And it'll make you feel better if she's at home with us."

"Thanks."

"You're welcome. Just a little longer, and we can get you both back into bed."

I turned to stare out the passenger window and watched the

lights blur and flicker as he drove through the city back to the apartment. All that filled my head were the people I could've fucked over enough to target Savvy and Amber. I didn't even factor in Marcel. This was personal, and I made a mental note to check my cases during my duty with the Organized Crime squad. Mob murders. The threats. Everything came down to that part of my career.

They'd planned for me to die the night they attacked, and since Savvy and I were too protected, they'd gone after an innocent toddler. They'd pay for that, but I just needed to throw a few more knives at the timeline.

DOUGLAS

COLD CASE
UNIT

"You're developing creepy habits in your old age?"

Donna's amused voice only distracted me from the sweet sight in front of me for a second. Simon was stretched out beside the trundle bed holding Amber's hand while she slept soundly. Savvy's arm hung over the side and held the little girl's other hand. I'd tried to talk him into sleeping in his, well, my bed, but he hadn't wanted her to wake up alone in a strange place. Amber had had enough of that. I'd relented, but only after I made him a thick pallet on the floor. Even the psycho cat was curled up at Amber's feet.

"I couldn't sleep. I wanted to make sure he and the girls were okay."

"You love him a lot, don't you?"

"Yeah, but it'll never work so...I'm okay with it." As hard as that was to admit, I'd accepted the painful truth. I'd love him, but he'd never feel the same for me.

"No, you're not."

"To keep him happy, I am."

"What about you, Marcel? What would make you happy?"

I swallowed around the lump in my throat because I knew

what would make me happy, but it was impossible. "Him in our bed, with our girls sleeping safe down the hall."

"Our?"

"He thought he was whispering when we were in the captain's office, but I heard. He's leaving the department after this case and adopting Amber. I don't have much time left, Donna. I understood that when this was over, he'd go back to the basement, and I'd return to Homicide, and we'd maybe run into each other. This is so much more final."

"Then tell him how you feel."

"I can't. He doesn't want a romantic relationship with anyone, not even me."

"You can't know that."

"He's Asexual. He doesn't have…"

"I'm sorry."

"We can't help our feelings, and I won't make him uncomfortable."

"Marcel, you do know that sex isn't that big of a deal for you, right? Me, fucking is the greatest thing in the world, but for you, it's all about the intimacy. The touches and the kissing, hell, you got me off to make me happy and then just laid there with a massive hard-on and was content as fuck. At nineteen and knowing the career we chose, it was like an explosion, but as you got older, you were just happy with my presence. Rubbing my hair as we watched TV. Making out for a bit while our daughter napped or was distracted. Just because he's Asexual doesn't mean he wouldn't like intimacy. Penetration isn't everything."

"I know that, but I don't see the way I feel about him reflected back at me. I want him to love me, but he sees me as his work partner, maybe a friend. He's been so unwanted for so long. Made to feel as if he wasn't enough. And all I want to do is let him know he's perfect."

"You'll do the right thing, but make sure it's the right thing for all of you. You can't ignore the fact that in that room is everything you need. Don't disregard that." She leaned up to kiss my cheek, and I lowered enough for her to reach. "Get some sleep."

I nodded but had no urge to move from that spot. I needed sleep, though. I'd found a few nightlights and placed them all around the apartment so Amber wouldn't wake up in the dark. Pushing away from the doorframe, I went to my room and slipped into bed in nothing but my pajama bottoms. I closed my eyes, and the bed smelled like him.

When our time ended, he wouldn't need me anymore. No more seeing him in my kitchen every morning making coffee or breakfast, all sleepy and mussed from just crawling out of bed. Helping him finish getting dressed, standing close to him, and feeling how warm and solid he was. I'd gotten to see him beyond the expensive suits or snarky attitude. I needed to keep all of that and not just the memories of it.

I turned on my side and hugged a pillow to my chest, reminding myself I still had time. A little was better than nothing.

"AREN'T you so adorable when you sleep."

Oh fuck, I opened my eyes to find Doc staring at me from the other side of the pillow. He was stretched out on his belly, with his legs up as he tapped his socked feet together.

"Please tell me this is just a nightmare."

"I'm hurt. Daddy!" I grimaced at his shout, and then Stevenson was rushing into the room. "He doesn't like me."

"Everyone loves you, my sweet baby." The big man scooped Doc up and left the room, but not before I earned a glare as Doc pretended to sniffle. That little brat was trying to get me killed.

I rolled out of bed and went to use the bathroom, brush my teeth, and pull on a t-shirt. By the time I made it to the kitchen, I froze in the entryway to see that the room was packed with the entire Cold Case squad. Remy was seated on the counter beside Doc, and their respective men leaned between their legs. Donna was looking amused, and Savvy and Amber were eating as Simon cooked.

"There better be coffee." I grumped and then smiled as Simon held up a travel mug. I crossed the room, stopping to kiss the top of Savvy's head as she demolished her breakfast, and as I straightened, Amber pointed to her head, and I gave her a quick kiss. I continued to the stove. "Thanks, baby." I stepped up behind him, settled my hands on his hips. Lowering my head, I brushed a kiss to the side of his neck, his curls teasing me before I straightened and turned. My arm went around the front of him, my hand resting on his opposite hip. "Why the hell is everyone in our kitchen?"

"Um, your guess is as good as mine. I got up to make the girls breakfast, and they *all* started knocking on the door like the cops were trying to break it down. Well"—he motioned over his shoulder—"and I told Doc to leave you alone, and you see how that worked. You better eat while you can."

He handed me a plate, and I set my travel mug aside because I didn't want to let him go. "Thanks, baby. You're making yourself one, right?" I noticed it was suddenly very quiet, and everyone was staring except Amber as she focused on eating. "What?" I asked as I stroked his stomach through his thin t-shirt.

"I don't know. They've been like that since they got here. It's annoying as hell. You're distracting me, go eat." He patted my forearm, and I stroked my hand over his flat belly.

I didn't move away, just stood there to have my breakfast.

"What do I owe for the disruption of our morning?" I held out my arm for the syrup, and Savvy handed it to me over Amber's head.

"We wanted to make sure Amber was okay, and we brought some files that y'all needed. Are we messing with this little domestic scene?" Remy batted his lashes as he draped his arms over Robert's shoulders.

I scratched my nose with my middle finger.

"Don't do that. Amber doesn't need to learn bad habits from you. At least not yet."

I laughed as he pinched my side, and I leaned over a bit to protect my ribs. "Fine, but you do understand we're not strict, right?"

"Quit arguing with me and sit down." I bit back a groan as he patted my stomach and then pushed me toward the last empty chair.

I sat down, and Amber touched my arm and tapped her fingertips to her mouth. Before I could ask her what she needed, a warm slender body pressed to my back and leaned over my shoulder to add a pancake to the little girl's plate.

"She wants more. We teach sign language to better assist our nonverbal members at the Outreach." Amber placed her fingertips to her lips and moved them forward. "You're welcome." I caught Simon filling his plate, and he turned to lean against the counter to eat at an awkward angle.

"Get over here." As soon as he picked up his plate, I stretched my arm to grab the front of his t-shirt and pulled him down on my thigh. "Eat. You're doing too much, and you already slept on the floor."

"Marcel, we're not having this—"

I didn't even think as I cut him off with a kiss and then went back to eating as everyone kept staring or smiling at us. Simon was right; they were all being annoying.

"As much as I'm enjoying this delightful and unwanted visit, what are y'all doing here?" I twisted to grab my coffee, and it was taken by Simon before I could get a sip. I rolled my eyes as he handed it back to me.

"We already said we wanted to check on everyone. We're a

package deal, man, you get one of us, you've got all of us." Stevenson arched a brow.

I was about to covertly flip them off again until Simon cleared his throat.

"Were there any fingerprints or anything at the scene?" Simon asked.

"No. They got some foot impressions at the scene because of the rain we had last night. We hit the streets. We did get reports of a vehicle pulling up and then speeding away not long before the call from Cree. Someone thought they'd gotten a partial plate, but we're still running it against stolen vehicles and-or plates. Everything is in the files. You also have emails from Coleman. He wasn't happy with seven detectives over his shoulder all night. It was beautiful." Remy's glee at Coleman's comeuppance made everyone laugh.

"And he'd know, my baby was snickering in a corner the entire time." Robert turned his head to brush a kiss to Remy's forearm.

I hadn't realized what an issue Coleman was until a month after I started working there. Everyone was clear he was bigoted, but I didn't understand how he kept his job. His bias should've gotten him fired long ago. I finished my breakfast and leaned back, rubbing Simon's lower back as he ate and catered to the girls.

"I'm out of here. I'm going to be late for school." Savvy got up, gave Amber a big, loud hug, and then gave me and Simon the same treatment before she was headed for the door. "Tony, get your ass in gear, man. I'm late."

"I don't think Carmine is going to get his enforcer back." Doc giggled. "Daddy, down," he whispered in Stevenson's ear, and he lifted Doc off the counter. "Come on, Amber, we'll play dolls and watch cartoons."

"Shit, our wall." I cursed and tried to get up.

"We helped Graves tack a sheet over it before Amber got up," Robert said as he turned his head to give his husband a kiss.

"Thanks. I should've thought about it before I went to bed."

"It's fine. We had a lot of stress last night." Simon soothed me, but I should've remembered. Savvy didn't even pay attention to it.

"Are you doing okay?"

"Yeah, she's safe here with us."

"She is. So don't worry."

"I am. What if this is all my fault somehow? What if—" I cupped the side of his face and turned him to look at me.

"Baby, we're not going to play the what-if game here. Someone got their ego hurt. Someone got time and didn't think they deserved it. You're not to blame for doing your job. Our girls are safe. Savvy is off to school, and Amber is in the other room playing dolls. We'll find whoever is doing this." I stroked my thumb across his lower lip.

"As much as we're enjoying this show, you might want to wait until we're gone," Stevenson said as we turned to find him smiling like a fool at us with his chin in the cups of his hands.

"Fuck you, Stevenson. We didn't invite you here."

"Wow, you'll just have to have your morning quickie a little earlier from now on. Until we find out what's going on, guess what?" Remy motioned with a sweep of his arms. "This is the Cold Case squad."

"Shit."

"It's your own fault. You've been hanging around the dungeon too long."

"Don't sound so amused, baby. It's not nice."

"I thought we'd already established that."

"Go take your shower. I'll come help you get dressed in a minute. You have a doctor's appointment this afternoon to see about getting your cast off and to schedule physical therapy."

"Clean up my kitchen."

"It'll be done, go on." I helped him off my thigh, and he was leaving the room.

"You've been holding out on us, Douglas," Remy said.

"No, I haven't. Nothing is going on, and nothing will. Don't give him shit either. I know y'all." I stood, and I started cleaning up, loading the dishwasher to start after he was done with his shower.

"We wouldn't do that to him. You're not so bad, Douglas, and this might sound weird, but he's looking happy here with his girls and you. Make sure you keep him."

"Robert, I'd do anything to keep him, but he's not mine to keep. He likes the affection, but I don't know. He seems touch starved, and I like touching him." I felt guilty that we seemed to give each other the intimacy we both lacked unconsciously. Yet I was also happier than I'd been in years. I knew the Cold Case Unit were affectionate with each other—a natural thing in their weird found family. I was accepted into the group dynamic. Intellectually, I understood that's all I'd ever get from Simon, and I was strangely okay with that. I just had to remember that when it was time for him to go home.

GRAVES

COLD CASE
UNIT

The cast was off, but my little and ring finger were still in splints to finish healing. My dislocated joints were stiff and sore, but the doctor said it would loosen up with physical therapy. I was going through my old notebooks while Marcel cleaned up from dinner. Amber was worn out and had gone to bed at eight. Savvy was off at Carmine's to hang out with Silvia. Donna was off with friends, and that left me and Marcel alone.

I was going through my case notebooks I had from my time in Organized Crime. Nothing stood out. Whether I busted someone or not, everyone had always seemed respectful. I think that sometimes had more to do with Carmine's word than my actions, but that aside, nothing was standing out. No obvious threats.

As much as I was trying to focus, my brain kept going back to that morning. He was touching me more the past week than any other time. And with everyone else, I'd tell them to stop, but I liked his easy affection. The way he kissed me. Why did I have to wait until my forties to start losing my mind over someone?

"Do the damn messages ever stop?" He grumped as he came out of the kitchen, and I smirked as he held out his phone.

"Welcome to the Cold Case Unit's message thread. I was added during the Fellows's case." I'd thought the messages would focus on the cases we worked on, but it was a lot of joking and get-together planning mixed in.

"And I think someone, namely Stevenson forgot this wasn't for sexting."

"Oh no, he knows." I snorted as he dropped onto the couch, and he turned to face me. "But he does it more since you were added."

"How the hell did I get pulled into y'all's craziness?"

"You didn't complain...much."

"Finding anything good?" He motioned to the stacks of notebooks.

"No." I let out of frustrated sigh. "I mean, nothing is standing out. This was years ago."

"Why did you choose Organized Crime?"

"I don't know. Figured it would be a challenge. Strange as it sounds, I enjoyed it. They cycled me out after two years and reassigned me to Homicide."

"Did you always want to be a cop?"

"I don't know. Maybe it was my first rebellion. When I graduated from law school, I just couldn't see myself as a lawyer. I was only twenty-two, so it's not like I didn't have time."

"I can see you as a lawyer. With your mind, you'd succeed at it. But I think you're more suited to what you're doing now. How's your hand feeling? Better without the cast?" He slightly leaned forward and stroked the back of my hand.

His fingertips were rough yet gentle. They reminded me of the way he'd looked at me and stroked my bottom lip. I'd spent so much time putting a physical distance between myself and others that I forgot I loved the occasional affection from Mama Sue and Doc, even my other friends. I wasn't heartless. I'd wondered over the years what it would be like to have, not a sexual relationship, but an emotional one with another person.

"Baby?"

"A little stiff and sore, but nothing too bad. Could've been a lot worse."

"Are you okay? You've been a bit quiet today."

"I'm fine."

"Baby, if something's wrong, talk it out. You've been beyond stressed the past month, with what happened with Savvy and now Amber. Nearly getting beat to death. Living in my craziness."

"Actually, the craziness isn't that bad. Could do with a little more room to spread out."

"Want to go back to your fancy house?"

"My house isn't fancy." I glared at him, knowing my house was a lot bigger than I needed. Maybe it had been a way to plan for a future, even one I didn't think I'd have.

"Uh-huh, keep telling yourself that."

"I bought it ten years ago. I don't know. I guess I thought my life would be different."

"Different how?"

I pondered his questions as I threw the notebook in my hand aside and tried to come up with an answer that wouldn't make me come across as pathetic. "During boarding school and university...law school...I guess I didn't have time for parties or dating. I was exhausted. And at the end of the day, all I wanted to do was go back to my apartment and crash. I thought once all the stress was gone, I'd find someone."

"Not everyone is happy in a relationship, baby."

"You were."

"I was, and I loved being married. I enjoyed the companionship, and I miss it."

"What do you specifically miss?" I turned, stretched my left arm along the back of the couch, and bent my left leg under my right.

"Let's see. I miss touching someone just because I miss the feel of them. Holding someone in bed and waking up with them. Feeling someone under me. The sounds they make because I made them feel good. Mainly I miss the intimacy of having a partner."

"You know sex isn't that hard to find." The words tasted bitter on my tongue as an image of him going out and finding someone else. Which was stupid because he wasn't mine. Yet I knew our time was coming to an end, and I wouldn't get those touches and casual kisses to my cheek, neck, and quick ones to my lips anymore.

"It's not the sex for me."

I frowned at him. "How is it not the sex?"

"Easy, I can jack off and get an orgasm. That was one of the issues between Donna and I. She's a very sexual person, and I was more about the buildup...the foreplay. I didn't learn that until I was older. Jerking off doesn't give you that physical connection. The kissing and holding. Some nights I would get her off and be content to just feel turned on, that ache, letting it linger to enjoy it. Orgasms are moments...the other stuff lasts a lot longer."

"Really?"

"Surprised?"

"Very. I've thought about the act. and it really..." I paused because I didn't know how to explain it. My talks with Doc and Vega were never detailed. How did you explain something you didn't fully understand yourself?

"Doesn't do anything for you. But what about intimacy? Penetration doesn't equal sex. Some people don't like intercourse, but enjoy everything else. I had an Asexual friend years ago who didn't like any of it. No need for the intimacy or the act."

"I don't know. I've never done any of it."

"Never?" I shook my head in answer. "You're..."

I laughed at the disbelief that was clear by his expression. "Why is that so shocking?"

"Because you're absolutely gorgeous. And under that prickly exterior, you're sweet, funny, and scary smart. I figured someone had talked you into it during your impressionable years."

"I won't say I didn't get offers. I got a lot of them, but never met anyone who made me want to do it. I thought that would change as I got older. It never did, though. It made me feel broken for a long time until I had a talk to Doc and Vega one night in the Pit."

"What did they tell you, baby?"

"That I was normal. That people can have relationships without sex."

"They're not wrong."

"But how do I...I've never done anything, and I don't miss or think about it. But I wonder sometimes if...fuck, I don't know."

"That it would be different if you met the right person? Is that what you think about?"

"Yeah, even if I don't think about the penetration part, would I like the other stuff?"

"Do you like when I kiss you?" I swallowed hard and nodded. "Do you like when I stand close and touch you?" I braved another nod. "Because I've thought about nothing else for months."

"What?" My voice broke. As he moved across the cushions toward me, I froze as he lifted his left hand to my cheek, and just like that morning, he stroked along my lower lip. His hip and thighs rested along my shin.

"You have this pretty little crease in the center of your bottom lip, and the top is a perfect bow. Your curls are so beautiful and soft. I take every opportunity to brush them back and kiss your neck so I can feel them against my cheek." As he spoke, he moved his fingers into my hair. "May I kiss you? Give you a real one?"

"Yes." As I submitted, I nodded my head. I dropped my gaze to his full, wide mouth, and I had no idea what to do. I didn't understand why my heart quickened or that I suddenly felt too hot and cold at the same time.

He shocked me when he breached the inches that separated our mouths, but instead of pressing his lips to mine, he brushed them first to forehead, another to the tip of my nose, one cheek, and then the other. With each caress, his salt and pepper beard tickled my skin. His big hands cupped my face.

"I thought you were going to kiss me." My face heated at the breathless quality of my voice, and I closed my eyes so I couldn't stare at him.

"I am, baby, not good enough?" I felt his smile against my cheek as he kept kissing me everywhere except my lips. "Is this better?" I gasped at the first soft press of his lips to mine. My shaking right hand rose to grip his wrist. "Baby, that is so much better."

If I was supposed to answer, it didn't happen as he drew my lower lip between his and nipped at the captured flesh so gently. He repeated the slow movements on the top one. I pushed closer when he tried to retreat. There was an odd feeling in my chest and stomach. People had kissed me before, but never like this. He wasn't pushing or forcing. This was seduction—very much like the kisses I've seen my friends share with their partners.

He moved his hand deeper into my curls and clenched his fingers into a fist as he angled my head, but he never changed the intensity or the subtleness of it.

"You look so beautiful, your cheeks turning pink. The way you're trembling. Can you straddle my thighs? I just want to feel you against me, chest to chest, as I kiss you some more. Nothing else."

"Okay." There was that embarrassing broken squeak again as I allowed him to maneuver me until I rested on his lap, my thighs squeezing his hips.

"Is this okay?" he asked as he gently slipped his hands under my shirt to stroke my lower back. He had to lift his chin slightly to reach my lips again. "Damn, baby, I knew you'd feel this good."

He flexed his arms until my chest rested on his. My body reacted but not a full erection, just a slight firming behind my zipper. I felt an odd tightness in my chest and belly.

"Marcel."

"It's okay, baby, just relax, just kisses. I could sit here with you all night, getting these soft kisses from you, and it's more than enough."

"This...this can't be enough for you," I whispered between gentle nips and presses.

"This is as close to perfection as I've ever been." He groaned as he stroked his hands up my back on either side of the indent of my spine. "Do you like the way I touch you?"

"Yes." I pressed in closer, shifting my hips, and felt the thick bulge of his hard-on. He hissed at the contact. "Did I do something wrong?" I asked as I tried to shift backward, but he gripped my ass to keep me in place.

"You're doing everything just right...too right. I haven't done this since my divorce."

"Why not?" My words were muffled as he kept pressing his mouth to mine.

"Because I hadn't met you yet."

I pulled away and lowered my chin. "Don't say that."

"Why? You're the first person I've wanted to kiss in years. And I aim to keep you, whether you ever let me inside you or not. Because that shit doesn't matter to me. Now, I want you to relax." He removed one hand from under my shirt, cupped the back of my head, and pulled my face into the crook of his neck. He hugged me to him tightly and scooted down to get comfortable. "I've been waiting for this...to have you right here. I'm going to enjoy it before that chaotic brain of yours tries to tell you that what I say isn't true. Because, Simon, I'm going to prove I want nothing more than this right here."

I kept my left hand on the cushion and hugged his waist with

219

my right as I inhaled the clean smell of his soap and his natural scent. My brain did try to urge me to get up, that this was a bad idea, but I couldn't. I just wanted that closeness a little longer. He was warm and solid. He felt safe and comforting. I was too scared to say it would last, but, fuck, I was going to be selfish for once.

DOUGLAS

I'd fallen asleep with Simon straddling my lap and his face tucked into my neck, and I hadn't awakened until Savvy came home. She'd touched my shoulder to tell me goodnight with a huge smile on her face, and I'd reluctantly gotten him up to lead him to bed. I'd wanted to crawl in beside him, but a first real kiss to sleeping together all night was a huge leap. Pushing him didn't seem like a good idea, no matter how badly I'd wanted to gather him into my arms and hold him until morning.

Part of me had expected some awkwardness, but he'd been his usually cute, sleepy self when I joined him in the kitchen for coffee. I didn't hesitate to cross the kitchen, grab his sides, and lean down for a kiss, but nothing too heavy. I hadn't thought his lips could be softer than they were the night before, but they'd cushioned mine.

"There better be coffee," I whispered against his lips.

"You so ruined the mood." He huffed as he pushed against my chest.

"At least I kissed you first before I irritated you." I softly chuckled as I tightened my hands on his hips.

"Yeah, yeah, and there's coffee."

"Thanks. Where are the Cold Case people, and why is everyone still asleep?" He didn't move, so I just grabbed a mug from the cabinet behind him and poured myself coffee. I laughed as he wrinkled his nose as I drank it black.

"Don't say it. You'll summon them, and I'm not mentally prepared yet." He groaned as he tucked his head under my chin.

I closed my eyes as his breath teased my skin. It felt like I'd waited forever to have him this close to me. I'd wondered if the light of day and a night's rest would send him back to being stand-offish. If he wanted me to back off, he was more than capable of telling me so, and strangely that's what I loved best about him. He didn't take my shit.

"They're your friends." My free hand came up to tangle in his thick curls. I didn't think I'd ever get used to the freedom to touch him or the way he allowed me into his space.

"No, they consider themselves family, which they believe gives them the right to annoy the fuck out of me."

"Seems about right. How's the hand this morning?" When I asked, he lifted his head and titled it back slightly.

"Still stiff, and my fingers hurt. But the over-the-counter meds are working. I was tired of being spacey all the damn time."

"You okay after last night?"

"Are you going to ruin it somehow by being your usual self?"

"That depends. What is my usual self?" I smirked as he rolled his pretty eyes at me.

He groaned. "That right there."

"Then yes, I'm going to ruin it."

"I'm going home."

"No, you're not. Although, we probably need more space, I didn't sign up for our apartment turning into Cold Case Central."

"Yeah, well, I didn't either. Us, Donna, our girls, and all the crazies, the boundaries have been shattered."

"Just wait until Vega joins them."

"Now, you really fucked up."

"You know, I would've rethought this attraction to you if I knew they came along with it."

"Don't be mean. Um, thanks for last night?"

"Thanks?"

"Not making fun of me when the big secret came out."

"The virginity thing?"

"Yeah, that."

"Why would I make fun of you?"

"What forty-three-year-old has never had the urge to do anything?"

"Maybe plenty of Asexual people never had the urge but gave into society's pressure. I wasn't lying last night that just the kisses and touches were enough." I set my mug aside. "Yes, I like sex, sometimes I even love it, but for me...I love the lead-up more. I learned that about myself as I got older. If all you want is the intimacy, I can take care of an orgasm myself."

"What if one day I want to...try?"

"Only if you're comfortable doing so."

"Everything is new, and I don't—" He let out a heavy sigh. "I don't, I mean, I've gotten myself off, but it's not like something I'm compelled to do."

"Again, we'll only do what you're comfortable with. Sex doesn't only equal penetration. But there is something that I really want."

"What?"

"Don't look so suspicious." I tweaked the end of his nose. "I want to sleep with you. I hated sending you to bed alone with me out on the lonely couch. You all cute and warm in my bed. Can I sleep with you tonight?"

"Yes."

"Thank you. Donna said I was getting a bit creepy watching you sleep."

"That *is* creepy."

"Now, you don't be mean. I was attracted to you a lot longer than you were to me. You really shouldn't be allowed to be this pretty." I smirked at the rolling of his eyes. "You know you're pretty."

"I've been told a time or two. I was told my looks were wasted on a cop."

"You could definitely make a better living as a model."

He huffed and tipped his head back. I took advantage and brushed my lips to his Adam's apple and then sucked lightly at his soft skin. He was beautiful. He'd tried to hide it with his buzzed head and all, but the curls and all suited him better.

"I'm rich. I don't have to make a living."

"What?"

"No one mentioned that I'm a trust fund kid with an amazing financial advisor and broker? My family bought their way to the levels they are now."

"Your parents are..."

"I know."

"Um, did I tell you they think we're married?"

"What?" He stared at me.

"They came to the hospital while you were there. The doctor said your husband and daughter were in the room with you."

"Oh, okay."

"That's all the freak out I get?"

"I was wondering why they haven't called to summon me to my weekly humiliation."

"Humiliation?"

"The day y'all couldn't find me, I was at breakfast with them. Mother handed me a card for her plastic surgeon to fill in the lines. They put me down for everything, my hair, my natural aging process, my job."

"Is that what you meant by the repercussions would be worse the night of the charity event?" He nodded. "There's nothing wrong with you at all. I could deal with a little less attitude, but I think that's your foreplay." I mentally patted myself on the back when he smiled. "My daughter loves you, and she's hateful to anyone she doesn't like. Donna threatened to steal you if I didn't get my head out of my ass. Months ago, I lowered myself to go to Remy and Robert for advice."

"What did they say?"

"That I needed to earn your trust and also to get my head out of my ass."

"Seems to be a problem for you."

"Maybe, but you weren't really giving me any *I'm interested* signals."

"I did let you into my personal space."

"I do like being in your personal space." I caught his gaze with mine and then lowered until my mouth almost touched his. "Does that mean I earned your trust?"

"Possibly."

"You're gonna break my heart, baby." I smirked as he tipped his chin, and his breath fanned my lips.

"I think you'll survive."

"God, is this what every morning is going to be like now?"

I turned my head, and Simon rose to his toes to look over my shoulder to find Savvy standing in the doorway still in her pajamas with a sleepy Amber on her hip.

"You wanted me to get a boyfriend. Now you're going to complain about it?"

"Boyfriend? You're jumping ahead a bit, aren't you?" he whispered in my ear.

"I don't think so. You love me, Simon Graves, and one day you're going to admit it." I gave him a quick kiss. "Who's making breakfast for our girls?"

"Simon's making breakfast. We don't have any leftovers for you to heat up since Papa Simon has been making us actual food and not take-out."

Simon hugged my waist as he chuckled at what Savvy said, but I glanced at him to find him staring at our girls, that haunted look no longer there. When he looked at Savvy and Amber, they were his, and he loved them, and he was happy knowing he didn't have to give them up. We made him happy, and we loved him without condition.

"Ouch, she's vicious, and that's all your fault. I'm going to take a shower while you decide on breakfast."

"Go get pretty." He pushed against the curve of my stomach with his good hand, and I staggered back.

I left the kitchen but stopped to drop a kiss on the top of Savvy's head, and then did the same for Amber when she pointed to the top of her messy curls. Then I continued to my bedroom. Part of me hoped I wasn't getting ahead of myself with Simon, but I also knew he had to feel something. Once this case was over, he'd be all mine, and we could build on what we had without the specter of an unknown number of killers gunning for us and our girls.

All I had to do was keep them safe and make sure my baby didn't blame himself for bringing this down on us. I knew he already did, but he couldn't tear himself apart for doing his job. I was also working against a timer quickly ticking down. If he left the force, I needed him to still want to be mine. And not just because he loved my daughter. I needed him to fall in love with me, too.

I'd just stepped under the hot water when my bathroom door opened all the way, and I peeked around the curtain.

"We got another body."

"Shit." I cursed as I quickly washed as I listened to the water run in the sink. "Do we know anything?"

"No, but this one's at the Outreach. Boss showed up to open, and it was left inside." I heard Simon spit. "Doc's already on his way. Tyson knows we're leaving any minute."

"Who's watching the girls?"

"Tony's taking them to Carmine's. I knocked on Donna's door, and it doesn't appear she came home last night."

"Yeah, she has an old friend with benefits. I think she was crashing at his place. I'll text her to let her know what's going on." I turned off the water and swept the curtain open to grab my towel as I stepped out of the tub. "I'll make us a few travel mugs to go." I held the towel in front of me as I lowered my head slightly to kiss the side of his neck. "You've got ten minutes to be ready." I patted his hip as I exited the bathroom to get dressed and listened to the shower turn back on.

We kept saying we needed another body but would this one be able to get us closer to the people involved or at the very least tell us what the fuck was going on. I needed this case over with. I wanted to romance my baby without the damn danger of attack always lurking too close by.

GRAVES

COLD CASE
UNIT

The shift in mine and Marcel's dynamic seemed almost too easy, and I wanted to question why, but I didn't have the time. I'd gotten the call of another body to distract me from my misfiring brain. The crime scene was right in the middle of what had been a safe area for years. First, it was Carmine's club, then Seamus's pub, and what the truce turned into a demilitarized zone, the Outreach, and strip. The victim wasn't just on our doorstep. It was right in the middle of our damn after-school area.

Boss had texted me separately to say they'd moved operations to another warehouse and blocked off all access to the affected area.

"Baby, it's okay." I turned my head to take in Marcel's profile as he squeezed my thigh with his big hand. "This may be the escalation we needed."

"I wanted that, but I didn't want it there. We put the truce in place for a reason. We wanted our children to always be safe."

"I know y'all did." He lifted his arm and wrapped his hand around the back of my neck to massage the tight muscles as we made our way to the strip.

The massive crowd at the crime scene tape made me tense, and the firming of Marcel's grip said he'd had the same reaction. He pulled into the space between two marked cruisers, and we both got out. Then we hurried forward to avoid the questions, especially the ones from the press who had descended like vultures.

"Graves, Douglas, this is bad." Stevenson jogged towards us and slowed as he matched our pace.

"What do we got?" I asked.

"Male victim, unknown age, someone caved his face in and removed his fingers. Doc's thinking they were removed with some type of small pruning shears. Before we go in—" Stevenson stopped, and we did too.

"What's going on?"

"This was more than escalation, man. They tried to destroy him. Doc doesn't even think Vega's skills can get us an ID on this vic. His head is almost flattened. Every facial bone is shattered."

"Does he think this is connected?"

"The vic has been re-dressed. This was so much more than them just wanting to delay identification. He's literally a skin bag of broken bones. Until they can do some form of reassembling him. We can't even tell you what height he is, except from his in-seam. He can be anywhere from six-foot to six-three. By the size of his suit, he's probably a man who used to be physically fit. I've never seen anything like it. Boss is inside talking to the forensic techs and a few uniforms about anything that may have been missing or out of place. Everyone's waiting for you inside."

I nodded at him as Marcel followed me through the propped open door, and I caught sight of Remy and Robert standing beside Boss. We headed for Doc where he was crouched down beside the victim.

"What's the word, Doc?"

"Whoever he is, someone was very pissed at him. Most of his teeth appear to still be there but mixed in with the facial bone fragments. I don't even think I have a good enough jaw to see about resetting them for dental comparisons. His fingers are nowhere to be found. He's nearly devoid of blood, but we have maybe a few smears. I think he's been dead twenty-four to forty-eight hours according to decomp, but I can't even be positive of that. There's so much tissue damage from the beating. So right now, that's two bodies we can't identify. Our last vic didn't get us any hits in any of the databases, not even partial matches."

I stared at the destroyed mass of tissue in an expensive tailored suit and noticed some black ink that peeked just above the collar of the blood-stained shirt. I squatted down and hoped like fuck I was wrong. "Give me some gloves." I held out my hand as Doc offered me the box. I pulled out one and used it to lift the right lapel to the side. I cursed as I saw the monogram stitched on the inside pocket. "Dekland Mancini."

"*The* Dekland Mancini?" Marcel lowered beside me as he asked.

"He has an old shoulder tattoo that went slightly above his collar. He normally covered it up. It was from an old crew he ran with back in his teens. Just kids trying to play tough. The monogram on his inside pocket, it's hand-stitched in gold thread."

"What the fuck is going on, Graves?" Doc asked me.

"I have no idea, but we got bodies dumped at Carmine and Seamus's places, one close to the border of the strip, and now this one right in our own house. Two attempted murders on me and Savvy, and the kidnapping of Amber. This is more than some warning. This is—" The yelling of my name made me jerk my head up, and I saw a uniform officer leaning into the door. "Yeah?"

"You got a guy asking for you."

I pushed upward, and as I neared the entrance, I recognized the bruiser behind the cop. Irvine Bastian, he was Dekland's right-hand man. I raised my good hand and motioned him to let Irvine through. Marcel was close behind me.

"Bastian, what are you doing here?"

"Is that the boss?" Bastian stepped to the side out of view of the people outside and kept his voice low. "We got word that a body showed up at the Outreach. Is it him?"

"What makes you think it's him?"

"He left three days ago. Said he had some business to take care of. Wouldn't let any of us go with him because it was a private matter."

"You got any idea what the private matter was?"

"Graves, you know how the boss is. Disrespect isn't tolerated. He's been losing his shit for about a year now. Got real cagey, secretive…secret meetings he wasn't even letting me in on. The organization is hemorrhaging money, he was damn near broke, and then he claimed he got a new partner."

"Broke? I haven't heard anything about him losing that amount of bank."

"There was this new taskforce. They've been busting our contacts left and right. Like the fuckers knew every detail. I think it was run by a SWAT commander, Sharp, always got a K-9, wicked-looking dog."

Marcel and I shared a glance, and then we brought our attention back to Bastian. We had no idea about a new taskforce. If they were targeting Dekland, they'd have brought in Organized Crime to be in on that. I'd have heard rumors about that since I asked a lot of questions.

"When did the taskforce make its presence known?"

"They started hitting hard about six months ago. Dekland had four shipments seized in the span of two months. But the thing was, he didn't seem paranoid about it. He didn't change procedure…no routine scans for bugs or tracking tags. If anything, he got cockier, and that's when all the private convos and meetings started happening. Even with the busts, it was just business as usual. We thought this possible unknown partner was gonna fix it all."

"Any idea who the partner was?" There was only so many people it could've been, but none of them had the funds to bankroll an operation like Dekland's. We'd notice any new faces who showed up around the strip. Like people have said before, everyone was pretty old school and territorial.

"No damn clue, just saying he was going to be running this city soon. No one would see it coming. Last two months or so, he's been...I don't know, man, he looked terrified, and you know Dekland, his balls are bigger than his brains. He never knows when to be scared. After you two paid your visit, the mask fell, and he was on his damn phone. He was screaming about what the fuck they'd gotten him into."

"You got any clue who they were?" Marcel asked.

"Nah, man, we've all been on edge. Dekland's use went way up. He had one of the guys bringing him powder daily instead of his usual few girls and some party favors on the weekends. So, is it him?"

"From his clothes and what looks like a tattoo, we have a tentative ID made by me."

"Shit." Bastian pushed his fingers through his short hair and leaned back against the wall.

"And you've heard nothing?" I asked.

"We've all been ready to jump ship the last few years, but the money was still coming in, so we stuck it out. It's a cushy fucking job. But Dekland wanted his cred. He was raging about Bianchi and Seamus, even Boss, tired of those three fags running this city. My boyfriend kept telling me to get out. A lot of the guys were thinking of finding employment elsewhere. Dekland was losing it, but we stuck it out because we got partners and families to think about. About four months ago, I sent my man and his kid to stay with his mama outta state just until I could figure something out."

"Did Dekland have any plans for Bianchi, Seamus, or Boss?" I wouldn't be shocked if he did. He always seemed to have some plan going. Dekland wanted to be king, and he wouldn't settle for anything less and that could've gotten him killed.

"Not that he was sharing, but he said their takedown would be epic, and he'd finally get the respect he deserved."

"Not many could get him the clout he needs. There had to be something. If he was that on edge, he had to let something slip."

"That's the thing, Graves. Dekland liked to brag…he wanted everyone to know how big he was or could be. But me and the rest of his inner circle? We were completely pushed out. He's always been a homophobic ass, that's nothing new, but it almost seemed as if he was weeding us out one by one…anyone who didn't fit the image he had of his organization."

"Maybe like he was setting up for a new image?" Marcel shifted and crossed his arms over his chest.

"Yeah, yeah, that, like a reinvention where he wasn't the old banger back in the old neighborhood. No matter the price of the suit or his new zip code, he was still a punk. I think that's what pissed him off the most about Seamus and Bianchi. They didn't let him forget it."

"Were there any new outfits making noise?" Marcel asked.

"Nah. This is a pretty old school city. A Bianchi was running the streets since the industrial boom. Seamus, mean fucker, but he earned his stripes as an enforcer, became the son Liam Ingram never had. That gave him respectability. You got your groups that have strongholds in smaller areas of the city, but they ain't playing no games to be more than what they are. They occasionally try for a bigger score here or there, but they ain't throwing down huge weight. The only one who'd have any clout would be the Darner family, but when he died, his sons made sure they were above reproach. Dekland took a major hit when Darner got taken out."

"Why are you talking, Bastian?"

"Because I got a nice guy and a cute kid, Graves. We've been living a pretty normal life the last few years, and I like it. With the proof of Dekland dead, ain't nothing keeping me from moving on."

"That would give you a huge motive to take him out," I suggested.

"I know it does, but if whoever the boss was dealing with scared him, I sure as fuck ain't staying around to work for them...none of us are. As soon as I inform everyone our boss is laying on a slab, we're all disappearing."

"What do you think would bring all this shit down on the Families and the Outreach?"

"What does this place have that no other area has?"

"What?" I asked.

"Prime real estate."

"He's not wrong. Bring up crime in an area...prices go down in order to sell quick," Marcel suggested.

"But Flo said there wasn't an influx of permits for renovation or new construction."

"They could just be buying everything up, let the heat die down before they start building or upgrading existing structures."

I hated to agree with Marcel because that would've meant someone was running an operation on our turf, and we hadn't heard about it. "We can look at property records to see what's been sold and when. Maybe for the past year."

"Vega would be the one to talk to."

I nodded and turned my attention back to Bastian. "Thank you, Bastian."

"I wasn't here. Until I'm out of town, you got no info from me."

"Understood."

He lowered his head and slipped his sunglasses back on as he disappeared back into the bright sunlight of mid-morning. I turned back to face the room and looked around the space that should be filled with volunteers and children running and laughing. Instead, a mangled body rested in the middle and tainted everything we'd accomplished.

"What are you thinking?"

"We didn't think it had anything to do with the Outreach. We revitalized the area. Crime is down. Drug offenses and overdoses are at an all-time low. So, what we've done here brought this on us."

"Don't think that, baby. What we have is someone connected to Dekland. We know that Sharp may have information for us. They may have panicked and took out Dekland, which means they fucked up."

"What if they didn't and taking him out tied up a loose end?"

"One of us has to think positive."

"Graves," Boss said my name, and I turned my head.

"I'm sorry, Boss."

"What the fuck are you story about? And before you try to take this onto your shoulders, we're not in control of other people's actions. You just find out who brought this on us." He placed his hand on my cheek and then kissed my opposite one. "Chin up, honey."

"I'll try."

"Remy and Robert are going to get Roo and then pick up your girls. We're all meeting at Mama Sue's for dinner later. We're all hitting our contacts and maybe come up with something."

"Thanks. I'll call Carmine and let him know Remy's picking the girls up. Tony will probably shadow them, though."

"Of course. Tony's getting some major shit about having a new boss."

I chuckled as he winked at me, and then he was headed toward his office. "Boss, anything messed with that you could see?" He stopped and turned on his toes.

"Nothing was taken. The security cameras just showed four

large males entering to drop off the body, and one broke away to access the hallways to our offices. They bypassed the alarm system, but I'm having Zero come in to run a scan to see if any of our computers were accessed and if anything was downloaded. I'll know more by tonight."

"Okay." I pushed a sigh through my clenched teeth. Doc was loading the body on a gurney with the help of two of the crime scene guys and told us that he was headed right back to the morgue to start the autopsy. I told him that we'd be right behind him.

"On the way to the morgue, give Vega a call to see if she can get us the call logs and any other information from his phone. We don't exactly have time to wait for court orders." He was right. We didn't have much time to spare. If getting rid of Dekland was tying up loose ends, we might already be too late.

"We'll request them, so if we find anything, we're in a position to use whatever we find."

"Sounds like a plan. Let's get going. Hopefully, Doc can find some clue during the autopsy, and Zero has something for us. Who's going to call Sharp to see about getting his cooperation?" Marcel asked with an innocent smile.

"Robert, they're friendly. A special taskforce needs the agreement of some pretty powerful people, especially one that's kept on the down-low." I shot a glare at Marcel as he poked my side. "I am not calling my father unless it means life or death. Any way we can circumvent that ball of fucked-upped-ness I'm all for it. If Sharp will talk to us even better. I can call a few of my contacts in Organized Crime."

"We have a lot to do before dinner time. Let's get to it, and maybe we'll even make it home to sleep in our bed."

"The day has just started, and I'm already exhausted."

"We solve this case, put all the bad people away, and you, me, and our girls go on vacation with no cell phones or dead bodies to deal with for two whole weeks."

I groaned. "Don't tease me. I haven't had a vacation in"—I paused and mentally cursed—"I don't remember my last vacation."

"That means you're due. And we can find something fun for Savvy and Amber to do. But at night, you're all mine." He sneakily patted my ass.

"Don't get handsy on the job, Detective Douglas."

"I wouldn't think about it."

"Uh-huh, you're already thinking about it."

"I definitely am."

I rolled my eyes as we walked outside as the coroner's van pulled out of the lot, and we headed back to Marcel's SUV. Before I had my seatbelt buckled, I already had my phone out and started making all the calls I needed to. Sending a text to our group to have Robert call Sharp and to tell him I'd fill him on why later. My brain started taking notes, moving the mental index cards around, and trying to fill in the information that we'd learned from Bastian. I needed to do more than throw knives at a wall. I needed definite answers because everyone I loved and cared for seemed to be in danger. When I found out who, badge or not, I'd make them pay for what they'd done.

DOUGLAS

"**M**ama Sue!" Savvy and Amber squealed as they ran into the older woman's arms, and she cuddled them to her. I shook my head. The woman still looked at me like my mere presence offended her. I stood back as Simon got in on the action. Closed for a private party sign marked the door, and I went to what I'd come to think of as our normal booth while my girls and Simon got love.

I'd kept him distracted all day, but we'd finally arrived at the moment of truth. Another squeal marked Roo's entrance, and she was pushing her way into the mix. Tony had posted up next to the door while Robert, Remy, and Carmine walked toward the booth.

"Bianchi." I greeted him as he looked around a bit uncomfortable. "Sweating there a little bit?" At least he was dressed casually in jeans, t-shirt, and a leather jacket.

"I never anticipated that I would willingly spend all my time with cops or cops' kids, but I must admit, my nieces are perfect." He slid into the booth, but Remy and Robert pulled up a chair for Robert to sit down and pull Remy onto his lap.

Doc and Stevenson entered, with Doc in his customary spot

tucked under his Daddy's arm. To be honest, like Carmine, I thought I'd have a straightforward life when I'd relocated. Except for the addition of being a full-time parent, I'd believed it would be business as usual. That hadn't been what happened. Boss was next to show, and he leaned down slightly to kiss Mama Sue's cheek loudly, causing the woman to giggle. Boss and Simon made their way to the booth, but the girls went with Mama Sue to the back.

"Mama Sue said she made us something special, family-style, and the girls were going to finish helping her," Simon said as he took the seat beside me, and I stretched my arm along the back of the booth. "Was Sharp willing to meet us?" he asked Robert.

"Yeah, he should be here any time. Said he was going to have to go home and change, feed Jupiter." Robert checked his watch. "Should be here any minute."

Stevenson and Doc sat beside Carmine, and then the last member of the team arrived. Vega came in with Zero. Hellos and hugs were exchanged, and Vega and Zero set up their computers on the next booth. Simon started laying out the files and index cards he'd taken off our wall at home.

"Anything come up in the computer search?" I asked.

"Nothing stellar that would give us any clue. They seemed to be trying to access volunteer records, but when Zero and I built the encryption program, unless they have world-class hacking skills, they weren't getting shit."

"Why such high-level security?" I asked.

"We have encrypted info for some people we've made disappear. Our very own Wit-Sec program. They did try to get into our financial records." Boss rubbed his hands over his shaved head, and he looked exhausted.

"Was clean-up a problem?"

Boss looked at me and shook his head. "No, we have a friend who does crime scene clean-up. By the time school was out, it was like nothing had ever happened. But most of my afternoon was spent doing damage control. Everyone really stepped up today, and on a good day, they go above and beyond." Boss jerked his attention to the door as the bell signaled someone entered.

"Anyone able to join the party?" Sharp asked as he approached with his canine shadow perfectly in sync with his every step.

"Thanks for coming, Sharp."

"Robert, your tone didn't sound like I had much choice."

"You're not one for orders."

"That's why I like being in command, but it's been a while since my undercover days and shady meetings." He shot a glance at Carmine.

"Nothing shady about it, Sharp. We came across some info in the course of our investigation. They said you were heading up a taskforce." As Simon spoke, I watched Sharp, but he didn't give anything away, not even a flinch.

"That's on a need-to-know basis, and you've got one of the bosses sitting at the table. I'm not inclined to assist."

"Dekland Mancini was tortured and murdered," I announced and looked for some reaction. Again, there wasn't anything.

"That hasn't been verified yet."

"He's definitely not being admitted to the club," Vega muttered without ever looking up from whatever she stared at on her laptop.

"Actually, it was. We're just not sharing the confirmation." Doc started to fidget, and Stevenson pulled out his phone, tapped the screen, and handed it to him. I could see a coloring app, and Doc was distracted.

Sharp groaned and grabbed a nearby chair and set it down next to Boss. As the commander sat, he pinched the bridge of his nose. "I'm really not liking you guys. Not long after I transferred here from Dallas, I was approached by the DA's office. They were forming a taskforce to start making hits on local organizations. Hit them where it counts, disrupting their shipments in any way possible, making it harder for them to bring in cash."

"Doesn't seem on the up and up," Robert said.

"We were told we'd be working in a clandestine fashion. The team they compiled was pretty much feral...a lot of undercovers who were in deep...years for some of them. We worked out of a warehouse near the shipyard. Any product we seized was kept at the warehouse as well, so we always had what we needed to run our busts. Mancini was our main target."

"Why Dek? He was mid-level at best. He couldn't come up with the amount of weight that would make an operation like that run. Seems idiotic." Boss commented.

"That was my thought, but I was just there to do the planning. Everything was calculated down to the second. Any degree of error wasn't acceptable."

"Who did you report to?" Simon asked as I saw the wheels turning.

"District Attorney Graves. It went from the unit commander, police commissioner to the DA. Thing was, we were told to carry on with our usual operations. I was still mainly performing my duties as SWAT commander. All the others were still deep undercover or detectives."

"That's spreading y'all pretty thin. Homicide is already an always-on job gig. Throw in the taskforce...that's giving no downtime," Remy said as he shifted on Robert's lap.

"Most of the cops are showing signs of extreme burnout. I'm pretty sure none of them could pass a drug test at this point. I wouldn't be surprised if our evidence was light."

"Then why the fuck are you still in?" Boss seemed to be studying Sharp pretty hard.

"I don't know who the fuck you are, but I take my job seriously." Sharp turned away from Boss, essentially dismissing him as a non-issue. "The unit commander isn't much better, so I went straight to the top, and the DA told me to do my job. I couldn't have an opinion unless he gave it to me."

"That didn't sit right with you?" I was sure I already knew the answer.

"You know fucking well it didn't. I started paying closer attention."

"We got intel that Dekland and his associates were well aware of the taskforce." Even as Simon spoke, I knew Bastian's name wasn't going to pass his lips at any point.

"Graves, they shouldn't have known shit. We're pretty much off the books when it comes to the taskforce. We're essentially operating on our own."

"Wrong, because they knew the cops had made the busts, but our confidential informant didn't seem to know anything about clandestine."

"We weren't even allowed to have a badge on us, and if we did, it was hidden under our clothes in the event we had to identify ourselves. But to be completely transparent. I've been out of the loop for about three or four months since my dressing down by the DA. I'm still in charge of recon and planning, but I haven't been in person for the ops. What's all this shit about?"

Everyone turned to look at Simon and waited for him to answer. "It all started for me with the second body dump at Carmine's club. My involvement began with someone handing over my card on what turned out to be Douglas's case."

"And?"

"Patience, we have a process, Sharp." Simon started opening files. "After the murder of the fourth man, we learned some information that they were possibly day laborers, picked up by construction companies. Three of them have been positively ID'd by an independent source. The fourth, he was unknown, still no information on his actual identity or where he came from." He slid the files across the table toward Sharp, and the other man picked them up and started flipping.

"They were all tortured in the same way. Tool marks and trace evidence were consistent with the same tools and location.

They all had a small amount of sedative in their systems. Not enough to incapacitate, but definitely enough to hinder any strength to resist," Doc said without looking up.

"They were busted for petty crimes, served short bids in county…no extensive prison time. Any searches I made on them didn't throw up any red flags or have the Feds coming down on me for hacking their servers." Vega still focused on her screen.

"You hacked federal databases when you already have access to them?"

"It was a test. They didn't make sense, so if they were officially working in some capacity for the Feds, they'd have shut me down. That didn't happen. And I made my presence known as obnoxiously as possible." She rolled her eyes like Sharp asking was weird.

"I'm going to jail for just sitting with y'all. How does Dekland getting taken out fit with the others?"

"During the autopsy, I did rush on his tox and found the same sedative, with an entire host of other party favors. He'd used shortly before his torture and eventual demise. To be honest, with his levels, I don't think he could've remained conscious for most of the damage inflicted." Doc answered as he cuddled back against Stevenson's chest.

"Our CI said his use had turned to a daily occurrence in recent months," I commented.

"You have five dead people. What else do you have? Except for some small fiber evidence and some tool marks, there's really nothing to link them." As Sharp spoke, everyone groaned, and he looked more annoyed than usual.

"We just figured it was a rival crew, a new up and comer who wanted to make a name for themselves by targeting body dumps at Carmine and Seamus's places, but no one's making any noise, and I mean nobody. You want to fuck with Bianchi and Finnegan, and you think you're succeeding, you're going to want to brag."

"What changed, Graves?"

"The attack on me. When they chased me from the alley with my daughter with me, well, they wanted to know where Douglas's brat was. I refused to tell them. They tried to kill me but they had shit aim. Then we pulled in our crew, and no one went anywhere alone. When they couldn't get to me, they went after Amber, the girl I'm adopting. Everyone was in safe houses. Savvy has a security detail provided by Carmine. They weren't getting anywhere. A few bodies turning up, in the grand scheme of things, how does that really affect us? But then they turned the Outreach into a crime scene...bad press for us."

Boss cleared his throat when Simon finished talking. "Several years ago, we negotiated a truce. The Outreach and surrounding portions of the strip were considered demilitarized zones. We'd all come to a peace agreement. No illegal or gang activity. This agreement held strong for several years. Then the murders started, the perimeter quickly decreased until it reached the Outreach. In the middle of our afterschool program area."

"You negotiated a ceasefire?" He looked at us like we'd lost our minds. "And you agreed?" Sharp shot a glare at Carmine.

"We respect what Boss does, Seamus and I. Some of the smaller crews readily agreed to respect the border. Dekland was a holdout but didn't last very long. He started getting the cold shoulder from suppliers who may or may not want to allegedly mess with more profitable business partners. So Dekland's bottom line was the only reason he agreed."

"Not that I'm in anyway condoning whatever this bullshit alliance is that y'all got going on, but y'all think you're the targets, why not just post a sniper and take you out at any time?"

"We don't think it's us. We think it's Graves that's the target. Not saying we don't got some pretty fucked up enemies," Remy said as she leaned back against Robert's chest. "They made it personal when they took shots at Graves and Savvy, but more so when they grabbed Amber. That means they were aware of how he felt about that little girl. They wanted to hit him where it hurt. Dekland's body dump, well, that was hitting him where he felt the happiest. These people want Graves to back off, but for what reason, we're still clueless."

"With my years in Organized Crime, I'd think someone would hold a grudge, but they'd think more like you, sniper, or just walk up to me on the street and put a bullet between my eyes. This production? I have no idea what it's for."

"Could it be a diversion of some sort?" Sharp asked as he patted his dog when Jupiter nudged his knee with his nose.

"My involvement wasn't guaranteed. Douglas was assigned the first murder, but me being in Cold Case, there's no hallmark of a cold case element that would've brought me in. The only reason I was called was because the female witness to the second dump gave the responding uniforms my card."

"Could she have been set up to get you involved? Rumor is Cold Case has a big presence. I've heard about the cards."

"No, the witness is pretty low profile. She doesn't like making waves. They threatened to take her in on solicitation, and as soon as they did, she handed over Graves's card," Boss answered.

I saw the wheels working. He was law enforcement through and through, so he'd try any angle that wouldn't make his fellow cops look bad, but I also knew he'd go with the evidence wherever it pointed him.

"Maybe whoever wants to set Graves up made it worth her while. Money makes loyalty lax."

"I know my people, asshole, and we're loyal, something I don't think you know much about." Boss's jaw clenched.

"You don't know shit about me, boy, so keep your opinions to yourself."

"I ain't nobody's boy."

"Behave, children present." Vega hissed as the sound of small feet running towards us sounded.

We all turned to find Roo and Amber hurrying to the table.

Amber crawled up next to Simon, and Roo climbed onto Remy's lap. Savvy was helping Mama Sue set out oven pans of food and baskets of rolls.

"Come on and make y'all's plates. Y'all ain't wasting my food." Mama Sue whispered something to Savvy, and she walked behind the counter to grab the stack of plates to place them on the surface and then the silverware tray.

"Sharp, we need your help on this. We've got our girls to keep safe. We have a lot to lose if they escalate more," Simon whispered as he hugged Amber to his side and looked at Savvy to share a smile.

"Give me a few days to poke around. I ain't guaranteeing anything. I'm still not sure how I feel about the people you associate with." Sharp glanced between Boss and Carmine.

Everyone got up to move as Mama Sue repeated her order to make plates, and Sharp got up, ordered his canine to follow.

"No, boy, I said make a plate. That meant you, too. I'll get your partner a bowl of water. No one ever leaves my place hungry." Mama Sue patted his cheek less than gently, and I swore I saw Sharp's cheeks turn a little pink.

Conversations about the case were ended, and it was like our usual unit dinners, people laughing and telling stories about the good old days. Simon and I catered to Amber, made sure she had everything she needed. Everyone was relaxed and comfortable, but I couldn't ignore the glances everyone was getting from Sharp. There was suspicion and something else there, but I couldn't quite figure out what. All we could do was hope he didn't betray us, and we had to add another person to the list of people we had to look over our shoulder for.

33

GRAVES

The apartment was quiet. Donna had gone to bed early as she had to catch a flight in the morning. She hadn't been able to extend her leave. Savvy and Amber were asleep after going into their food comas from Mama Sue's dinner. She'd even sent home leftovers for the girls to have. As much as my mind was distracted by the case and the safety of Savvy and Amber, there was something more present that was making me nervous.

The shower was running in the master bathroom, and I was laying in the middle of Marcel's bed. I'd showered earlier while he'd spent time with Donna before she had to leave. She had a car coming for her at three AM. I was somewhere between excitement and embarrassment that this would be the first night I'd ever slept with someone else in the bed with me.

I didn't want to seem awkward, but if that was the case, I wasn't succeeding. I'd just put on baggy pajama bottoms to sleep in, but I kept nervously adjusting the sheet and comforter that I'd neatly folded to lay across my belly. He said we were just going to sleep. That it wasn't going beyond that, but I still didn't know what to expect.

Oh God! I yelled the words in my head as the shower turned off and as my mentally counted seconds turned to minutes, and I started to get out of bed. I couldn't do this. My feet barely hit the floor when I heard Marcel chuckling.

"Escaping, baby?" he asked, and I glanced over my shoulder to find him shirtless, wearing only gray sweatpants.

"No, I was just..." I flipped him off as his laughter turned louder. "Asshole."

"You know, I can easily go sleep on the couch like normal. You may have said yes this morning, but you can revoke consent."

I turned back around, rested my elbows on my knees, and then buried my face in my hands. "I don't know what you want from me." My voice was muffled. I laid my cheek on my good hand and watched him as he lowered onto the mattress beside me.

"I want you to feel safe and ready, and if me sleeping in the bed with you makes you uncomfortable, well, I can sleep on the couch, and we can do this another time. We can lay in this bed on opposite sides, or we can share the middle while we cuddle. As much as I want to hold you all night, if you don't want that, I'm okay."

"I still don't understand how that's enough."

"You're painting me with the same brush as your friends. They're highly sexual people in the physical sense. I won't lie and say I don't love sex. But honestly, like I've told you before, I can get myself off. Orgasms are easy to get. Whether that's solo or with a hookup. I miss the freedom of intimacy. A stolen kiss. And if we ever do have sex, it's most likely not going to end with me fucking you. I know it's shocking, but penetration isn't everything. Some people don't even...wait for it...like it."

"Now you're just being snarky."

"Simon, before I even met you, I wasn't the casual type. Getting my dick slick wasn't my favorite thing in the world. Nothing about you being Asexual changed what I do and don't like. As romantic and sexual partners, what we are meshes perfectly for me. Like I said, I just need you to figure that out."

I fell backward and stretched my arms out on the bed, and stared up at the ceiling. "I'm almost forty-four years old. I shouldn't be nervous about sleeping with someone."

"Just because you feel you shouldn't be doesn't mean you aren't." The mattress dipped slightly as he stretched out beside me, and his hand spread over my belly as he laid his head on his upraised hand.

"I took you for an uncommunicative masculine man."

"Baby, I'm raising a daughter. I'm teaching her what to expect and demand. That toxic masculinity bullshit flew out the window about the time I let her put sparkle polish on my nails and stick floppy bows to my bald head. Don't even get me started on the makeup. I've worn so much makeup. And I'm almost fifty, and my give-a-fuck broke a long time ago. Outside my job, I don't know. All that other shit just isn't important. Yes, I'm a perfectionist about my job, but until recently, I tried to leave that at the door when I came home."

"If we're too much trouble, me and Amber can go home."

"Not a chance. If you two go, me and our kid go with y'all. So, what's it going to be? A goodnight kiss and me headed to the couch, or us curling up in this big bed?"

"I'm not having sex with you."

He smirked. "I didn't think you were. I'm just tired of half an apartment separating us at night. You know something that surprised me?" he asked as he scooted a bit closer and then lowered his head until his mouth almost touched mine.

"What's that?"

"This." He combed his thick fingers through the hair on my chest. "Figured you for the waxing type or naturally smooth."

"I tried, I waxed once, couldn't keep up with it, never made a second appointment, and then I trimmed, shaved, and all that did was drive me insane."

"It suits you," he whispered as he gently brushed his lips to mine. My eyes closed as his right arm slipped under my head, and I turned until my chest pushed flush to his. "I thought about this all day." His big hand rested on my side, and his thumb stroked the pale skin of my belly.

"If it's not enough, you have to tell me," I said softly between tender presses of our lips and his hard cock pressed to my softer one. He didn't try to rut our bodies together or push me to my back—he didn't push at all.

"More than enough, baby, hard or not, you don't owe me a damn thing except this…" He gave me a bit of his weight as I twined my arms around his neck, and he stroked his hand along my ribs until he tucked it under my arm. His thumb circled my nipple, and I felt that same odd feeling in my belly I'd gotten when we'd made out on the couch the previous night. Our kisses alternated between easy and demanding, but he never tried to get closer than we were.

"I'm not—" I tried to keep the embarrassment out of my voice. He was ready, and my body just wouldn't, but I didn't want him to think I didn't like it. Yet I also didn't want to lead him on that he'd get more than another make-out session like the first time. Fuck, I didn't know what I wanted.

"Oh, baby, you don't have to be. That isn't what this is about. We're just loving on each other a little before we got to sleep."

"But you are." I whimpered as the tip of his tongue teased mine. He made me feel good—it felt good. I loved when he touched me, but nothing happened but a slight firming.

"I like being turned on. We'll cuddle while I enjoy it. All you have to do is get me where I'm on edge, and if it's too much, I'll go to the bathroom to take care of it. Be selfish for me."

My natural inclination to fight warred between my belief that what I had to offer wouldn't be enough and the fact that for the first time in my life, I wanted this closeness. Maybe not the physical act, but the intimacy of connecting with someone, or it could just be Marcel. As much as my friends said I was fine as is, they didn't want to fuck me.

"Quit thinking so much. We're just fine."

The second I nodded, his thick fingers twisted in my curls, and the kiss turned from teasing to something else. I felt safe to say no, that all I had to do was push against his chest or whisper stop, and he'd back off instantly. My lips felt swollen and bruised, and my skin was made sensitive by the brush of his beard against my smoothly shaved chin and cheeks.

I wasn't hard, but I felt...needy. I arched into him, and his body was big and radiating heat where it was pressed to mine. He lifted to position himself between my thighs, and his arms were braced on either side of my head as his hips bore mine into the mattress. His cock was hot and hard where it notched with my soft one through our pants.

"God damn, you feel good, baby." He slowly rutted against my lower belly, and I dug my fingers into his bowed back as his movements became uneven. "Touch me, just a little, please."

I stroked my right hand around to his smooth chest, caressed downward over the hard curve of his belly, under his sweats, until my fingertips teased the slick head of his cock. I gently circled it as his possession of my mouth became rougher—more demanding as his hips moved in the circle of my hand. I tightened my thighs on his waist, carefully curved my left hand around the back of his neck, and flipped him until I was on top.

He stretched his arms over his head and gripped the top sheet and comforter in his hands. His barrel chest quickly moved with every labored breath, and he was staring at me through the slits made by his lowered lids. His eyes widened as I slowly removed his pants to leave him naked, and then I was back to straddling his thighs. I tested the silky length of his shaft, to the base and lower to cup his tight sac, and his legs shifted open slightly. I teased the hair around his hole, and his back arched almost violently.

"Again," he demanded, and he groaned as I did what he asked.

Until him, I'd never touched someone in a sexual way, never craved it the way I did with him, but my only intention was to make him feel good. I took in the contrast of dark to pale, lean to thickly built. I pushed at the flexing muscle, gently and pre-cum pooled on his dark brown skin as just the tip breached his hole. He was so big and gorgeous and completely at my mercy, and I felt so powerful.

"Jerk me off. I need it, baby."

I lightly drew my fingers back over his taint, his balls, and along his pulsing length until I wrapped my fingers around him. I did as he asked. I gave him what he needed, and some foreign compulsion in the back of my mind bid me to growl *mine*, but I bit it back as I leaned forward to slam my mouth against his as I stroked him in a slow, firm rhythm. Our tongues tangled, and he let out the sexiest, little whimper as I sped up my strokes until he froze and told me to stop.

I didn't hesitate. I stopped and stared down at his sweaty face and heavy-lidded eyes. "Doesn't seem like that was enough."

"Fuck, it was almost too much. I love this. The almost painful need." He shook beneath me. "Always on edge. The denial." He cupped my face tightly in his hands. "And you are too fucking good at it. Just the tip of your finger nearly had me going off. Now, let me hold you until we fall asleep."

"Marcel, are you sure I'm enough?"

"You're fucking perfect."

34

DOUGLAS

Donna had snuck into our room to say bye. I'd awakened instantly to find her smiling down at us. She'd kissed my cheek, whispered she was happy for me, and would call when she landed. It was on the tip of my tongue to ask her to stay, but the military was her life. She'd never wanted to do anything else, and it would be selfish to ask her to. She was going to get Savvy during the summer. After I'd watched her leave, I'd dozed a few more hours.

It was an hour before sunrise, and I laid in bed for the first morning in a long time with a warm body curled up to my side. God, my Simon was perfect. I knew he worried that what he could offer me in the way of sex wouldn't be enough, but the teasing hand job before I made him stop took me exactly where I needed to go. I'd stretched out on my back with him drawing circles on my heaving chest as I tried to catch my breath as my cock pulsed a frantic rhythm. Edging myself had never been that fucking good. Pre-cum had pooled on my belly as I enjoyed the ache. I swore that need still burned in my lower belly.

That one four-letter word that I wanted to say just wouldn't form on my tongue. Not that I didn't love him, I knew I did. But what we had was still too new for him, at least. We had the case, Amber's pending adoption, and the unknown person or group that wanted to destroy us.

"You're thinking too loud." Simon groaned as he tucked his head under my arm and pulled the covers up to hide under.

"It's almost time for us to get up."

"No, it's not. The sun isn't up yet."

"You're adorable when you whine."

"You're an asshole in the mornings."

"How will my heart take all this sweet-talking you're doing?"

"I want to break up."

I laughed as I scooted down and slipped under the covers with him. "No, you don't." I groaned as my naked body pressed flush to his, and I lifted his lean thigh to rest over my hip. "I told you, you're going to love me, Simon Graves." I kissed him and stroked his stubble-covered jaw with my thumb.

"Delusional," he said even as he snuggled to get closer to me.

"I've waited months to get you right here. I'm not giving that up." I rested my forehead on his.

"Was last night okay?" I heard the insecurity in his tone. I'd never seen myself as the submissive one in bed, but with Simon, I'd have let him do whatever he wanted to me.

"My answer hasn't changed from last night. It was perfect."

The frenetic raps on the locked bedroom door, what sounded like both girls trying to break in, broke us apart with a groan. "Dads! Breakfast, people, breakfast."

"My mornings used to be so quiet." He threw the covers off us, and then he was rolling from bed. He stretched his leanly muscled frame and then bent to grab our pants where we'd thrown them the night before. He tossed my sweats to me and then pulled on his as he strolled to the door.

I barely got myself covered up with the sheet before he threw open the door to find two adorable, smiling girls.

"The sun isn't even up yet."

"Amber was hungry." Savvy cheekily grinned.

"Uh-huh, and that's not your stomach sounding like the roar of an avalanche?"

"Not me, Papa Simon. I'm too delicate and lady-like for that."

He stepped out and turned Savvy with Amber clutching her neck. "Did you at least start coffee?"

"Nope."

"Why do we even keep you around?"

"Because I'm cute."

I chuckled as I listened to their snarky morning conversation slowly fade as they headed for the kitchen. Fuck, that's what I missed about having someone, the normalcy of it. My partner in bed. Kids interrupting us for food or just to be bratty. Some people wouldn't see what I had as an ideal, but to me, my partner and family were everything.

Yes, there were a few more challenges having Simon as said partner. He was a stubborn brat. His thought process was a mystery. And I was his first relationship ever. At least I'd developed a wealth of patience to deal with him. I waited until I heard him and our girls talking in the kitchen before I got up and put on my pants.

After I used the bathroom, I headed to join them in time to see Savvy running with a travel mug for the front door. Tony always took over at six AM. The neighbors were starting to question the big dude posted outside our door, but most knew I was a cop, so they didn't get too nosy. Maybe it would be better if we moved to Simon's where we'd have more space. Tony already drove Savvy to school, did whatever he needed to do, which I didn't want to know about, and returned to pick her up.

I waved at him through the open door as he accepted the mug from Savvy. I entered the kitchen to find Amber making a mess of mixing batter for waffles or pancakes. They were Amber's favorite. I kissed the top of her head as she pointed as she always did when giving me permission, and then I brushed my lips to

Simon's bare shoulder as I picked up my mug he'd already poured for me.

All of it was so domestic, and the thought made me smile. I got a hug from Savvy. Our usual morning routine began, the girls helping with breakfast and my man growling at me if I messed with his order. He had three plates overflowing with pancakes on the table.

As we were about to sit down, a knock sounded at the door, and I got up. I groaned as I saw who was standing on the other side.

"Sharp, a bit early for a visit."

"I haven't gone to sleep yet. It's late for me. Your doorman almost got introduced to Jupiter when he tried to frisk me."

"He's serious about Savvy and Amber's safety. Come on in. Second pot of coffee should be done." I turned away and felt him following, and then the door closed. "You had breakfast yet?"

"No, I don't want—" Savvy jumped up with a mouth full of food to grab another plate and mug she handed to Simon. "I could eat."

I took my place, and he sat on the opposite side of Simon as Savvy retook her place beside Amber. Sharp ordered Jupiter to rest, and the dog curled up under the table. Sharp made a plate as Simon filled his mug.

"What do we owe for the early morning visit?" Simon asked.

"I did some poking around last night. Maybe we can talk when the children—"

"I shot someone," Savvy announced proudly.

"You did, sweetie. Finish your breakfast so you can get ready for school." Simon looked very much the proud dad, and I shook my head. "Did you find anything interesting?" he asked.

"Inventory was a lot lighter than I first suspected. We were short about eight kilos. Only three are officially checked out for a supposed deal Sunday at the shipyard."

"Typo?" I asked after I added more food to my plate.

"No."

"Who were they checked out by?"

"Stelman."

Simon and I both groaned, and Sharp shot us a glance.

"Not a friend of yours?" he asked.

"Stelman is a bigoted asshole. I didn't think he would be dirty, though. I've met his father a few times. He used to work Homicide, and while he was a nightmare to work with, he did take pride in the job." Simon ate but paused when Amber signed that she wanted more, and he leaned across the table to add an Amber-sized pancake to her plate. "I think Stelman Jr tried to organize a party when the four of us moved to the basement."

"He's a half-assed cop. The most he talks about is the amount of"—Sharp cleared his throat—"ladies he dates."

"Man-whore." I nearly choked on my swallow of coffee as Savvy muttered.

"Savvy." Simon warned as there were some words Amber didn't need in her lexicon yet.

"Sorry, Papa Simon." She rolled her eyes, but Simon didn't call her on that.

"Was anything else light?" I asked to change the subject.

"Not inventory-wise, but like I said last night, I think most of them would come up dirty on a piss test. No. I went specifically to the files to check for any notes on Mancini. Everything for the last three months was missing, hard copy and computer records. I didn't want to search too deep in case my credentials were flagged. I'm sure you have someone who could possibly bypass the security protocols."

"Possibly."

"I gotta go get ready," Savvy announced as she jumped up, put her plate in the sink.

"Could you grab our phones from beside the bed first, please?" Simon asked, and Savvy was running from the room. She came back a few minutes later and handed them to me.

"Boss, we're gonna be late if you want to pick up your friends before school and hit the drive-thru for coffee," Tony yelled from the open door and then slammed it.

"Boss?" Sharp asked with an arched brow.

"Carmine isn't getting his enforcer back," I said.

"I think he likes working for Savvy more anyway." Simon grinned as he took his phone that I handed him, and a few seconds later, my phone started to chime several times.

"And so it begins." I noticed Sharp's confused expression. "If they ever say they'll just add you to the group text, say no or start blocking numbers. It goes off all day, every day."

"Vega says she's on it, but also added Zero so that he can do the search so nothing can be traced back to us if the searches are flagged."

"How the hell does all that even work?" Sharp asked, but I motioned to Simon for him to answer.

"Back during the Fellows's case—"

"The serial case?"

"Yeah. I learned that Remy had known Vega and Doc for decades along with Boss. Not my story to tell, but you can discover the rumors if you ask. A few of the cases were on my desk before Robert and Remy pulled them into their investigation. I pushed my way into the case, and I got added. They're like this really weird family. We have an entire message thread, and we message all day."

"But what's with Carmine and his enforcer? I don't get it."

"I met Carmine back in my days with Organized Crime. We developed a respect for each other, and he's always been respectful, and I returned that. When I got hurt, Savvy was with me, and I called Carmine to pick her up while I led the attackers away. Tony became Savvy's security. I think my oldest daughter is a bit...corrupted with power."

"Didn't think you two were an...item."

"We weren't until recently. I had to wait for Simon to get his head out of his ass." I chuckled as he flipped me off by scratching the side of his nose. "Hey, I get in trouble for doing that in front of our youngest."

"That's a rule for you, not me," he told me with his brattiest grin.

"But back to the subject at hand. What did they have on Mancini?"

"We were mainly keeping an eye on drug trafficking business, and I was kinda confused as to why we weren't paying closer attention to his other side hustle. We took down two shipments, a total of twenty females aged fifteen to twenty-one, but all the busts and info that we had, charges still weren't brought against him. There was more than enough evidence to put him away...he would've died in prison. Someone was keeping him out of jail, but I can't figure out why. The DA would have one helluva right to brag. Part of me was thinking Mancini was an informant. It was the only explanation, and after it was discovered he was taken out, I thought it was payback."

"You don't sound too convinced," I said as Amber finished eating. I cleaned her up, wiping down her sticky face and hands, and then she was off running. She and Moriarty would watch cartoons. That psycho cat loved the girls, especially Amber, who could carry him around and dress him up if she wanted.

"Well, if we were supposed to focus on Mancini, we could've arrested him months ago. Bianchi and Finnegan weren't even on the taskforces radar, which never sat right with me. I mean, yeah, take out the easiest target, which is obviously Mancini. He doesn't have the power the other two have. A few of the smaller gangs were busted first. Everyone's aware of what Mancini and his crew were up to. He didn't exactly cover his ass."

"Are we talking some form of police corruption?" Simon leaned back in his chair.

"If so, I'm going to be pissed. They made me complicit by association. But I hope I'm not going to offend you, but if they are running their own criminal organization from inside the taskforce, then it goes as high as the DA."

"I won't argue in opposition. There isn't much I wouldn't put past my parents, but being seen above reproach is also important to them."

"Hypothetically, what would be their motivation?" I asked Simon.

Simon sighed heavily and scrubbed his hands over his face. "Well, in front of the cameras, they praise what's going on at the Outreach, but behind closed doors, they very much see the strip as a blight on their city. There's been some talk about trying to legalize sex work and changing drugs statutes to make anything under a certain weight as a sentence for treatment rather than jail."

"When did that start?" I hadn't heard anything about that, and that was a huge change. Narcotics would be out of business.

"A few years ago, talks started between Boss and several local politicians about running on a legalization platform. The model works elsewhere. Regulating sex work would make it safer for the workers as well as clients. The Outreach would become a hub for regular testing, which, to be honest, we already do. We have an almost hundred percent testing rate for the local sex workers. Drug offenses and overdoses have fallen to an all-time low in the last few years. With all that, my parents would rather see the entire strip along with the Outreach disappear. As I said, they always run on a platform that mirrors the moral majority. But I don't see them going to the extreme of murder and attempted murder."

"What would happen if both became legal?" Sharp asked. "What would be the consequences for the DA and State's Attorney?"

"They pride themselves on law and order. Under my father's tenure as DA, he's definitely lobbied for harsher sentences even for misdemeanors. Sex workers and non-violent drug offenses have increased convictions rates. If Remy was here, he'd do an entire lecture on bias in our judicial system, but I wouldn't disagree with him. Although the election is coming up, Father's approval rating is down, and he has about three other people running for the position."

"Does seem to be rather extreme for an election stunt." Even as I said it, I saw the wheels start turning, and those mental knives were being thrown.

As we finished up breakfast, I gathered everything to clean while Simon showed Sharp to the door. Why the hell would Simon's parents go to such an extreme? Also, taking out Mancini no matter how low on the hierarchy he was, was still a risky move. We'd waited for an escalation mistake, but if Simon's parents were behind whatever production this was, could we even prove it?

Arms looped around my waist as I washed dishes.

"Everyone's going to be here soon. I'm going to get dressed and get Amber ready." From his tone, I knew what he was thinking, and I decided to let him process. No matter what, I knew he had to work everything out on his own. He'd explain when he was ready.

35

GRAVES

COLD CASE
UNIT

The sweet little lady smirking up at me always amused me. Flo Danners was all cotton and demure dresses, but as soon as she was done with work, it was latex and stilettos. "Hey, Miss Flo."

"You're looking good, Detective. Still want to play hard to get?" I sensed the flirting coming, but it instantly stopped as I had a toddler wrapped around my legs.

"Honey, let your Papa Simon work." Marcel came up behind me and reached around me to extend his hand. "I've heard a ton about you. I'm Marcel." He spread his hand over my belly and gave me a squeeze before he stepped away. I listened to his footsteps fade as he walked to the kitchen.

"Well, well, well, how the times do change. I want details later when there's no little ears around." She winked at me.

I shook my head as I motioned her inside, and Savvy skipped into the room. "Papa Simon, you want me to distract Amber?"

"Would you? I just need about half an hour."

"Of course. Mom's about to do a video call. She wants to see my sister's adorable face."

Amber easily went to Savvy, and I wondered what would

happen when we separated and went to our different homes? My girls would be devastated by the separation. I would be, too. I got so used to being a part of a full-time family that included Marcel and Savvy, Amber and me. But I pushed the thoughts away for another time.

"You want coffee or something to drink? I think Marcel has some beers."

"No, I'm due at a party in about two hours. A coffee would be good, though." She held up a thick folder. "I got that information you asked for from the property tax clerk."

"Let's go in the kitchen." As soon as we entered, I saw Marcel pouring three coffees. He made mine the way I liked and placed one on the table. He pulled the half-and-half from the fridge and set the sugar bowl beside it.

"We have some leftovers if you're hungry."

"No, Marcel, that's nice of you. But like I told Simon, I have to be at a party. I knew this was important, so I wanted to get these records for you two."

"What did you find?" I asked as she started emptying the folder and making piles and then doctored her coffee.

"About a year ago, some of the foreclosed and condemned properties on and around the strip started getting purchased. They went for cheap to get them sold. A few of them have permits pending for complete demolition of the structures that are still standing. This pile"—she tapped the thickest one—"is the condemned and foreclosed properties. Now, this one is much more interesting." She pointed at one that was only slightly thinner. "This is all the low-income housing. But from our records, those are all rent-controlled or sliding scale. Six buildings in total with a ninety percent occupancy."

"What's interesting about that?"

"The company, Travers Investments, bought said properties, but that's not the interesting part. Travers Commercial Investments deals mostly in high-end properties such as condos or those chic warehouse spaces that typically go for high six figures or low seven. There's no way a company like that would purchase those buildings to keep them as low-income housing. Sure as fuck ain't getting that price on the strip."

"Travers...I've never heard of them." Mingling with people at the parties my parents ordered me to attend, but that was a name I'd never heard of, and rich people sometimes loved to brag about acquisitions.

"Probably because the place only exists on paper, through a PO Box, and a website that, in their mission statement, claimed they deal with life's ultimate luxuries. I tried to find if it was a dummy company for a larger entity, but I hit a brick wall. Vega or Zero can get you what you need, I'm sure."

"How many properties in total have they bought in the past year, and it didn't cause a stir?" I asked.

"Fifteen properties on the strip, another twenty in the surrounding areas and around the waterfront. They haven't caused a fuss among the residents because nothing has officially been announced. It's gentrification at its finest. They're going to come in, put up luxury properties, Trendy boutiques, and everything else to drive up housing costs and slowly push out the smaller businesses and make it nearly impossible for the people who live on and around the strip to make ends meet. These very rich people are not going to want the unwashed masses and the sex workers roaming around their properties."

"So if there was a rise in crime, commercial and residential prices would plummet," Marcel said as he picked up stacks and started flipping through the pages.

"And this Travers can come in and buy up those properties for next to nothing and can develop these high-end properties, and their profits would be astronomical." I mentally cursed. I mean, we'd had an idea something along those lines was in the works, but Boss and other advocates pushed back. Yet we didn't have as much funding or enough power in city hall. That's why we'd started to develop relationships with politicians to get more in office that had similar values as us.

"Exactly. It's not a secret that in the last five years that the politicians have been developing this plan to make Winston Harbor the next destination for rich professionals and being able to court large companies to open branches here. As much as the Outreach has done to turn the reputation of the strip around, it's centrally located and prime real estate. And Boss has kept a tight hold on the area, but there's only so much that he can do to stop the progress the powers that be want."

"I've heard about people coming in and planning small petty crimes, but to plan murders that seems extreme." He moved on to the next stack, but he never looked up from what he was reading.

"The deaths of who they probably consider nobodies compared to hundreds of millions in profit? Greed is a powerful motivator. And there's also the status that comes with that amount of money. That can open a lot of doors for you."

"Jackie's sons run an investment firm, and she's fond of you. Do you think she could have some information for us?" Marcel asked.

"It couldn't hurt. She did provide all the information we needed without question. The Darners are the people that you want to rub elbows with in this city if you want to make connections." I crossed my arms over my chest. "Is there anything else that stood out in your search?"

"The records I found for Travers only go back four and a half years. They've amassed a very who's who of clients. There were testimonials and pictures of clients in front of their properties. But the pictures of the executives looked like images downloaded from those stock sites. Very handsome and generic, a whole lot of pretty, white male folk."

"Baby, I'm going to call Vega and see if she can come by to pick up the new info."

"Thanks." He kissed my cheek as he set the papers down and

went to the living room where we'd left our phones on the coffee table. "And no permits were filed under anything to do with Travers?"

"No, darlin'. I cross-referenced addresses with permit filings, and was only two permits connected to any of the properties Travers purchased and those were complete demolition. I think they're biding their time until they get everything they need. These apartment buildings are registered as sliding scale apartments. They're going to have to go through a lot of red tape to start the eviction process, especially at the scale they need. I ran a check, and they've purchased the buildings around Boss and the Outreach. It's like they're going to strangle him."

"But Boss hasn't received any threats. The only thing that happened was Mancini being dumped at the Outreach."

"But, honey, they have a better way of taking Boss out..." I frowned as she pointed at me. "You. You're connected to the DA, you're a cop, you're on the board of the Outreach, and anyone who can access your financials knows that you can fund the Outreach just on your own. And some months you have."

"No one's supposed to know that."

"No one's supposed to, but that doesn't mean it stays a secret. My brother is well aware you put your time and money into his program."

"Shit."

"Don't be like that. Boss knows you don't want anyone to know, so you're just the anonymous donor. And don't tell that man I claimed him as my brother."

"You two still on the outs?"

"Darlin', he's sixty and still in love with a ghost. That Outreach is his permanent love letter to Juan. I called him on it, and he doesn't like to be reminded that he's been living in the past for over thirty years. I just want him to live for something other than his people and the memory of his first and only love."

"You two are always fighting about something. He'll get over it, and you two will be besties again."

"I know, but it's getting harder to fight against this perfect memory. To him, nothing could be better than Juan. I don't think it helped that when Juan was murdered that he lost his lover and Dominant, and then he was set adrift. I better get going. I have calls into a few more friends, and they said if they heard anything, I'd be the first to know."

"Thanks for this." I walked around the table and gave the petite woman a hug, and I chuckled as she grabbed my ass. "Was that your payment?"

"What I really want in payment would get me arrested for solicitation."

"I'm getting really tired of everyone trying to steal you away." Marcel's amused voice came from the doorway, and Flo and I both looked at him and laughed.

"If I really meant it, I wouldn't have to try too hard." She stepped away, and I stayed in the kitchen as Marcel showed her out.

I shifted to stare at the papers strewn across the table, and that feeling of doom grew in the pit of my stomach.

"Talk it out."

"If my parents are behind this, not only did they try to kidnap and-or murder Savvy, but they were also well aware that they were the reason I was in the hospital when they showed up. I understood that they didn't care about me other than what I could represent for them, but to try to destroy everything I love...why?"

"Baby," he whispered as he twined his arms around my waist and rested his bearded chin on my shoulder. "I know there's nothing I can do or say to lessen the pain of what they may have done. You're a detective, an amazing one. All we have right now is theories. We have to wait for proof."

"I know, I do, but the problem is the theories match with what

I already know about the people who created me as a prop. Do you know that's one of the reasons I didn't think I'd make a good parent?"

"You're an amazing parent. Just ask our girls. They love their Papa Simon."

"Thanks."

"No need for that. Why don't we go see if we can say hi to Donna? I think our daughters are still talking to her. Tomorrow, we'll come up with a plan to solve the murders but also to save the strip and Outreach. What y'all do is way too important not to fight for."

I closed my eyes as he turned his head and nuzzled my neck, and I hugged his arms tighter to my stomach. He was right. We had time the next day to put a solid plan into place. If my parents were behind all this, I would destroy them to keep everyone and everything I loved safe. If there was one thing my parents had taught me was where to find someone's weakness and exploit that for my gain.

I chuckled as he tightened his arms around my waist and lifted me off my feet. He turned and walked from the room with my feet dangling as he tickled the side of my neck with his beard. He made it so easy, and maybe that's why I was so scared to accept what was happening because nothing in life ever came easy for me.

DOUGLAS

COLD CASE
UNIT

"Would you snitch me out for drinking on the job?" I asked Simon as we listened to the unofficial tap on his parents' phone, home, and cell phones. DA Graves and his breathy mistress were making me sick to my stomach.

"You? This is one of the people who contributed to my DNA."

As I opened my eyes, I rolled my head on the headrest to find him glaring at me. Zero had worked his magic and got us connected to every phone, even the secret lines. Savvy and Amber were at Carmine's while me and my baby tried to find something that would get us more official means to run surveillance.

"Does your father's girlfriend have asthma?" Vega asked over the laptop, and I heard Zero snort and choke in the background. The pathetic phone sex lowered until it was just a drone.

"Why is this a conference call?" Simon asked.

"What else were we going to do? The rest of the team is buried in files that Zero and I sent, and we needed a bit of amusement. Man, don't take this from us!" she yelled.

"Fine, anything interesting?" Simon asked and then took a sip of his coffee.

"No, but Jackie, by the way, I adore that woman. She's so vicious for looking so much like a demure grandmother. She had a talk with her sons, and they said Travers came out of nowhere. They attempted to compete with her sons' firm and failed spectacularly. I can connect her."

"I'm sure she'd prefer not to suffer along with the rest of us. Did you find the people behind Travers?" Simon refilled his cup from his thermos of sugary elixir that didn't even taste like coffee.

"Whoever they have covering their tracks is an artist, but not as good as me and Zero." The faint tapping of keys punctuated Vega's pause. "Grantham Consortium. They own about a dozen investment firms. Their business layout is more complex than my genealogy charts. Backtracking from Travers took me through three other companies on one line. But Flo was right. Most of these companies are ghosts. No real board of directors exists for any of them."

"What's the fucking point then?" I asked.

"The point is, other than their real estate holdings, nothing's overtly illegal, and even that's questionable. They all fly pretty low under the radar. One of the dummy corps comes in, buys up all the properties, and as soon as they're done renovating or building, they disappear like a dad in a wife-beater going out for smokes and never coming back. They cycle through at regular intervals. Only one company is active at any one time. Most outfits like this, it's money laundering. They bring in an investor or group of investors who need a large amount of cash cleaned, Grantham takes their cut, and investors are free to walk away with their ill-gotten but laundered money."

"Vega, still not making sense that someone who wants to fly that low would resort to murder and possibly bring major heat down on them."

"Douglas, Douglas, we have to get you to loosen up. Zero, my man, explain the good part."

"Couldn't you have started with the good part, Vega?" Simon huffed.

"Where would the fun be in that?"

"Okay, here's how it plays out. Grantham shows several sales in the last decade. These dummy corps being snatched up... someone's paying for a name. A strict quiet business model. A way to do business without putting yourself out there. What Grantham is essentially doing is covering their ass by off-loading the now useless company with a pretty makeover and giving it to someone else who needs a cover for a short period of time. Travers doesn't show that the company was sold to anyone. Grantham operates in non-extradition countries and offshore, mostly in international waters. They have several virtual addresses, PO Boxes, so there's no physical location. It's just all servers and nothing else.

"So, say someone wants to do something shady, like, shall we posit a guess, perform a coup without seeming to. Hypothetically"—we all groaned at Zero's amusement—"a group of politicians operate under this umbrella, nothing to connect them, not even paperwork. But people like to brag, especially rich, entitled people. Travers takes the heat, but since Travers doesn't exist except with a very weak electronic data trail, there's no one to prosecute."

"So you're saying in your very long-winded conspiracy theorist way that hypothetically, a group of businessmen, politicians, or such, move all this money around, revitalize an area with luxury real estate, and sell for extreme profit, and clean any dirty money involved."

"God, you make it sound so boring, Graves." Zero groaned, and Vega cackled.

"They're your friends, baby. I'm not claiming them." I poured another black coffee from my separate thermos.

"But in this case, we have corruption of the highest order. Your old man is up for re-election. The better the strip and

Outreach are doing, the more his approval rating has tanked. I'm talking it can't get much lower. His constituents are losing faith in his ability to hold to his campaign promises. It's no secret that your parents would love to nuke the entire strip and do away with what they consider the pestilence of the residents. Also, with the new legislation for regulated sex work and the treatment-slash-fine changes for non-violent drug offenses is getting a lot of support. Old-fashioned eugenics, my friend. They make it look like crime is on the rise around the strip, and the efforts of the community activists are failing. It works two-fold, your parents and their partners, whoever they may be, make a ton of cash that can't essentially be traced back to them, and they turn Winston Harbor into the moral jewel."

"I still don't fucking understand it, though. My parents have more money than they know what to do with. My mother's great-grandfather amassed a fortune that he passed down. My grandchildren would still benefit."

"Your parents are almost broke." Zero piped up.

"What?"

"Yeah. They look rich on paper, but about a decade ago, they lost a good portion of their wealth and never recovered."

"Darner?"

"Yep. Darner had this brilliant idea about a private investment just for an elite few. He said that they would triple and, in some cases, quadruple their money. But what Darner was actually selling was an empty promise and filling his coffers for his buy-in to the glamorous world of organized crime. Their money is locked into their portfolios, and the market is so unstable if they try to sell they're going to take a huge loss, not to mention taxes."

"What about my money?"

"That money and investments were transferred to you. It's yours free and clear. Your grandfather's will and specifications for your trust stated the money couldn't be touched unless you had siblings. It would be divided equally, but as the only child, you received the bulk on your twenty-fifth birthday. You're still a very wealthy man, but what happens when you die, Simon?"

"All of my assets will be sold, and any proceeds will go to a few charities and the Outreach. My lawyer suggested that I put a stronger plan in place in the event of my death, especially being in law enforcement." He cleared his throat. "Could you send me all their financials?"

"Sure, you'll have it in a few minutes." She paused for a few seconds. "So they won't get anything?" Vega asked.

"I mean, if they have a life insurance policy on me, sure. But my assets? My attorney made sure it was iron-clad."

"When did that happen?"

"About a year ago." I caught a frown crease Simon's brow. "I met with my financial advisor. I live off what I make, so my money's just been sitting there growing. The only purchases I've ever made are vehicles and my townhouse. There's also my monthly donation to keep my programs going at the Outreach. And because I didn't have any children, they suggested I make more definite plans."

"Do your parents know?"

"Hell no."

"Is it possible they think they're going to make a killing by you ending up dead?"

"Vega." I made sure the warning was clear in my voice as I saw the realization and horror on Simon's face.

"It had to be asked, Douglas. You have two people who are going through their reserves at alarming rates and living way beyond their means. It wouldn't be the first time someone killed a family member for profit or did some pretty shady shit to cover up the fact that they're running on fumes. Which his parents are at this point."

"The real estate is to refill what they've lost. The murders and threats are for one or both to remain in office and to keep their public persona intact." Simon scrubbed his hand over his hair as he dropped his head back against the rest.

"I didn't say your parents were in possession of common sense by any stretch of the imagination." The screen flickered, and Vega and Zero's faces filled the screen. "Desperation makes people do stupid things."

"But taking out Mancini was a monumental mistake." I heard it in Simon's voice—he was just pulling straws and hoping he didn't come up with the short one. His parents were in all likelihood prepared to kill him and demolish everything he believed in and treasured to the ground.

"From what we learned, Mancini seemed to be getting increasingly paranoid. His drug use increased. What if he discovered what was going to happen? They were courting him as an asset but were going to burn him the second the deals were finalized. They catered to his pride and ego, promised him he was going to take Bianchi and Finnegan's places at the top of the food chain. What if all this started way back with Darner? Is there anything you can think of that would have given this away?" I asked.

"No. I see them for my weekly humiliation every Sunday. Other than the times I have to mix with them at parties and fundraisers, they barely acknowledge I exist. We do quite well avoiding each other. The only times they claim me are when they're in front of cameras."

"Maybe something about your switch to the Cold Case Unit spurred them into some kinda action. Darner's case was moved to Cold Case about three years ago. Since it was so high-profile, they kept up the pretense for a while. The unit is closing cases at an impressive rate in the last few years, the Fellows's case, the kidnappings and murders. What if they were playing the long con, and we started making them nervous?" Vega arched a brow and took a sip off her energy drink.

"There was no evidence in the Darner case. By the time his body was found, any evidence was too degraded to test. And it was pretty much written off as he'd crossed the wrong person. A lot of the people he fucked over were the who's who of the Winston Harbor society page...no one wanted to attempt to accuse any of them of the murder."

"I liked this case better when it didn't make any sense."

I stretched my arm out to massage Simon's thigh as he became more miserable. There was a difference between accepting your parents' neglect to finding out they possibly wanted you dead. I'd witnessed their disconnect at the hospital when they just ordered someone to tell Simon to call them and went back to their party. I wasn't as close to my dad and my siblings as I had been when I was younger. Yet I knew that if I ever called, they'd drop everything for me...for Savvy. There's no way I could understand what they were doing to Simon. Savvy was always my number one. To Simon, Amber and Savvy were everything he wanted. He wanted kids and family.

"We're still digging. They have tighter encryption the closer we got to Grantham. We're hoping to find a money trail that leads back to any one of our players, but I will say we're fucked if they hit one of those cushy little tax havens."

"Thanks, Vega."

"Not a problem. Enjoy the wheezing, and we'll check in later." She cut the video feed, and I shook my head as the volume on the computer returned to the audio from inside the house.

"Are you okay?" I asked as I raised my hand to pinch his chin and turn his head until he looked at me.

"Well, the knowledge my parents want me dead should've come with a little more shock on my part. My parents' careers and appearances mean everything to them. To be viewed as lesser than, would kill them. Generations of my family were all independently wealthy. I could've been the typical trust fund kid, but I wanted to work my ass off. I always sensed they could cut me off at any time. I didn't even know the full extent of my trust fund until I received it."

"This isn't on you, baby." I leaned to the side until I could brush my lips to his. "Any mistakes they made was their poor planning." I gave him a small smile as he stroked my bearded cheek with the backs of his fingers.

"I know. But when I think they can't treat me any worse than shit on their shoes, they prove me wrong. I didn't ask to exist, Marcel."

"Don't do that. Think of what you have. Savvy and Amber, me when I'm not annoying the fuck out of you. You got friends... family that would choose you any day of the week."

He tilted his chin down and rested his forehead against mine, and I listened to the weariness of his sigh.

"We'll take care of this, and it'll be back to life as normal."

"That's what I'm scared of, Marcel. My normal wasn't at all happy. When this ends..." He gave me a quick kiss. "Is there still an us?"

"Oh, baby, you're not getting rid of me. You'll be back in Cold Case, and I'll be sneaking down from Homicide to find a corner of our own. Let's take care of what we need to do, and then we'll go home to sleep. When we wake up, we'll go get our girls and have a family night for a bit a de-stress."

"I'd really like that."

We separated, and I turned the volume up as we listened to the silence between his parents, the berating of the staff by both Mr. and Mrs. Graves. And I tried to imagine Simon growing up in a house that seemed nothing but cold. But he hadn't. It had been nannies and boarding school, and then college. No wonder he was insecure about whether I wanted to keep him or not. He'd never been put first, not even by his parents. He had no idea what a loving family was. Until the Cold Case Unit and the Outreach, he's mostly spent his life alone. Simon may take a bit more effort, but he was worth everything I had to do to prove that he was mine. He deserved everything, and I was going to make sure I gave it to him.

GRAVES

COLD CASE
UNIT

There's a lot you can do when you have the right help. After an evening spent with Marcel and the girls, my head was clearer. I'd put somewhat of a plan in place, and after a week of working out the details, I was ready to close the case. When you had a friend who bordered on anti-establishment and worked as a lawyer, and a hacker with a gray moral fiber, there wasn't much you couldn't fake.

I knew my parents were on the edge of foreclosure on the family home that they'd remortgaged two years ago to cover some of their debt. Right now, I had paperwork that I'd bought the debt. The glitch would disappear after twenty-four hours.

"You ready to go this far?" Gladys asked as we pulled into the horseshoe drive of the pretentious house that I was raised in for the first five years of my life.

"I just need to bluff to make them lose their cool and send someone after me. If I hit them out of blue, maybe the panic at losing status and all that will make them mess up."

"You know I'll do anything for you. You're family. And you do know as soon as DA Graves sees me, he's going to be on high alert. We've never had a polite interaction."

"I know." Even before I knew Gladys was Robert's ex-wife, I'd heard her name enough when my father would complain about her.

She worked for one of the most prestigious firms in the state, and her win rate on her pro bono cases was out of this world. She terrified most of the people in the DA's office when they realized they had to argue against her.

"Gladys, um, between you and me, this might be my last case."

"Because of Amber?"

"Yeah. I mean, I have my law degree. I just have to get my license to practice. As a single dad, I don't think I can leave every morning, even in the Cold Case Unit, and be worried about coming home to her."

"As far as I know, you're not single. You have a very sexy boyfriend, which, to be honest, kinda shocked all of us. Douglas isn't exactly...one of us. He's very much rules and regs, and we look at how to bend said rules and regs a lot."

"He's not so bad, but we were forced into this close proximity. What if it doesn't last beyond the case? I love Savvy and..." I sighed as I turned to look out the window.

"Does that love extend toward her dad?"

"Yes, I think, I don't know. I'm forty-three, and he's the first person I've *ever* been intimate with. He says the Asexuality isn't an issue, and I believe him, but I'm just, I don't know."

"You're scared. Most people are at the beginning. You think Shine and I had it easy? Hell, I was scared for over a year about giving myself away and facing the rejection. She made the first move. Over thirty years of marriage, and even Robert had never kissed me like that. We have our issues, she's dealing with her trauma, and I'm being supportive, and she gets mad that I don't get mad or frustrated with her. I was married to a cop. I had plenty of anger and frustration to last me a lifetime."

"But you and Shine fit so well."

"I think so, too. But I'm just saying it wasn't easy. She's the first woman I was ever attracted to, and I grew up in a home where being LGBTQ-plus wasn't acceptable. I had my own issues to get over, but Robert falling in love with Remy helped a lot with that. You and the rest of the unit have this weird way your brain processes stuff. You just have to let it do its thing, and it'll all work out. Let's go take down one of my least favorite people and end my day on a high note before I go home to my woman."

I nodded and got out of the driver's side, and I rolled my eyes as Gladys didn't wait. She never did, but it was ingrained in me to try to open the door. She straightened her expensive suit and smoothed her nearly flawless bun of silver hair, and we slowly made our way to the door. I raised my hand to knock. Even I was supposed to be announced by the housekeeper.

It had taken me forever to get used to just walking into a friend's place when I found the door unlocked. The austere housekeeper, Mrs. McWhorter, opened the door and gave me a disapproving snarl.

"Young Mr. Graves, I was unaware you would be visiting. Are Mr. and Mrs. Graves expecting you?"

"No, but if you could announce me, I have some business to speak with them about."

She reluctantly motioned us inside but told us to wait by the door.

"Such a warm welcome," Gladys muttered.

"Every damn time."

The housekeeper returned moments later and told us to follow her. We were led to the formal living room. Just being in the house made me uncomfortable, especially wearing my faded t-shirt and jeans with my boots. I was out of place. Gladys looked like she belonged there more than me.

We were told to have a seat and that my parents would be in shortly. I knew what they were doing. They'd make me wait in order to build up tension and keep me on edge, but that wasn't what was happening that day. I held the manila envelope in my right hand with the fake paperwork inside.

They'd arrive any minute in their perfect evening wear like some *Dynasty* couple, the woman lazing around strewn with diamonds and the man wearing a smoking jacket and his customary scotch. I swear I couldn't wait to see them in their newest fashion of lock-up orange.

"Simon, I'd say this was a pleasure, but we weren't expecting you or a…guest." My mother came in decked out in a white silk pants suit.

My father was next, but he didn't say a word, and, yes, there was the crystal rocks glass of scotch.

"Let's cut the shit. Your home went into foreclosure seven hours ago. I bought the home for the price of the mortgage outright. You have twenty-four hours to leave the property. I think this will explain everything."

I tossed the envelope on the coffee table as my mother dramatically collapsed onto the couch, and my father stormed over and set his glass down to pick up the envelope. I held my breath. This had to play out to keep them off-balance, and I couldn't have them thinking clearly.

"What the fuck is this?"

"As my client has said…"

"You're a criminal attorney. You don't know shit."

"I beg to differ. But as you dared to interrupt me, I'll repeat myself. It has come to our attention that your accounts were emptied to pay for an excessive amount of debt that you've seemed to ignored. Your creditors have grown tired of your failure to make good. Simon has bought the family home to keep it in the *family*. With a growing family with two daughters, he really does need more…space for them. I'm here to represent his interests, and his wishes are that you are to vacate the premises within the allotted time, or we will file for an order of eviction. Either way, you're broke, and lawyers expect payment, unless you're going to represent yourself, but you're just a lowly criminal attorney, wouldn't want to chance it."

Mother was unnaturally pale and almost looked as if she were going to puke all over her expensive carpet, and father was several shades past a ripe tomato as he angrily flipped through the papers. They looked official enough. Even I couldn't tell at first glance. With his rage, he probably wasn't paying attention to the details.

"What's it going to be? I know some apartments on the strip that are available. I could make some..." The shattering of glass as he threw his drink caused my lips to slowly curve into a smile.

I'd pay for this, I knew I would, but as I paid for it, they'd go down, and that's all I cared about. They looked down on everyone, judged all people on how little they had in their bank account, the shade of their skin, and the jobs they worked just to make ends meet. The thought of being broke made my mother physically ill and my father angry.

I needed that rage and fear. I needed it to fester until they did something stupid. I needed action, not planning.

"You'll pay for this." He spat the threat between his clenched teeth, and he snarled his nose.

"I've paid for it quite a bit in my forty-three years. What else do you have to throw at me to join the hate and neglect? That's all you've offered. So, tell me, Father, what do you have for me? Remember, there's a witness in the room."

"Get out. You're not getting my house."

"First, it was Mother's house. *Her* home where she grew up, and you lost that. You shouldn't be too scared of what I'm going to do. I know just how cruel she can be when you cross her. I look forward to hearing from you."

I motioned Gladys out first, and then I turned my back on him and my mother. No threats they could give me mattered. To them, I wasn't even a child—I had been a possession. To be honest, I was less than something they owned because they cared more for the items they purchased, made everything all shiny to impress. Me, they could never make me perfect enough.

Gladys was already in the SUV, and I walked around to the driver's side. As soon as I closed the door, slender arms circled my neck.

"How did you stand it?"

"I lived in the UK and went to boarding school. I just had to deal with their neglect. They didn't care enough to do anything else." I cleared my throat. "I'll take you home, and then I have to go to my townhouse. Marcel is staying at the apartment with the girls in case they do decide to retaliate physically."

"You got protection, right?"

"Carmine sent one of his security details. They'll be inside and outside to catch anyone. The last team they sent for me was sloppy. Let's hope they didn't upgrade since they tried to kill me last time."

"Don't joke about that." She straightened as I turned the key. "When it's time, and this case is solved, come to me, and we'll discuss your exit plan."

I nodded. I had too many decisions to make, but first, I had to take down whoever it was that was endangering me and mine. Part of me hoped that it was all a bunch of coincidences, and my parents weren't behind it. Yet I wasn't holding my breath. I had twenty-four hours before the clock ran out on this op, and I had to figure out something else.

DOUGLAS

COLD CASE
UNIT

I glared at everyone telling me to remain calm, especially Stevenson, who I'd told the same thing to over a year ago. Amber hugged my neck tight enough that if she were bigger, she could've choked me out. Savvy was quietly crying where she had her face buried against my ribs. My girls wanted their Papa Simon back.

The plan he'd put into place, as much as I'd wanted to fight him on it, people like his parents needed to be hit where it counted—with their bank account and appearance. The bank error that showed all their personal accounts were empty, and their home officially foreclosed on hit hard and fast. All credit cards were maxed. We'd wanted to see if they did a funds transfer from any secret accounts to cover what went missing.

Zero monitored all activity, but as of yet, nothing was moved. It hadn't helped us out any when Sharp arrived to tell us the warehouse had been empty, any and all records were removed or destroyed, and the taskforce commander told them it had been indefinitely suspended. They were in cover-up mode. They had to get rid of anything tying them to everything to do with the clandestine unit.

The only other thing that needed to be destroyed was Simon. He was our ace in the hole. In order to keep the girls out of the impending collapse, he'd gone to his townhouse. He hadn't gone unprotected. Carmine had sent in a security detail with him. Ten minutes after one missed status update, a second team arrived to find two men critically injured and two deceased, and no Simon in sight.

Carmine and Seamus were both on the warpath. As much as I didn't trust Seamus, both the men had put out no-touch orders on Simon. Someone had disregarded that command and they couldn't allow that to stand.

"I scouted the perimeter," Sharp said as he disconnected the call that he'd taken moments after arriving.

"What did you find?" Remy asked as he leaned back against his husband.

"Four-man team, muddy footsteps on the pavers, and some deep impressions in the damp soil of the grass said we had four distinct footwear patterns. They also entered in formation and policed any brass. They were a highly trained entry team, but my guys would've watched their feet. Either they were crunched for time, or they didn't care."

"How did they get a jump on the guards?" I asked.

"They had two at the rear in the garden area and two inside to watch Graves and counter any entry from the front. They fired through the wrought-iron fencing, taking out the first two men. Once they reached the rear door, they popped the standard lock, and entered. They went with blades because they didn't know where in the house Graves was and wanted a quiet search. They silently took out the two inside guards. From evidence left at the scene, Simon had drawn his weapon, and they tasered him. The contacts, his weapon, and phone were left at the scene."

"Anyone see a vehicle?" I asked.

"No, but they must have parked at the end of the alleyway

behind the row of townhouses and carried Graves to their vehicle."

"What about his tracer?" Vega asked.

"His what?" Sharp shot Vega a glance.

"Each member of the team has one. We implemented it after Doc got snatched. It's inside something they'd wear all the time but also could be switched out. I think Simon's is under the insert of his boots, and occasionally concealed under his watch. We don't typically use them when we're not on duty, but in this case, he may have it."

"His watch was a no-go since his hand injury. Can you pick it up? I don't know if he was wearing his boots or not. I know that's what he had on this morning when he left." I said, but then every member of the team pulled out their phones.

They all rattled off coordinates and then all of them cursed in unison. "That's in the middle of the damn harbor. They stripped him and dumped his shit," Stevenson said as he put his phone away and cuddled Doc, who didn't look as if he were holding up.

"If not, I'll get a dive team out to check the location," Sharp announced, and I glared at him as Savvy cried harder. "It had to be said. We don't know what his usefulness to his kidnappers is." Vega threw a pen at him as he walked to the kitchen to make the call.

"Who would know to dump his clothes or that he could even be traced?" I adjusted Amber on my shoulder as I felt her body go limp. The stress and crying for Simon had exhausted her.

"No one that I know of. I didn't go through official channels for them. I had a friend build and code them for me. It was just personal protection for our unit. If they have some sort of functioning brain cells, they'd have to think that maybe it was a set-up and dumped the items as a precaution." Vega spun her Mala between her fingertips. I'd noticed the habit when her thinking was more chaotic than normal.

"The team that tried to take Savvy and attacked Simon didn't seem as if they were a professional team." He'd said they were muscle, and they'd barely tried to conceal the bodies they dumped, and the only thing they did that was smart was cover their tag.

"Then they have a boss that has some knowledge."

I nodded at Vega. "Savvy, I want you to take Amber to your room. I have something I need to take care of."

"Are you bringing Papa Simon home?" Her bottom lip shook.

"I'll do whatever is in my power to get him home where he belongs, okay?" She just nodded and took Amber. I watched them until they disappeared down the hall. "Where are his parents right now?"

"The men I have sitting on their house checked in and said that the mother is home, but the father left about an hour ago. One car trailed him to an upscale hotel, and he went inside. They talked to the receptionist, with some monetary compensation, my man was told he had a standing reservation. Should my men interrupt the romantic interlude?" Carmine asked.

"Do it," I said as I left the room. I grabbed my tactical gear from my closet and started to change.

"Marcel, think before you act, man," Robert said from behind me.

"They have him, and from the bodies we found, they don't show any mercy."

"Yeah, but you have Savvy and Amber to take care of. You go off and do something you regret, and Simon won't forgive you." Robert was trying to talk sense into me, but all I knew was Simon was out there, and I had no idea where he was or if he was even alive.

I turned as I tightened my black belt. "What do you want me to do, Robert? Just sit here?"

"No. But let us handle lead on this."

"He's right, Douglas," Sharp said as he entered. "I have a small team organized, nothing that will cause much notice. My second in command is already in motion to secure us transport, and any paperwork will call it a training op. I'm famous for pulling surprise ones on my team a few times a month. We'll take lead. You take care of our six and be there to get Graves out."

"I shouldn't have let him go."

"Man, Graves was gonna do whatever he had to do. Your man isn't one to back down. In order for him to have everything he's always wanted, this was the only option." Robert gave me comforting slap on the back.

"Douglas, we got a problem." Vega ran into the room.

"What fucking now?"

"We picked up some chatter from the house. Zero has been monitoring incoming and outgoing calls and emails from the home. The mother has contacted a divorce attorney about fifteen minutes after the father left the house for his booty call."

"And that's a problem why?"

"She made a call to a friend. In the call, she was talking about the DA fucking up everything. His mistresses. The money. She made it sound as if she had no idea what her husband was actually up to and that she didn't know they were broke. Yes, significantly less wealthy but not broke. I think everything was news to her earlier."

"So, the DA was trying to save face?" That made the weight in the pit of my stomach expand.

"Exactly, it seems that Mrs. Graves has no monetary reason. She logged into several personal accounts that prove she's going to be doing quite well. These accounts were opened and funded with transfers from foreign banks when DA Graves made the investment fuck-up." She looked at her phone again. "The DA was trying to keep this from everyone, including his exceptionally high-maintenance wife. Her daddy apparently gave her a backup plan when he died. He had several accounts that were willed to her separately, mostly in the UK where her family was from. Ones that appear DA Graves had no knowledge of."

"His life and career are going downhill. He wanted quick money and partnered with Mancini and went into business with Grantham. He created this fucked up mess. And when it all seemed as if it was imploding around him, he needed to take out his biggest threat, Simon and the power we all have through our contacts and the Outreach. Once the news came out about all the properties being purchased, he knew Boss would contact us." Robert wasn't being helpful.

"And that wasn't going to work in his favor." As soon as everyone knew about the properties, they'd go into protection mode and try to save the strip."

"The murders were a diversion. One carefully orchestrated to keep us focused on Bianchi, Finnegan, and Boss."

"That's why there wasn't a real pattern to the victimology. They just knew the best place to pick up vics that wouldn't cause a stir when they were found. Then we went to interview Mrs. Darner, and then Mancini, we started asking too many questions."

"Yep, now, that he thinks Simon owns the house and that his bank accounts are completely dry, if he's going down…"

"He's going to take Simon with him." I finished Vega's statement.

"That's the best-case scenario for him, but he's unaware that we've been investigating him." Robert combed his fingers through his hair, and I saw the strain it was taking on him and the rest of the unit.

"Yes!" Vega yelled. "I got the DA! We pinged his phone. He's at the old packing plant on the other side of the bridge."

"Let's move." I grabbed everything I needed, and headed to my girls' room.

When I entered, they were curled up on the bed, and I crouched beside it. "I'm bringing your Papa home, I promise. Carmine and Tony will probably take you to Carmine's to stay while we go get Simon. I love you both. Be good, and me and your Papa will see you soon." I kissed Savvy's forehead and then did the same when Amber pointed to hers. I straightened and stepped out into the hallway where Carmine was waiting for me

"We'll take them to my place. We'll keep them distracted. And if official channels don't work, I don't mind coming out of retirement."

"Thanks."

"Any time. Just know your girls will be safe and sound until their dads come home."

I hoped like hell I wasn't lying to Savvy and Amber. Savvy understood that things could go wrong, but Amber, all she knew was that Simon, me, and Savvy, we were her safe space. She'd always have a home with me no matter the outcome, but I didn't want any of us to lose Simon, especially the two girls who'd become ours.

GRAVES

COLD CASE
UNIT

When I woke up that morning or the previous one, pacing the inside of a shipping crate after being stripped down to my pink-gray briefs from a laundry mishap hadn't been on my to-do list. I really should rethink my life's aspirations. Maybe I should be scared, but I was pissed, and that was mostly because my girls would be terrified. I'd promised them crepes for breakfast. And I hated breaking promises to them.

I scratched the marks on my chest where the taser contacts had struck me as I'd reached for my off-duty *Sig* and stared at the pulley with a hook hanging from the ceiling. The grating of metal on metal, and the loud reverberation of the lock disengaging made me pivot on my bare toes. Stelman's smug face was the first one I saw. He was the one who had taken the taser to me. As soon as he'd lifted his mask when he'd entered my bedroom, I hadn't been shocked, but the cynical part of me expected to see Sharp when the other men were revealed.

The fact they allowed me to see their faces told me I wasn't leaving that container alive. I shouldn't be so calm about more than likely ending up murdered and tossed in the harbor. What could I say? I'd never been the most excitable person around.

I was about to speak when my father entered, looking as put-together as usual. Not a hair out of place or a wrinkle to crease his brow.

"DA Graves, what a pleasure to see you. But I was not summoned to this meeting in a very gentlemanly fashion."

"You couldn't leave it alone. Everything was perfect, Simon. Your mother would've never known that her lifestyle was about to become one that belonged to the people she despised. But you had to come in with that attorney. How did you do it? That *woman*, the computer girl, did she empty my accounts?"

"Actually, no. If you'd checked at six AM, your balances would've been restored, those pesky computer glitches. I just knew how to hit you where it hurt." For a second, the veneer slipped, and I saw he realized he'd played into a trap. Yet that didn't change my situation.

My friends had no idea where I was, and when they'd tossed my boots, the GPS tag went with that. They'd have a general direction, but Winston Harbor wasn't a small town. There were plenty of places they could hide me, and I'd never be found. I just had to hope Vega or Zero had a few tricks up their sleeves to get me out of this.

I didn't even know how long since they discovered I'd been taken. I'd only come to a short while earlier. "Why? I know you can't even fathom how to be poor, but why? My girls, you could've done anything to me you wanted, but you went after my daughters."

"Daughters?" He coldly chuckled. "My people failed. Neither of them were supposed to survive, but what did you do? You called in Bianchi. You didn't leave me a choice. Your death would've gotten me everything I needed to recover. Then you had to shame me and your mother, Douglas, those mixed brats."

"I won't survive what you're about to do to me, but I can guarantee if you insult my girls, you'll be dead before those guards of yours take me down."

"Get him ready."

That was all he said as Stelman and another cop I recognized but didn't know the name of came at me with a rope. My left hand was still useless, but I swung at Stelman, my fist connected, and snapped his head back. Yet before I could throw a punch at the second man, he grabbed my injured hand and squeezed. As I struggled, they both twisted my hands behind my back, secured them with the rough ropes, and I grimaced as I heard the chain slide through the pulley.

There was a tug at the ropes, and a hard jerk drew my arms toward the ceiling, bending me half. I tried to stand on my toes to relieve the pressure.

"You know if you had just done as we asked of you, Simon, married a nice girl, produced the next generation, but I should've known better. You were always a failure."

Father's shoes came into view, and I spit on the expensive leather. I barely felt the knee connecting with my ribs as I listened to my father curse.

"You're nothing more than an animal, Simon. And what's the only way to deal with something of your kind?" He paused as if he were really waiting for me to answer. "We put it down. But I have it under good authority that Stelman wanted a repeat of what he did to Mancini. He took a lot of pride in putting that animal down as well. That's all the other men were, too, and killing them was merciful. What happiness could they have being the way they were?"

"You talk too fucking much." I hissed as the tension cranked upward, and fire burned in my shoulders.

"Drug him, do what you have to do, and report to me when you're done."

"Police, get down, down."

Yelling came from outside the container, and then I heard shots fired. Voices were raised. Screams rang out, and the chaos seemed to be getting closer. I turned my head to find Stelman getting ready to shit himself, and Father hadn't moved. The door opened with a grinding of the hinges, and I couldn't maneuver enough to see who entered.

"DA Graves, what a pleasure to see you again." Marcel's voice was cold, and even when we weren't friends and bordered on enemies, I'd never heard that tone. "Hi, baby."

"If you tell anyone about this, I will kill you in your sleep."

"I missed you, too."

"Didn't think this was your thing, Graves." Remy was a brat, and I'd pay him back for this.

"Cute undies. Didn't take you for the pink type." Stevenson actually laughed. Bastard.

"I'm killing you all. I can get away with it. I'm rich. They'd never convict me." I growled. I should've just pissed them off earlier and let Stelman kill me because I was never living the rescue down.

"No, no, I'd put that down if I were you, Stelman. Before you're able to raise that gun, our sniper will put one right between your eyes." Robert, the voice of reason, I loved him more every day.

"I was about to call. They wanted to ransom…" A round of gruff laughter cut off my father's excuse.

"We've been monitoring your phone, you received no calls, and you slipped out of the back of the hotel where you were going to meet one of your mistresses. She was very willing to talk to us. You really should've picked a stronger alibi." Marcel's voice was back to the chilly tone, and I wanted to see his face.

Even when he irritated me, I still found comfort when he smiled at me. I'd never admit that out loud, but I wanted everything he promised me. Us. The girls. A family and I knew I was trouble, and I couldn't always keep my mouth shut. Yet he'd told me I was just right, and no matter how crazy that that's what filled my head right then, I needed to see him look at me the same.

I flinched as a gunshot echoed off the metal walls, and the unknown cop fell backward. "That's one, you're next, Stelman. What's it going to be?" Robert asked.

I saw the movement from the corner of my eye as Stelman began to raise his weapon and a scream followed the exploding of his right knee.

"I've been waiting years for that." Robert let out a satisfied sigh.

"Daddy, don't make me jealous. That sound is just for me."

"I need new fucking friends," I muttered, but all my friends laughed so they'd heard me.

My father's protests and the clichéd, *do you know who I am* actually came out of his mouth, and there was a scuffle as I assumed they took him into custody. Stevenson came into view as he jerked Stelman off the floor and dragged him limping to the door.

As someone approached, all I saw was thick legs highlighted perfectly in black pants and feet encased in huge boots. I sensed who it was even though they hadn't said a word. "I know those legs, Marcel."

"I was just enjoying the view. Maybe we can try some bondage? It's like cuddling but with ropes. Extreme cuddling, shall we say, Shibari. It'll spice up our snuggling game."

"I'm breaking up with you and taking my girls and going home." As soon as the tension released from the rope, I straightened, and Marcel unknotted the binding.

"You okay?" He looked around as he asked and then lowered his mouth to mine. It was a soft, quick brush.

"Embarrassed of me?"

"No, and you didn't answer my question."

"I'm fine. How are my girls?"

"Okay, I promised them I'd bring their Papa home. I was scared I wouldn't be able to keep my promise." He stroked my cheek with his big hand.

"I'm good. A few minutes later, I can't guarantee I wouldn't have had more broken bones. Give me your pants," I demanded.

He chuckled. "I'm not giving you my pants. I'm not as sexy pants-less as you. There's clothes for you in the car. When the divers found the weighted down bag with your clothes, Vega bought you some sweats and a t-shirt."

"Here, you're making my men uncomfortable," Sharp yelled, and I looked up in time to catch a blanket. "It's my dog's blanket. Feel privileged he's sharing." He disappeared.

"We're not claiming him, right? He's just a temp."

"Vega doesn't like him, so he's definitely not sticking around."

"You don't sound too confident."

"She didn't like me at first either."

"Shit. Let's get this over with. The indignity should be treated like a Band-Aid and just ripped off."

"The pink really works for you." I elbowed him in the ribs, and he laughed as he took the blanket from me to wrap it around me.

"I'm in pink underwear and wrapped in a dog blanket. This is not how I saw my life."

"Admit it. In some small, demented way, you're actually enjoying this." He winked as I didn't answer. "Come on. We agreed you could read him his rights and push him in the back of a cruiser."

"I can?"

"Oh yeah, my brat gets what he wants, and you've been living for this moment." He draped his arm over my shoulders and led me from the container.

Everyone was off to the side as if they were giving Marcel and me a minute alone. Stelman and my father were both on their knees. The defeat on my father's pale face said it all. It had finally sunk in that he wasn't getting out of this. His actions had brought disgrace to him and my mother. Everything he'd held onto with a steely grip disintegrated in a matter of minutes.

He was a broken man, and my mother's career probably wouldn't survive either, but she was a born politician, so she would work an angle and come out looking completely innocent. I wasn't sure how innocent she was. All of that didn't matter at that moment. The final nail in my father's coffin awaited, and I was really looking forward to reading him his rights.

I stepped up to him. "Mr. Graves, you have the right…"

DOUGLAS

COLD CASE
UNIT

C aptain Tyson paced the width of the Cold Case Unit, cursing under his breath as me and every member of the Cold Case Unit, including Doc and Sharp, tried to appear as if we were truly children waiting to be chastised. The night had dragged on as we worked the scene, divided of the paperwork, and it was already mid-morning. Most of us were running on empty and ready to go home.

"So." He turned on his toes and crossed his arms over his chest. "For months now, you've been working a multiple murder investigation, the attack on your fellow detective, and I had to hear about you arresting the DA and several highly decorated cops on the morning news. With a nice image of one of the detectives in pink briefs splashed across the screen."

"I didn't have any clothes, and Marcel wasn't parting with his shirt to cover my oh so delectable ass, his words, not mine." And there was the British accent. "And they weren't pink when I bought them. Savvy threw a hot pink shirt in with our grays and ta-da."

I noticed everyone in the room except me and Tyson rolling

our lips between our teeth and coughing to hide the choked laughter.

"You may think it's a joke, but the higher-ups are getting inquiries as to why a forensic genealogist, the senior medical examiner, five of my best detectives, and our newest SWAT commander was running an unapproved op with a supposed assist from an alleged hacker, and a mob boss to take down the District Attorney."

"Um, there was no hacker or mob boss involved...that was all speculation, Captain Tyson." Vega sounded so innocent—it was weird.

"Vega?"

"Yes, Captain?"

"I will arrest you just for my amusement."

"Yes, sir."

"Detectives Kauffman, since you two are in charge of the heathens, what do you have to say about this development?"

"Daddy, this is all yours." Remy stage whispered and pivoted on the corner of the desk trying to put distance between him and us. Traitor.

"Over the course of our investigation, it came to our attention that there was possible police corruption involved. As the commanding officers of this unit, it was our decision to keep the knowledge that we were looking into DA and State's Attorney Graves among our unit."

"And Sharp's involvement?"

"Captain Tyson, I was asked to join a secret taskforce by the Police Commissioner and the District Attorney. I was given strict orders that any actions taken by said taskforce were on a need-to-know basis. At the point when the taskforce became common knowledge by the Cold Case Unit, I was asked about it, and I concluded that they needed to know, and no one else."

"Doctor?"

"Daddy made me do it." Doc squeaked and then slapped his hand over his mouth.

Tyson choked out a laugh and shook his head. "Jesus Christ, I'm glad I don't have to deal with y'all all the time anymore. You're all suspended for a week without pay. It'll be a nice vacation for the rest of us. And I expect your transfer papers on my desk by the end of the week, Douglas."

"Transfer?"

"You're hooked up with a Cold Case Detective. You're going to either transfer or work down here anyway. We'll just cut out the middleman. And just so y'all know, when you return, there's going to be about forty cold cases waiting for you from other precincts. Congratulations, you're officially the entire Winston Harbor Cold Case Unit."

"We didn't sign up for that!" Robert protested.

"I know, Robert, I did it for you. Thank Vega. She put in requests for those forty cases to be reexamined. Since we're the only precinct with funding for a full-time Cold Case Unit, you're the lucky ones. Now I don't want to see or hear any of you for a week."

"What about my team?" Sharp asked.

"As they were only following orders, they'll be assigned to another team for the duration of your suspension."

We all waited for Tyson to leave, and then we looked at each other until we broke down laughing.

"We really needed a vacation. Remy and I wanted to take our girl and grandkids camping. She wants to join some scouting thing."

"Daddy, I told you my idea of camping is a motel without room service."

"You've gotten so spoiled. You used to live in abandoned houses. Three days without electricity won't hurt you." Robert wrapped his hand around the back of Remy's neck and pulled him off the desk as the older man took his husband home.

"What about you and Stevenson, Doc?" Simon asked.

"Sleep, lots of sleep. A week without bodies to examine will do me good."

"And I think a short vacation. I have a friend with a sailboat, and my baby's wanted to go." Stevenson smiled at Doc, and Doc blushed, throwing himself into Stevenson's arms. And as always, the bigger man carried his boyfriend away.

That left us alone with Vega and Sharp, and Sharp looked confused. "That seems a bit anticlimactic. A week?"

"We set a precedence. And in the grand scheme of things, this ain't that bad. I'm going to go pack. Cash is off on a week and a half gig, and I'm going to surprise her. Glad you're still alive, Graves." She gave Simon a hug and punched me in the arm with all her tiny might, and pulled out her phone as she headed for the door.

"So, what's it like to be considered one of the Cold Case ghouls?" Simon asked.

"I don't recommend it. I should've known y'all would be trouble when I helped out with Doc's rescue. Although, I gotta say, a week of no middle of the night calls doesn't sound too bad."

"Got a partner bitching at you?" I asked with a smile. Sharp wasn't one to ever look relaxed or share too much information.

"No. My husband left about four years ago. My job isn't always easy on relationships, especially civilians, and I refuse to date another cop. Especially one in the closet. Made that mistake once."

He was about to say something else, and then our phones and his started chiming. We looked, and Simon and I started laughing at Vega's message.

Vega: *Welcome to the chaos, Sharp*

"How the fuck did she get..." He groaned as he realized she was a computer geek and was friends with a hacker. "I'm so regretting this already." He ordered Jupiter to follow, and then it was just me and Simon.

"You okay, baby?"

"Well, my father wanted me dead, and I was about to be drugged and used for batting practice, but better than expected. What about you and the girls?"

"Savvy sent a selfie of her, Amber, and Silvia to let me know they were okay. Her and Silvia were watching some movie, and Amber was curled up between them. I want to talk to you about something?" I took a deep breath. I should've had the balls to do it before he was taken, but I wasn't going to make that mistake again.

"I can move out as soon as we—" I cut him off with a rough kiss, holding his face tightly in my hands.

"No, you go, we go. I know this shit with us is new, and you're still processing how you feel about me, but I love you. I want us to live together and raise our girls, and fight and be snarky. If you don't feel it yet, that's fine. I just needed you to know."

"When?" he asked where his lips almost touched mine.

"A lot longer than you liking me. The attraction on your part is new, and I know the way your beautiful brain has to process. So you say it when you're ready."

I noticed his eyes closed when he nodded, and his hands gripped my shirt tightly. I gave him a minute, and then he tilted his chin up to push his mouth to mine. I'd never get tired of him being close. Being the one he wanted to be intimate with.

"Why don't we go home? Both take a long hot shower, get some much-needed sleep and then order take-out. Tony's dropping Amber off early in the morning and then taking Savvy to school."

"But I wanted them at home."

"And Savvy said I should have you to myself for the evening. We can video call them while we wait for dinner to show up. Your oldest knows that you're going to put her and Amber first, just like you did with her when you were in the hospital."

"My oldest. I'm never going to be tired of that. I'm thinking of leaving the force. Gladys and I talked."

"I heard you say to Fran that this was your last case. You love being a cop, but you love the girls more, so whatever you decide, I'll support you. We have an amazing support system, and Amber will never run out of babysitters."

"I was so sure that's what I wanted, to retire and fall back on my law degree, but I'm not sure."

"Then just think about it. With this case off your shoulders and a weeks' vacation, you'll have time. Now, let's go home and enjoy a child-free afternoon and evening of just you, me, and cuddles."

"Um, what if I said I had a surprise for you?"

"I'd ask, what is it, but from that bratty smirk on your face, you're not going to tell me."

"You're right about that, Detective Douglas."

"Brat." I pressed my lips to his smile.

"I like when you call me that, but I will deny it if you ever tell anyone."

"Then that will just be between you and me, brat." I took his hands and stepped back, leading him from the room and out to the parking lot. I wanted to get home and reconnect. In those hours of looking for him, I'd realized how attached I was to his presence, the way he made me feel, and I needed that back.

GRAVES

He knew just how to distract me, the stress of the kidnapping, the almost beating, and right then, I didn't care as I took in the strained lines of Marcel's face as he held his legs open. The plug disappearing into his well-stretched hole. I'd bought it as a surprise when I noticed the way he jumped, and his breath caught just so when I barely brushed his entrance the few times we made out. He whined the first time I slid a single finger inside him, and then he'd held his breath.

I didn't have any urge to get off. I felt pleasure when he'd jerk me off or rubbed his cock against mine, but my body didn't strive for a release. We didn't mind, but I knew what he needed. I'd edged him for days just like he enjoyed, and his restlessness told me he wanted to come. His submission gave me a sense of power and rightness I'd never felt before him.

Kink or power exchange never really interested me since it didn't seem to fit my Asexuality and my lack of interest. That was until him. Months of arguing, snark, and believing him to be my greatest nemesis had all culminated to this point. He accepted everything about me, even the parts of me I'd considered broken until my friends helped me realize I wasn't. I tapped the base of the plug as I sucked at his sensitive nipple,

"Quit teasing, brat." His voice went gruff, and as I brought my gaze to his face, I smirked at him.

"Now, Detective Douglas, I thought you liked the teasing." I removed his hands from behind his knees, and as he stretched out the left one, I straddled it. I spread my left hand on his chest and braced my weight on my right. Lowering my upper body until his quickened breaths teased my lips.

"But you're just being mean."

"Mean would be leaving you like this. I have no intention of doing so." I nudged the flared base of the plug with my knee, and his hands flew up to fist in my hair. I took in the way he squeezed his eyes shut. That sexy hitch in his breathing before he froze.

"You better not."

"Do you like your surprise?"

"You know I do," he said, stuttering, and I relished the sound of him losing control.

When it was just us, he let the mask fall away, and all he needed was me to play with him a bit. He groaned as I rubbed my soft cock against his hard one. I loved the feel of him. The strength and size of his form under and against mine. I took any opportunity to straddle his lap and make out when our daughters went to bed, and it was just us and the intimacy of the moment.

"Shit, I want you to get me off. Will you?"

I didn't answer. All I did was crawl between his strong, thick thighs and rest my hips on his. He tilted his pelvis, and as always, we were obsessed with the kissing. I loved on his mouth as I rolled my hips, rubbing my belly and cock against his, as my movements shifted the plug. Each time I rolled my lower body, he'd pull my hair, and the slight sting made me smirk.

"I'm buying you more toys." My voice rumbled against his lips, and he started grunting and letting out these beautiful high-pitched whines as he almost violently held me to him. His body trembled and arched, meeting each downward movement of my hips.

"Don't fucking stop, oh, fuck, baby."

The agony on his face made my heart beat faster, sweat beaded my skin, and it was there in every harsh breath, each bruising grip that the way I loved him was enough. I was enough, just me. I gave him what he needed freely, and he expected nothing else, just my touch and attention. He let out a shout and his back arched, bowing mine in the process as wet heat spread between our bellies.

He gripped my ass and rubbed me against him as his entire body jerked, and he was the most beautiful sight I'd ever seen. He collapsed under me, and I gave him my full weight. I stroked his cheeks with the backs of my fingers as we lazily kissed.

"I love you, you know, right?" I whispered, and his eyes opened wide.

"What?" His voice broke.

"I knew for a while, but I was scared. I wanted to be enough for you. Just me, all my snark and brattiness. My weird brain. I just...I love you, our family. I just wanted you to know."

I'd never seen him smile as bright in all our months of knowing each other. "It broke me thinking you'd never love me back. In the hospital, I came so close to losing you, and I tried to accept it."

"You've loved me that long?"

"Probably longer, but when I almost lost you, it hit me. Especially when you asked who needed you. Me...I needed you."

"What happens now?" I asked.

"Well, we get to be together, we get to raise our daughters, and we're going to be very happy. Maybe I can actually take you on an actual date. We haven't been able to do that yet."

"What about Mama Sue's?"

"You didn't like me when we had our dinners there."

"Maybe I kinda liked you the second time. I did share my desserts with you."

He snorted. "There is that. Come on, baby, we're about to get very uncomfortable. We'll clean up, get some uninterrupted sleep, and then we figure out what to do for an entire week off."

"Like Doc said, sleep, so much sleep. I have about four years of sleep to catch up on. Maybe three now, since I've actually been sleeping full nights since I moved in here." I gave him another quick kiss and rolled off him, seeing the mess he'd made of us.

Never in my life did I anticipate that I would love the smell of another person on me, their release smeared across my skin. It was odd and also comforting because it was Marcel. I couldn't imagine having this with someone else.

"You're thinking too hard again."

"I was just…it's odd. Before you, I never thought I'd be naked in a bed with someone after getting them off. The thought was always distasteful to be that close and intimate with someone. With you, it feels right. I feel safe knowing that you'll never demand or push me for more than I can give you physically."

He rolled to his side. "What you give me physically is just fine with me, so maybe I won't ever get to fuck you, feel how tight you are around me, or you inside me. I'm perfectly okay with that. I can get an empty orgasm anywhere. I can jerk off in my bed or shower every day, but that doesn't give me what you can. Kisses and affection. And that's more than enough. Now, get that pretty ass out of this bed, and we can clean up. You're going to complain later when that dries in your stomach hair."

I rolled out of bed and glanced back over my shoulder as he did the same on the opposite side. For the first time, I let myself enjoy looking at another person, study the way the muscles moved beneath his skin. The roundness and the slight softness of his ass.

"I was serious earlier."

"About what, baby?" He groaned a bit as he walked, and I knew the plug was shifting.

"I'm going to buy you all the toys. I may not be able to be inside you, but I'm going to see how you like being fucked one day."

"Give you a little power, and you turn into a demanding top." He playfully rolled his eyes.

"Hey, that's what happens when I find out my boyfriend has needy bottom potential."

"Ha-ha. Get your ass in the bathroom. You gotta take the plug out. If I try, I may go for a solo round two."

"Needy," I whispered as I entered the bathroom with him growling behind me.

I could get used to this. I could even picture years of us together, and where in the past I'd have expected fear, all I had was a sense that with him and our family, I was right where I needed to be.

EPILOGUE

DOUGLAS

COLD CASE
UNIT

L ife had changed so much in a year. Simon and Gladys had started their own practice specifically for the strip and Outreach. My transfer to the Cold Case Unit happened quickly, especially with Simon changing careers to be home more with our daughters. He'd changed his mind ten different times before he'd decided a new job would be better for him. I'd always told him I'd support him whatever he chose to do, and he was happier. Our youngest went to work with him every day.

We'd moved everything to Simon's house where we had more space. Savvy still had a permanent security detail until Simon's father was tried for orchestrating the murders of five men and the attempted murder of Simon and Savvy. They were still looking into accomplices and investigating to see if his mother was innocent or not.

I would've complained a bit more about a mob boss, his husband and kids, and his enforcer spending so much time at our place, but until we knew how far the corruption went, we had to be careful. Plus, as weird as it was, they'd become family, too. Savvy and Amber loved their honorary Uncles and Sylvie.

Simon was still dealing with the betrayal. Although, since he had almost no healthy emotional connection to his parents, it was more about them trying to hurt the people he loved. They considered the strip a blight on their city. The Outreach was standing in their way of progress, and it stood on prime real estate. Simon had blamed himself that he hadn't seen it sooner, so I'd suggested a vacation for the four of us, and part of that was bringing them to meet my family.

We'd put it off as long as we could, but it was time my dad met Simon and our new daughter. I hadn't called to warn him, which was probably a monumental mistake. Yet I didn't want my brothers and their families to descend until later, or we were safely on a plane home.

"Um, there may be a little something I have to tell you."

"What the fuck didn't you tell me?" Simon glared at me, and our daughters joined him. Amber and Savvy had Simon's personality down pat.

"Dad doesn't know we're coming."

"So, we're here, you have your pretty soon-to-be husband and a bonus granddaughter, and he doesn't know?" I knew that tone, and it didn't bode well for me when we were alone.

We had a snarky relationship, it worked for us, but the occasional real argument would happen. Trying to talk my Asexual boyfriend into makeup sex wasn't a ploy I could use, so I had to buy him lots of snacks and coffee to make up for me being an asshole. I'd readily admit to myself that most of the disagreements were my fault, but I'd never say that out loud.

"I didn't want my brothers in on the first meeting."

"This is going to be fucking amazing. He does know you're Pansexual, right? At least he'll know there was a boyfriend possibility."

"Quit being such a drama queen, they know I'm Pan, but I'd never expected to bring home a pretty lawyer."

"Just wait until I tell Doc and Vega about this one."

Just what I needed, a threat about my baby's besties, and if they found out, Carmine would, too. I pushed the doorbell as I continued to earn damning stares from him and our daughters.

"I'm so looking forward to what Uncle Doc and Aunt Vega do to you." Savvy hissed, and a perfect smile curved her lips as the door opened. "Grandpa!" Savvy threw herself into my dad's arms.

He was the same height as me, with heavy muscles from still working construction, but the lines on his face were a bit deeper than I remembered. It had been a while since I'd come home. Not that we'd ever had a bad relationship, I knew he loved me. Yet being a single father, there wasn't always enough time for him to be the always present parent.

"What's with the surprise?" he asked as he shot a glance at Simon with Amber on Simon's hip.

"We're on vacation, and I thought it was time you met Simon."

"Come in." Dad kept his arm wrapped around Savvy as he stepped back.

Shit, I knew that tone, and I was about to get yelled at like I was sixteen again. I placed my hand on the small of Simon's back and gave it a comforting stroke as we walked inside. My childhood home hadn't changed, and except for the upgraded furniture, it was the same. My dad led us back to the kitchen.

"Simon, meet Ernie Douglas. Dad, meet Simon Graves and our daughter, Amber."

"Daughter?"

"Yeah, the adoption became final last month for both girls." When Dad reached for her, Amber held her hand out and said no. "We don't pick up or touch without permission." I got the old school *are you insane* expression.

"It teaches body autonomy, especially for girls, and makes them more comfortable with telling people no. And demanding strangers, and even family, respect their boundaries." Simon explained as he always had when the girls set boundaries and people thought it was over the top.

"And we know we can say no when our peers try to pressure

us into sex before we're ready," Savvy said as she held out her arms for her sister, and the girl went right to her.

She definitely missed my dad's eyes widening at his granddaughter casually mentioning sex. This was going to be an amazing visit. I shot a look at Simon to find him looking at his girls with pride. To him, they couldn't do anything wrong and had made sure Savvy's assertiveness grew, and I could already see the confident woman she'd become.

"New-age bull—" My dad's teeth almost snapped together as Simon and Savvy pinned him with twin looks daring him to finish. Fuck, I was just glad I wasn't the recipient of those like normal.

"Amber has to go to the bathroom," Savvy announced and carried Amber from the room without breaking her angry stare at my dad until she disappeared.

"She's gotten more bossy."

"The correct term is assertive. Should I take our girls back to the hotel while you visit?" Shit, my baby was irritated.

"Baby."

"I won't have our girls disrespected, possible Father-in-law or not."

"Father-in-law?" It was almost comical the way my dad's voice rose a few octaves.

"I did say I was getting married again when we talked last time."

"Him?"

I chuckled as my baby almost growled. "Yes, him."

"What does he do?"

"Well, *he* is standing right here. Now I see where you get your atrocious attitude from." There was my brat I adored.

"He's a lawyer and on the board of an Outreach program," I answered with pride. With his career change, he had more time to devote to the Outreach, and Boss was ecstatic about that. It gave Boss more time to devote to more community activism.

"Impressive. How did you two meet?"

"I picked apart his cases because, as your granddaughter loves to say, I'm a perfectionist asshole."

"Savvy's assessment is flawless."

I turned my head to smile down at him. From our first meeting, I didn't think a little over a year later that we'd be planning a wedding. More kids weren't off the table as an option, adoption or foster, maybe both. "Of course it is. She takes after you and Donna."

"Donna's a joy. I don't see why you complain so much."

"Um, my husband-to-be and my former wife shouldn't be such good friends."

"Who says? I like her more than you most days."

"Now I see how Robert feels about Gladys and Remy." I looked away from Simon to find my dad staring at us, and I didn't miss his amusement.

"I like him. You've always been too big for your britches."

Simon gestured wildly and let out a heavy sigh. "I know, I've tried to tell him countless times, but he doesn't listen to me or our daughters when they agree with me."

"He was never one for listening at all."

"You should've introduced me to your dad before I said yes to your proposal."

"It's too damn late now."

"I'm calling your brothers, their wives and the kids will want to meet their new cousin and see Savannah."

I groaned, and Simon chuckled at my obvious reluctance. My brothers and sisters-in-law, and all my nieces and nephews had one volume—loud. It was chaos personified, and I hoped like hell Simon and Amber were ready.

THE SECOND BED in a hotel room was empty as my dad decided to keep the girls overnight to catch up with Savvy and learn more about Amber. Savvy knew the rules, so Simon had only given a short-list and reminded him about consent, but Amber had her big sister to advocate for her. I'd felt proud when Amber had given us hugs and waved at us as we left. She was confident and safe, and Savvy was growing up so much. Compassionate and intelligent, she knew her mind, and who she was, and when I said we did good with our kids, I could say Simon and Donna had done the most. Amber loved her stepmom, Donna.

She'd started calling Donna mom since Savvy did, and since Savvy was her big sister, she figured Donna was Mom. Donna had just smiled and hugged Amber tight. My eyes were closed as I reclined against the pillows with Simon leaning on my chest.

"It's weird, isn't it?" he asked.

"What's weird, baby?" I played with his chest hair, wrapping the curls around my fingertips.

"The girls not being with us. It's always the four of us."

"Enjoy some quiet and take advantage of my dad spoiling them a bit. I'm sorry I didn't tell him."

"Hell, I'm kinda glad you didn't, especially after your brothers and their families showed up. I wouldn't have wanted to walk into that. Amber would've freaked out."

"I still should've said something. But up until we pulled up to the house, I didn't even know if I was taking you and Amber to meet him."

"Why? Ashamed of your pretty, husband-to-be?" He turned his head and laid his cheek on my chest as he looked up at me from under his thick, dark lashes. I cupped his cheek in my left hand and stroked his skin which had the pleasing texture of stubble after a day. He was beautiful, and I loved him.

"Never. But me being Pansexual to my family was kinda this abstract concept. I'd never brought a man home or even mentioned dating one. It's like this constant coming out process. Sometimes it's tiring."

"Try being Asexual. I'd tried dating a few times, but—"

"They wanted you to give it up."

"So fucking much." He let out a heavy sigh. "I thought you'd lose interest."

"Never happen. I know sometimes it's in the back of your mind, but I love cuddling you at night. You love all the things I enjoy, and you're not shy about helping me out with orgasms. And when you do want to get off, I'm not shy about giving my man blowjobs."

"I love you, Marcel, I really do. I don't think I'd want all this with someone else. I didn't before you."

"That just makes me extremely lucky." I gave him a kiss, and then he turned his head. I laced my fingers with his and reveled in how enough we were for each other. He liked the romance, the dates, and the affection that I'd always craved. Once upon a time, I considered him an enemy, but I wouldn't change anything about us. We were always just right.

COLD CASES AND BRUISED HEARTS

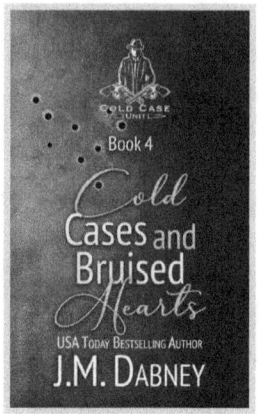

When your only goal is to save the world who's there when you need to be rescued?

Boss

Most of my life I'd been the savior, the one everyone came to in trouble. Could be to atone for sins of the past. Could be because I was a natural caregiver. Whatever it was I didn't understand how to do anything else. My Outreach Program cared for everyone in the city you needed help and I wouldn't say I hadn't made enemies, but I'd never had one like SWAT Commander Dolan Sharp before.

Dolan

No one did anything for free or out of the kindness of their hearts. That wasn't how the world worked and it was always survival of the fittest. I didn't care what anyone said about the man named Boss. I had no problems with breaching the perimeter of a hostage negotiation, but I was ordered to pick up

Boss from the Outreach. There was one thing I was sure of, I didn't like him and I damn sure didn't trust him

There's always threats at every turn, it's just a matter of when they catch up with you, but when one jaded man and another with a seemingly deep death wish have to work together who's going to survive the aftermath?

ABOUT THE AUTHOR

Two time USA Today Bestselling author J.M. Dabney is a multi-genre published writer of Body and Fat Positive Romance & Fiction. They live with a constant diverse cast of diverse characters in their head. They live for one purpose alone, and that's to make sure everyone gets the happily ever after they deserve. There is nothing more they want from telling their stories than to show that no matter the package the characters come in or the damage their pasts have done, that love is love. That normal is never normal and sometimes the so-called broken can still be beautiful.

The author is Non-Binary and uses the pronouns They/Them.

ALSO BY J.M. DABNEY

Cold Cases Unit

Cold Cases and Second Chances

Cold Cases and Dark Secrets

Cold Cases and Bitter Enemies

Cold Cases and Bruised Hearts (Pre-order coming soon)

Cold Cases and Zero Witnesses

Sappho's Kiss Series

When All Else Fails

More Than What They See

Dysfunction it its Finest Series

Club Revenge

Soul Collector Prophecy

Twirled World Ink Series

Berzerker

Trouble

Scary

Lucky

Brawlers Series

Crave

Psycho

Bull

Hunter

Executioners Series

Ghost

Joker

King

Sin & Saint

Trenton Security

Livingston

Little

Gage

Pure

Masiello Brothers

The Taming of Violet

3 Moments Trilogy

A Matter of Time

The Men of Canter Handyman

Black Leather & Knuckle Tattoos

Chance at the Impossible

Bloody Knuckles Bar & Grill

Clipping the Gargoyle's Wings

Standalone

By Way of Pain (Criminal Delights - Assassins)

Christmas, Bloody Christmas (By Way of Pain Xmas Story)

Waited So Long

An Odd, Little Girl

Claiming Whisper

Adoring Beast

A Yuri Sorenson Mystery

Not Another Statistic

Permanent Freebies

Has the Honeymoon Ended? (Brawlers Short Valentine's Story)

Once Upon a Bear Claw

The Scars She Bears (Executioners Short)

WRITING AS SIOBHAN SMILE

Little Love

His to Own, Hers to Claim

Shug's Daddy

Mama Didn't Sign Up for This

Butcher's Babygirl

The Story Began Once Upon a Time